SORRY FOR YOUR LOSS

Also by Jessie Ann Foley
The Carnival at Bray
Neighborhood Girls

SORRY FOR YOUR LOSS

JESSIE ANN FOLEY

HARPER TEEN
An Imprint of HarperCollinsPublishers

HarperTeen is an imprint of HarperCollins Publishers.

Sorry for Your Loss

Library of Congress Control Number: 2018968292
ISBN 978-0-06-257191-5

Typography by Catherine San Juan
19 20 21 22 23   PC/LSCH   10 9 8 7 6 5 4 3 2 1

First Edition

For my daughters: Roisin, Sheila, and Aine

THE FLANAGAN FAMILY

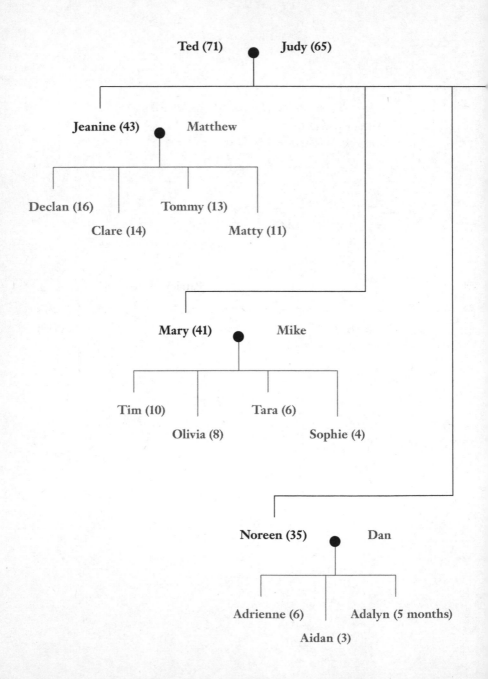

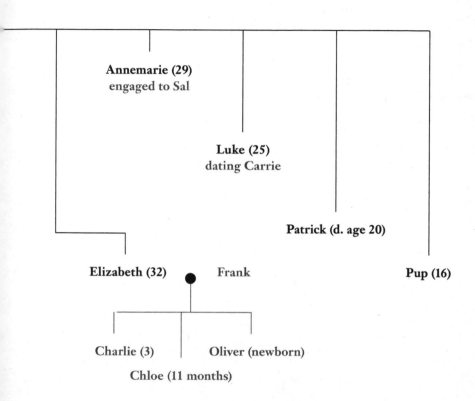

● *denotes marriage*

Annemarie (29)
engaged to Sal

Luke (25)
dating Carrie

Patrick (d. age 20)

Elizabeth (32) ● Frank

Pup (16)

Charlie (3)   Oliver (newborn)

Chloe (11 months)

As we descend into the deep, the pressure increases
relentlessly, and the light from above all but disappears.
Yet, incredibly, there is life.

—**DAVID ATTENBOROUGH**, *Blue Planet II*

The basic elements of art are as follows: shape, line, space, form, texture, value, and color. In order to succeed in this course, you will need to understand these elements and apply them to your own work.

—*Studio Art I syllabus, Mr. Van P. Hughes, Abraham Lincoln High School*

SHAPE:

a flat, enclosed area of two dimensions

1

LATE ONE FRIDAY NIGHT AT the beginning of May, Pup Flanagan sat slouched in one corner of the couch in Izzy Douglass's basement, staring with great concentration at the cracked screen of his phone and trying to ignore the slurpy tongue-on-tongue sounds coming from underneath the striped blanket in the other corner.

Pup wanted to leave, obviously. But he couldn't. After watching a piece on the *Today* show about teenage sexuality, Mr. and Mrs. Douglass had announced to Izzy that she and her horrible boyfriend, Brody, were no longer allowed to be in the basement alone together. A third party—someone who was honest, trustworthy, and had nothing better to do on a Friday night—must be present at all times. Pup fit all three of these descriptions; plus, Izzy had the kind of power over him that made him incapable of refusing her a favor, even one he dreaded.

"But how will your parents know we're not having a threesome down here?" Pup had asked. "I mean, I'm *also* a hormonal, sex-crazed teen, aren't I?"

"They're not going to worry about us having a three-some."

"How do you know?"

"*Because*, Pup," Izzy had said. "I mean—no offense—but it's *you*."

Which stung. Though she had a point.

Born when his mom was forty-nine and his dad fifty-five, he was Pup the Surprise if you asked his mother, Pup the Accident if you asked his seven older siblings. He was almost seventeen and had finally, his pediatrician thought, stopped growing. He stood six feet three inches tall and weighed 142 pounds, even in a sweat suit and Nikes with a Taco Bell Triple Double Crunchwrap sitting in his stomach. This height-to-weight ratio made him look less like a human being and more like a redheaded, buck-toothed praying mantis; in other words, not the kind of boy you had to worry could tempt your daughter into having a threesome.

A hand had wormed its way out of the blanket and was now feeling around the couch for something to grab; it landed on Pup's outstretched leg and began gently caressing the knuckly bones of his ankle.

"Hey!" Pup gave a kick, and Brody's hand slithered back inside. "Sorry, dude," came the muffled apology. "Wrong leg."

Pup pressed himself into as small a package as he could manage, folding his limbs beneath him like he was disassembling a tent, and squinted more intently at his phone. A trill of giggles broke his concentration, followed by a soft moan. Pup sighed loudly, as a pink-and-red-checked bra was tossed from beneath the squirming mound of blanket and landed at his feet.

"Okay," he said, kicking the bra away from where its strap had looped around the toe of his Nike. "I'm leaving."

"Wait!"

Izzy's flushed face, framed by a pile of tousled hair, emerged. Her naked shoulders were dusted in a constellation of pale freckles.

"Just give us ten more minutes. Please?"

"No." Pup shook his head, averting his eyes from her bare shoulders. "This is gross, and anyway, I should already be in bed by now. I have to be up super early tomorrow."

Brody's head emerged now, also flushed and tousled.

"With those artsy chicks, right?"

"Yeah."

"You trying to hit any of that? That girl Maya Ulrich was in my French class last year. She's *hot*, bro."

"Hey." Izzy smacked his arm, but not nearly hard enough, in Pup's opinion.

"What?" Brody said innocently. "I didn't mean she was as hot as *you*, Iz." He leaned over to start kissing her again.

"*Anyway*," Pup interrupted. "I'm not trying to *hit* anything. I'm just taking some pictures with them so I don't fail art."

"You're getting your ass out of bed at five a.m. to watch the sun rise with a bunch of girls, and you're telling me you're not even working any angles? Sunrise is when the *magic* happens, baby. The *romance*."

"I think that's actually sun*set*," Pup pointed out.

"Sunrise, sunset, what difference does it make?" Brody shook his head sadly and worked up a loud belch from his diaphragm. "The problem is that you have no game."

"What can I say, Brody? I guess I just don't have your charisma."

"Can't you stay just a *little* bit longer, Pup?" Izzy had gathered the blanket around her shoulders and was watching him hopefully.

"No." Pup avoided her gaze. "School's out in a couple weeks and I need this grade." He stuck his phone in his pocket, stood up, and hurried up the basement stairs without turning around and risking becoming ensnared in those green-flecked eyes that could make him do anything. He slipped past Izzy's parents, who were sitting across the kitchen table from one another, typing away furiously in the glow of their separate laptops. Pup wondered whether the Douglasses had seen any specials on the *Today* show about the negative effect of workaholic parents on their teenage children, but thought it best not to ask.

On the short walk back to his house, Pup took his phone from his pocket and called his sister Annemarie. It was almost midnight, but he knew she'd pick up. Annemarie always answered Pup's calls, even if she was at work, even if she was out with Sal, even if she was in bed and half asleep. In big families like the Flanagans, everyone pretends like they all love each other equally, but of course that isn't true. Pup loved Annemarie the best, and he liked to think that she felt the same way.

"How bad was it?" she said, picking up on the second ring. Pup could hear papers being shuffled around in the background.

"Are you still at *work*?"

"I'm *always* at work these days," she said. "Do you have any idea how much flower arrangements cost?"

Annemarie was getting married in the fall, and Pup, after having been a ring bearer about eight thousand times, was finally moving up in the world: he'd been promoted to groomsman. Sal, Annemarie's fiancée, was cool and all, but Pup still worried that after they got married, things would change between him and his sister. Then what? Each of the eight siblings in the Flanagan family had his or her role, and each role had its complementary partner: Patrick was the saint and Luke the sinner; Mary the practical-minded, no-nonsense paramedic and Jeanine the highlighted, manicured former sorority girl; and Elizabeth and Noreen, who were both too good-looking to understand the struggles of normal people. Though there were thirteen years between them, Pup and Annemarie were the two Flanagan children who no one really knew what to *do* with; Pup was the quiet afterthought of a sibling, seven years younger than the next-youngest child, and even though Annemarie was a successful corporate lawyer, she was also covered in tattoos and had renounced organized religion before she'd even graduated high school. She and Pup were the two outcasts of the family, and outcasts needed to stick together.

"So how *bad* was it?" Annemarie repeated now.

"Well, you called it."

"They hooked up right in front of you?"

"Under a blanket. I couldn't see anything. But I could hear stuff. And I could *imagine*."

"Oh, Pup."

He sighed. "I just don't *get* it."

"I'm sorry," she said. "I don't get it either."

When Izzy and Brody Krueger had first started dating, Annemarie had predicted it would last a month, two, tops. She was usually right about stuff like this, but Brody and Izzy were now going on month seven of their relationship, with no sign of it letting up anytime soon. Pup still couldn't believe Izzy could *like* a guy like Brody. Sure, he played the drums, so he had that going for him, but his grades were even worse than Pup's, he always had Dorito breath, and he talked with a fake California accent. He used words like "gnarly" and "rad," and pronounced "taco" like "taw-go." Not only that, he had long, dirty fingernails, evidence that he was a secret slob, like that guy from *The Catcher in the Rye*, one of the few English-class books that Pup had actually read (almost) all the way through.

But there was no point attempting to explain all of this to Izzy. Her attraction to Brody was an enigma wrapped in a puzzle, wrapped in one of those shrink-wrapped plastic covers they put around video games that are practically impossible to open without using your teeth.

"Pup," Annemarie began gently, "you're not going to like what I'm about to say."

"Please don't tell me to move on." He turned up the path to his house.

"It's just, how much longer are you going to *wait*? She *knows* you, Pup. And if someone *knows* you and still doesn't *want* you . . ."

"Wow. Harsh."

"Look, I'm sorry, kid." On the other end of the line, Pup could hear more papers moving around. He pictured Annemarie in her big-shot office on the twenty-third floor of the Aon building, stockinged feet kicked up on the desk, pinstriped blazer covering the tattoos that snaked up both of her arms. Flowers. Mermaids. Sal's name around one wrist, Patrick's name around the other. The Flanagan family tree, twenty-eight names and counting, blooming across the entirety of her back. She liked to joke it was a good thing she was on the chubby side, otherwise she'd already have run out of space. "I'm just tired. Listen. I love you, okay? So it's just hard for me to comprehend how somebody else doesn't."

"Doesn't *yet*."

"Right. Yet. Good night, Pup Squeak."

"Don't call me that. Good night."

He turned the key in the lock and tiptoed into the front room. As usual, his parents had dozed off on the couch in front of their favorite program, *Antiques Roadshow*. As images of a Chinese enamel porcelain vase—valued at $4,000!—flickered over their faces, Pup unfolded the worn green quilt that hung over the radiator and placed it gently across their knees. He picked up the empty teacup that was balanced precariously next to his mom's elbow on the rounded arm of the couch, then crossed the room to switch off the television. In the kitchen, he rinsed the cup in the sink, wiped away the grease from his mother's ChapStick, and put it away in the cabinet. Before heading upstairs to bed, Pup opened the fridge, chugged some milk from the gallon, and stood for a moment in the quiet stillness of the house. White light from the full moon poured through the window above the sink, illuminating the faded yellow tiles of the floor. Pup sometimes felt, in moments like these, that late-night silences held secrets, and that if he only listened hard enough the secrets would reveal themselves. He stood in the middle of the kitchen, listening, the milk handle cold in his hand. But then, from the front room, his dad let out a loud, burbling snore, and the mysterious stillness was shattered. He put the milk away and headed to bed.

2

THERE WERE EIGHT STEPS UP to the Boys' Room, that big, smelly, attic loft with its row of three twin beds, outdated concert posters, and carpet faded in places all the way through to the linoleum. On the wall above each step hung a framed middle-school graduation photo of each Flanagan child, in order from oldest to youngest. Each Flanagan child, that is, except for Patrick, whose photo had been replaced with one of those old-fashioned paintings of an angel. For almost three years now, Pup had grown to hate that fat, pink-cheeked, blond-haired, dead-eyed cherub on the seventh step. He hated its dimply legs, its pinprick nipples, its dumb harp, its golden, feathery wings, and every time he passed it on the way up to bed, he gave it the finger. It was fine, he guessed, if his parents wanted to think of Patrick as an angel in heaven now, but even if Patrick *was* an angel, he certainly didn't look like *that*. Patrick's hair had been jet-black, for one thing, and for another, he'd never touched a harp in his life.

Pup reached the top of the stairs, flicked on the bedroom

light, and was about to throw himself onto his bed, when he noticed that the crescent window on the other side of the room was shoved open as wide as it would go, held in place with the handle of an old toilet plunger. Outside, he could hear the tinkling of music coming from the tar ledge that jutted out from the roof of the first floor. He went over to the window, peered out, and saw his brother Luke out on the ledge, lying on his back in sweatpants and a hoodie, arms folded behind his head, phone on chest, staring up at the sky and its faint spread of city stars. On his right was a twelve-pack of beer, and on his left, a pint glass filled with a cloudy-looking brownish liquid.

"Hey." Pup leaned over the sill and stuck his head into the night air. "You're home?"

"Yeah," Luke said, not looking away from the sky.

"On a Friday night?"

"On a Friday night." Luke's words were just on the edge of slurring. Pup could see the twelve-pack was mostly finished, and he knew that his brother wouldn't call it a night until every one was empty.

"You want a beer?"

"Sure." Pup didn't drink, but if he accepted the bottle, that meant one fewer for Luke. He would nurse the beer, as he always did in these situations, then dump it off the side of the roof when Luke went inside to pee. He stuck one stork-like leg through the window, scraping his knee on the sash with a soft curse, and folded himself through. Luke uncapped a beer and handed it over. Pup took it and sat down with his back against the sun-warmed bricks of the house and followed his brother's gaze to the crisscrossing patch-work of roofs and power lines, the hazy skyline of the city in the southern distance.

"Carrie working tonight?" he asked.

"How should I know?" Luke glanced at his younger brother, his face curling into a strange smile. "She dumped me."

"*What?*"

"Yup." Luke finished his beer and upended the empty bottle in the cardboard carrier. "You heard it here first."

Pup was speechless. Luke and Carrie were, like, LukeandCarrie. They'd been together for eight years, ever since they'd gone to senior prom together back when Pup was still in fourth grade. Luke was graduating from law school in a month; he'd been planning on proposing once he passed the bar. And, even more than that, Luke Flanagan was *Luke Flanagan*, which meant that he was everything Pup wasn't: good-looking. Built. Confident. Super smart. Sure, he had a reputation for drinking too much sometimes—a reputation that had gotten worse over the last couple years, if Pup was being honest about it—but that hadn't stopped him from killing it at DePaul Law with his 3.8 GPA and his clerkship with a prominent circuit court judge. If Annemarie was Pup's favorite sibling, Luke was the one whose respect he most desired. Sometimes Luke would dole out little bursts of affection, which felt to Pup like suddenly stepping into a warm current in the freezing waters of Lake Michigan on a summer day, but then, just as quick, Luke would suddenly snatch it away with a sharply observed but devastating comment, always delivered offhand, which was exactly like realizing that the warm current you were just enjoying was actually someone else's urine.

"When did this happen?"

"Last week." Luke reached for another beer. "She said she's *tired*."

"Tired?"

"Oh, yes. Poor Carrie is *exhausted*. Because I'm '*inaccessible*.'" He jabbed his fingers into air quotes. "And I'm '*immature*.' And I'm '*just so negative*.'"

Silently, Pup agreed with all those things. Not that he was siding with Carrie or anything.

"I'm sorry, man. Are you okay?"

"Of course I'm okay. But thanks for asking, Dr. Phil." Luke opened his beer and flicked the cap off the side of the ledge. It clattered faintly on the sidewalk below. "Not the worst thing to ever happen to me, you know?"

Which, when he put it that way, was true.

Pup pointed at the brownish glass of liquid.

"What's that?" he asked.

"Oh, this?" Luke scooted to a sitting position and picked

up the glass. "You'll never guess. I was going through the back of the closet, trying to find this weed I hid a while back when mom was cleaning our room. Never found the weed, but I *did* find this."

"But what *is* it?" Pup picked up the glass and held it up to the moonlight.

"It's one of Patrick's protein shakes!"

Pup was so surprised he nearly dropped the glass. It had been over two years since he'd heard Luke so much as speak Patrick's name.

"I found a big jar of his protein powder, and I looked at the bottom and it wasn't expired so I figured—what the hell? And I made one. It's absolutely terrible. Taste it?"

Pup took the glass from his older brother, closed his eyes, and took a sip. He thought, for a wild, hopeful moment, that the taste of the protein shake would somehow bring back the feeling of Patrick, the way a smell from childhood can sometimes conjure a memory so strong it was like being immersed in the past. But all he could experience now was a chalky mixture of metallic-tasting chocolate. He leaned over the ledge and spit it into his mother's peony bushes.

"My reaction exactly," Luke laughed. "Now I understand why he never stuck to his 'fitness goals.' You remember those?"

Of course Pup remembered. Luke had found the list in the boys' sock drawer when Patrick was home from college for winter break. They had teased Pat about it mercilessly.

"One. Eat clean," Luke said, counting off on his fingers. "Two. Do butt clenches during Cellular Bio lecture." Pup smiled, remembering. God, how they had tortured Pat when they found his fitness goals, and the best part was, Pat didn't care. He had laughed along with them. He was the rare type of person who was so good-natured he was nearly impossible to embarrass, an essential survival trait when you're growing up with a brother like Luke. "Three. Expand calf circumference. Four. Go to Zumba."

That one was the one that always killed them: picturing their tall, goofy brother trying to shake his hips at a Zumba class.

"Did he ever actually *go* to Zumba?" Pup asked.

"I don't know," Luke said, "but I *really* hope so."

"And *I* really hope that someone, somewhere, has a video."

"The thing with Pat," Luke went on, "was that he could Zumba and lift and drink protein shakes all day, and he'd never be able to bulk up his skinny ass. He was like mom's side of the family. Me, I'm stocky, like dad's side. But you're like Pat. And the older you get, the more you're like him. Sometimes I look at you in a certain light or whatever and I almost think . . ." He didn't finish his thought.

Pup held his bottle to his lips and pretended to drink. He held it there until the sudden pain faded and the sting went out of his eyes.

"The only difference," Luke said, "is that he was taller than you. Dude was six foot six, and somehow he still managed to suck at basketball."

"He didn't *suck* at basketball."

"Okay, he didn't suck. But he wasn't as good as me. And he should have been, because he was so much taller than me. Tallest ever in our family."

"Hey, who knows?" Pup laughed. "I might still claim that title. I could still keep growing. I'm only sixteen, remember?"

Before Pup knew what was happening, Luke had tackled him.

"You *better* not," he panted, his hot beer breath an inch from Pup's face. "Don't you *dare* grow taller than Pat. What, you think you're better than Pat?"

"I was *joking*," Pup said, squirming in vain against Luke's vise grip on his shoulders. "And I can't even *help* it if I—"

Luke relaxed his grip and rolled away. "Nobody was better than Pat," he said softly. "Nobody."

Then he began to cry.

Pup didn't know what to do. It was not an exaggeration to say that he had never seen Luke cry. Not even once: not as a child, not as an adult, not at the hospital or the funeral, not during any of the awful weeks that followed when tuna casseroles and trays of Rice Krispies treats were piling up on the front stoop from well-meaning neighbors, not when their mother stopped coloring her hair and a gray line grew and grew from the top of her head until all the red was gone, not even late at night when he thought no one could hear, like Pup himself did, muffled into the pillow across the room of their shared attic.

"It's okay," Pup said uncertainly, reaching around to pat Luke on the back. "Everything will be okay."

"Just stay out here with me," Luke begged, his voice almost unrecognizable, muffled by the fabric of Pup's T-shirt. "Please. Just stay with me for a little while."

Pup had to be up in three hours to make it to Albion Beach by sunrise, or he would probably fail art. But what else could he do? He stayed.

3

PUP WOKE UP SHIVERING and covered with a fine mist of dew. Beside him, Luke was curled up in a snoring ball, his arm thrown around Pup's waist, most likely a habit of sleeping next to Carrie for all those years. Pup gently lifted away the arm, which was dead weight, and rolled out from beneath his brother. Luke didn't even stir. It was still dark, but the sky had a translucent, purple quality, and as soon as Pup saw it, he didn't need to look at his phone to know that he was already late.

"Shit!" He bolted upright, knocking over the full beer he'd pretended to drink the night before, which fizzed in a widening puddle, creeping closer to Luke's sleeping head. Pup stood up, his knees cracking, and crawled back through the window into the bedroom. He changed into the first semiclean T-shirt he could find, raked a toothbrush over his teeth, and ran back to the bedroom to grab the 35mm film camera he'd borrowed from his art teacher, Mr. Hughes. Just as he was about to make a run for it downstairs, he caught sight of his brother through the frame of the crescent-shaped window, curled up in the dawning light. The image stopped him in his tracks. Even in sleep, Luke didn't look peaceful; his eyes and mouth were screwed tightly shut, his fists were balled, his whole body seemed tense, ready to defend itself. His arm reached out, wrapping around a girlfriend who was no longer there, as if his body retained the memory of love even if his waking mind denied it. The light above him was spreading from deep purple to goldish pink.

Pup squatted before the windowsill, squared Luke in the frame, and pressed down on the shutter release. Then he ran down the stairs, grabbed the keys to his dad's Buick, and slipped out the door into the dawn.

By the time Pup arrived at Albion Beach it was 6:27 a.m. The sun was already hanging brilliantly over the rippling lake, and, as he sprinted across the sand, the four members of the Lincoln High School photography club were already packing up their equipment.

"You missed it," Maya Ulrich said without turning around.

"Crap." Pup panted, resting his hands on his knees.

"I *knew* you'd be late. Kim, you owe me two bucks."

Kim Strickland, a girl Pup knew from the hallways of Lincoln by her silver-dyed hair, black, smudgy makeup, and a septum piercing that he couldn't look at without wincing in imagined pain, glared at him, then dug into the pocket of her ripped jeans and slapped two bills into Maya's hand.

"Remind me why you're here again?"

"My final project." Pup untwisted his camera strap from around his neck. "For Studio Art. Mr. Hughes told me I could tag along with you guys and maybe, you know, pick up some techniques."

"Well, honestly, I think it's rude." Maya placed her camera carefully back in its pink pouch that was monogrammed with her initials. "I mean, we did you a favor letting you come on our shoot. And you show up an hour late?"

"Oh, relax, Maya," said Abby Tesfay, brushing the sand from her knees as she got to her feet. Pup remembered Abby from his freshman year English class. She'd been transferred out to the smart kids' class at the end of the first semester. He smiled at her gratefully, but she ignored him.

"I *am* relaxed," Maya retorted, reaching up to tighten her thick, lustrous ponytail. "All I'm saying is, it's just kind of annoying that Mr. Hughes asked me to invite some guy who's failing art to come shoot with us. I mean, who fails *art*?"

"Mr. Hughes isn't exactly an easy grader," Abby pointed out. "He gave me a C once because I *very* slightly overexposed an image, even though the composition and everything else was on point."

"That's different. You're in AP. The standards are super high." She turned to Pup. "*You're* in Studio *One*. You guys literally make ceramic bowls and draw flower vases with pastel crayons."

"We didn't make bowls. We made coasters," Pup said.

"Whatever. I'm out of here. I need my coffee." She looped her camera case around her shoulder and huffed away toward the boardwalk with Kim hurrying along behind.

"I really am sorry," Pup said, turning to Abby. "I just overslept."

"Don't worry about it." She folded her tripod under her arm. "This is a photography *club*. Just a fun thing to do outside of school. Those two act like we're photojournalists on the front line of a war or something."

"Yeah," Pup agreed. "Honors program kids are such dicks."

"*I'm* an honors program kid," Abby said. "Please don't overgeneralize."

"Sorry." Pup felt the heat rush to his cheeks.

"You can still get some good shots in this light," she said. "Try using a wide-angle lens, and shoot the sun off-center. See that walkway there?" She pointed to her left, at a circle of sandstone columns beneath which two empty benches looked out at the water. "If you silhouette those columns in your shot, you'll give your viewer something for their eye to latch on to, make the composition more interesting. Make sense?"

"Yeah." Pup smiled at her. "Thank you. Really."

"See? Not all honors kids are dicks." She gave him a little wave, then ran off to catch up with Maya and Kim.

Alone on the beach now, Pup turned his attention to the scenery. The late-spring air was cool and damp, but with the promise of heat later; the fog had already burned off and the sun was so strong on the water that when he looked out toward the horizon his vision filled with black spots. He played around with the controls on the camera, taking some shots of the trees and the sky, the water and the sand, trying to follow Abby's advice and shooting off-center with the sandstone columns on one end of the frame. But, even with her help, it all felt sort of pointless. After all, how many millions of people—people who were actual professional photographers—had already taken pictures of Lake Michigan before him? What was unique about Pup's perspective? The guidelines for the final project, on which his passing or failing depended, were one sentence long: *Create a piece of art that represents your personal aesthetic, using any medium of expression you choose.*

The problem was, Pup didn't *have* a personal aesthetic. He had only signed up for Studio Art because he thought it would be easy, and Intro to Guitar was already full. As for his medium of expression, that had actually been chosen for him, by Mr. Hughes, who had called Pup up to his desk earlier in the week for a conference regarding his terrible grade.

"Pup, when I review your work over the course of the last year," Mr. Hughes had said, opening a large manila folder to glare at the stack of garbage that comprised Pup's Studio One portfolio, "a few things are clear to me. One, you can't draw. Two, you can't paint. Three, you can't sculpt, hew, chisel, stitch, craft, smudge, or cut with a scissors in a straight line."

He'd gotten up then, and unlocked the tall metal cabinet that stood behind his desk. He reached inside and dug out a loaner camera attached to a frayed strap and stamped all over in big letters: PROPERTY OF ALHS.

"Photography is the last remaining mode of artistic expression practiced in Studio One that you have left to attempt," he concluded, "and I certainly hope it works out, because despite what people may say about me, I really *don't* enjoy giving Fs."

"And despite what people may say about *me*," Pup had replied, "I really don't enjoy *getting* Fs."

Mr. Hughes leafed one last time through the various pieces in Pup's portfolio—a smudged, incoherent charcoal self-portrait, a disastrously sloppy needlepoint sailboat, a runny watercolor painting of what was supposed to be a dog but that Mr. Hughes had mistaken for a turtle.

"There's nothing I would love more than to be proven wrong about you," he had said, handing Pup the camera. "So I guess you better get snapping."

Feeling overwhelmed now by his usual sense of dejection when it came to his schoolwork, Pup sat down on a stone bench at the edge of the path that led to the water. The sun was warm on his back and the waves moved in their ceaseless, rhythmic push and pull. Pup leaned his head back and was just beginning to doze off when he was suddenly jerking awake again as a memory that he hadn't known was there dislodged itself from his mind.

He had been to this beach once before.

He was very young, maybe four years old, so his memory was not anything but shards of images and feelings. He was there with his brothers and Annemarie, who'd been left in charge of the boys for the day. Luke would have been thirteen, Pat, eleven. But Annemarie and her friend Andi (whatever happened to Andi? Pup now wondered) had wandered off into the circle of sandstone columns to discuss some teenage-girl thing in private, leaving Luke in charge of the two younger boys. Pup, while playing in the surf, had stepped on the sharp edge of a rock, or a bottle, or a shell, he couldn't remember, and cut open his foot. He'd crumpled to the sand, howling. Luke had come running over and lifted Pup into his arms. He carried Pup to the bench where right this moment he was now sitting, and Patrick had knelt down and examined the wound. Pup could see it clearly: Patrick's dark head bowed over Pup's injury, the white, puckered bottoms of his feet and the blood seeping out and mixing with the sand and water. Pat had declared that the wound could become infected if something wasn't done immediately. He took Pup's little foot into his hands and said, "This works with rattlesnake venom," and then he sucked the blood out of the cut. Pup could remember it so clearly—the feeling of his older brother's lips on the bottom of his foot, the tickling pain, the feeling of relief as Pat had sat back on his heels, spit into the sand, and said, "You're cured," while Luke fell on the sand laughing with delight at the absolutely disgusting thing Pat had just done.

Pup kicked off his shoes, peeled off his socks, and lifted his right foot to his lap. His adult-size foot was plank-like now, practically as long and thin as a child's ski, and sure enough there it was, on the sole of his foot just below the big toe, a thin white scar, shaped like a fishhook. Pup ran his finger over it. It was about an inch long and very faint, nothing more than a razor-thin ridging of white on white, located on a part of his body that he never had cause to look at. He dropped his foot back into the sand and sat back, satisfied. The scar was physical proof that there were still things in his own memory that he had yet to mine; so many ways of bringing Pat back if he could only trigger them in the right way.

4

WHEN PUP GOT HOME, his father was still fast asleep on the couch, while Luke, he assumed, was curled up on the roof ledge sleeping off his hangover. His mother sat at her usual place at the kitchen table, drinking her coffee and penciling carefully in one of her adult coloring books.

"Hi, honey," she said, glancing up at him in surprise as he walked through the back door. "*You're* up early."

"Hey, Mom." Pup drifted over to the fridge. He found some orange juice and poured himself a glass. "I had a school thing. Photography club."

"How wonderful! I didn't know you liked photography."

Pup sipped his juice. There was no point in telling his mom about his failing art grade. Why add to her stress? Besides, one of the perks of having aging parents was that they didn't annoy him about school. It wasn't that Ted and Judy Flanagan didn't care about their youngest son's grades or his future. It was that neither one of them owned a smartphone. They had one joint email account—set up for them by

Annemarie—that could go months without being checked. While his friends' parents got text and email updates for every tardy or detention or plummeting chemistry grade, Pup enjoyed almost complete immunity. If everybody else's parents were helicopter parents, hovering around their children and managing their every activity, Pup's parents were more like space-shuttle parents: watching over him, sure, but from a very far distance, and living, for the most part, on a different planet.

"Do you want some breakfast?" His mom closed her coloring book. "I was just about to make some scrambled eggs."

"Sure, Mom. Thanks."

She got up and began rummaging around the cabinets looking for a skillet, while Pup handed her the carton of eggs from the fridge.

"Hey, Mom," he said. "Have you talked to Luke lately?"

"Luke? Of course I have. He's my son, isn't he?" She cracked an egg into a bowl and tossed the shell in the trash.

"Well, does he seem . . . okay to you?"

"Does he seem *okay*?" She cracked another egg. "Well, he's Luke. So, has he been a little Lukier than normal lately? Well, now that you mention it, I suppose maybe he has." She whirled around suddenly, the shell crushed into her palm. "Why? Is something wrong?"

"No!" Pup handed her the butter. Okay, so she definitely didn't know that Luke and Carrie had broken up. Which meant that none of his oldest sisters knew, either, because Jeanine and Mary and Elizabeth and Noreen were basically a single entity of prying older sisterhood, and anything *they* knew, Pup's mother would soon know too. "He's totally fine."

"Well, then, why did you *ask?*"

"I was just making *conversation*, Mom. Calm down."

"Fine," she said, whisking the eggs with a vigorous arm. "So, how was the party last night?"

"What party?"

"Noreen told me you were going to a party." She dropped a pat of butter into the hot pan and began swirling it around with the edge of her knife. "With that girl Izzy you've been seeing."

"I'm not 'seeing' her," Pup said, slumping down into the nearest kitchen chair. "And she didn't have a party. She just had people over."

"Isn't that what a party *is*? When you have people over?"

"Not really." Pup sighed. "Can you maybe make me some bacon, too?"

"We're out of bacon. I'll make you pork sausages instead." She poured the eggs into the pan. "So you're *not* seeing this Izzy person? Does that mean you two broke up?"

"We did *not* break up." Pup put his head in his hands. If it weren't for the promise of pork sausages, he'd be halfway up the stairs by now. "We were never *together*. We're just friends. Why does Noreen act like she knows my life?"

"Well, maybe I've gotten my facts wrong. It's possible, at my age." She pointed at him with her spatula. "But honey, if something's on your mind, you should tell me. You can *always* tell me if something is bothering you. You know that, right?"

"Yes, I know that," Pup said, even though of course this was not even remotely true. Pup's mom moved very carefully through life these days. She avoided anything that could disrupt the delicate balance of her emotions—she didn't follow politics, didn't go to parties or public events, had abandoned her beloved true-crime shows, didn't drive during rush hour, quit her bowling league because it was too "competitive." When the Cubs had won the World Series, while the rest of the family had gathered inches from the big-screen television in their matching blue T-shirts, Pup's mom went and hid in the bathroom during the late innings, unable to bear the thought of possibly having to watch them lose. And she *most certainly* did not want to know if her children were suffering from anything worse than a mildly rumbling stomach, a problem she could instantly fix with a large plate of scrambled eggs and pork sausages. He could not talk to his mother about his pathetic relationship with Izzy. He could not talk to her about his crappy grades. And most of all, he could not talk to her about Patrick, about how much he missed him, and how bad it got sometimes. Even if he *wanted* to tell her about these things, it wouldn't matter because she wouldn't want to hear them. She just couldn't handle it.

At that moment, Luke himself, glassy eyed and greasy haired, appeared in the doorway with his laptop bag slung over his shoulder.

"Morning," he growled, without meeting Pup's eyes.

"You're just in time for breakfast," said his mom.

"No thanks," Luke said. "I'm running late for study group."

He grabbed a bottle of red Gatorade from the fridge, stuck it in his bag, gave a general wave, and went out the back door.

"Poor boy," Pup's mom said thoughtfully, watching through the screened window as Luke hurried across the backyard and disappeared through the back gate. "He *does* look stressed. It's probably all this business with the bar exam. You know how hard he works."

She picked up a pencil then, and continued to work on a half-finished mandala in her coloring book, swirling with blues and greens and pinks, while Pup ate his breakfast in silence. He already knew what he would find when he went upstairs to put his camera away: the laptop Luke had bought for himself when he'd started law school three years earlier, forgotten, as usual, on the nightstand. And he already knew what he would do when he found it: he would pick up a magazine from the floor and toss it casually over the forgotten computer, so that if their mother happened to go upstairs she wouldn't see it and grow suspicious. Pup had his own suspicions, of course, about Luke's weekend study groups; about his shaking hands and bloodshot eyes and untouched notebooks stacked on the floor next to his bed. He would never ask his brother about it directly, though. He couldn't. That just wasn't the way their family worked.

5

MR. HUGHES WAS A WALKING stereotype of an art teacher. He had graying shoulder-length dreadlocks, a thick pair of black square-framed glasses that he was always tearing off his face to squint more closely at his students' work, and a stubby set of charcoal pencils that he carried around in the breast pocket of his yellow-armpit-stained open-collared shirts. The artsy kids at Lincoln whispered about how legit he was, because he'd had one of his installations displayed at the Museum of Contemporary Art and he'd lived in New York for like ten years.

On Monday morning, as soon as Pup walked into class, Mr. Hughes, who was standing on a ladder hanging a stack of papier-mâché kites from the ceiling, beckoned him over.

"Flanagan. How was your shoot with the photography club?"

"Pretty good." Pup stood next to the ladder, at eye level with Mr. Hughes's tattered Birkenstocks.

Mr. Hughes pointed a kite down at Pup. "You showed *up*, right?"

"Of course." Pup tried not to concentrate on the yellowish-ridged outcroppings of Mr. Hughes's toes. "I mean, I was a few minutes late, but yeah, I was there and I took a bunch of pictures." He unzipped his backpack and pulled out his borrowed camera. "I just need to have them developed."

"Good." Mr. Hughes looped the kite string around an exposed pipe in the ceiling. "Darkroom key is hanging on a hook on the wall behind my desk. Get to work! I want that camera back ASAP, and I want that photo on my desk a week from today!"

"Darkroom?" asked Pup. "But how do I . . . ?"

Mr. Hughes yanked off his glasses and stared down the ladder. "I went over that in the fall, when we did a photography mini-unit for extra credit. Don't you remember?"

"Uh, absolutely," Pup lied. "Of course." Where had he been in the fall? Oh, yes. The Chicago Cubs had won the World Series for the first time in 108 years. For the duration of the playoffs, Pup and the other twenty-six members of his immediate family had squashed together in the front room, wailing over the losses, screaming at the victories, eating vats of queso cheese and spinach dip and drinking inordinate quantities of root beer. The sky itself could have come crashing down all around him, and Pup would still be watching on a loop the replay of Kris Bryant fielding a Michael Martinez grounder and then firing it to Anthony Rizzo for the series-winning final out. How could he have been expected to worry about extra credit at a time like that?

Pup headed over toward Mr. Hughes's desk now, the black camera hanging around his neck like a noose. On the way, he passed Marcus Flood's desk. Marcus, like Pup, was a known slacker, and if there was a shortcut to be had, Marcus was the one who would know about it. Right now, Marcus was whistling contentedly to himself and molding a lump of clay into a one-hitter. "Hey," Pup whispered. "See this camera?"

Marcus stopped whistling and looked up. "Yeah. What about it?"

Pup glanced around to make sure Mr. Hughes was out of earshot. "If I took the film into the one-hour photo at Walgreens, do you think they could develop it for me?"

Marcus burst out laughing.

"Dude, don't you pay attention in this class at *all*? The only way Mr. Hughes will give you credit is if you develop that film in the darkroom. Weren't you there that day he showed us how to use it?"

Of course Pup had been there that day. He just hadn't been 100 percent *listening*. He'd been too busy mentally and emotionally preparing for game three of the NLCS, which was being played the next day in hostile territory—Dodger Stadium—with the series tied one game to one.

"I was there," he said. "I just wasn't . . . you know, *there*."

"I totally understand," Marcus said, reaching up and patting Pup on the shoulder. "You have my sympathies. But you're screwed, my friend."

"Hey," Pup said, forcing a smile, "how hard can it be, right?"

Marcus put the one-hitter to his lips and blew into it, sending a plume of stale breath into Pup's face.

"Famous last words."

Pup left Marcus to complete his illicit pottery project, grabbed the key, and headed out into the hallway. The darkroom, a former utility closet, stood adjacent to the art room; Pup had never actually been inside. He fumbled the key into the lock before realizing it was unlocked already.

"Close the door!" The voice, sharp but embroidered with a soft accent that sounded familiar but that he couldn't quite place, startled Pup so much that he stumbled backward, bumping against a hard surface and sending some metallic-sounding objects crashing to the floor.

"Sorry—I—shit." Pup's eyes adjusted to the weak red light that lent an eerie cast to the tiny space. Standing a few feet away from him was Abby Tesfay, one of the photography club girls.

"You have to be careful in here," she said, turning her back on him now and tending to a counter lined with big plastic jugs of liquid. "There's a lot of super-delicate equipment and Mr. Hughes will kill us if we break any of it."

"Sorry," Pup mumbled, bending down to pick up the plastic bottles and stacks of metal pans he'd knocked over in his idiotic entrance. "I just need to, like, develop this film and then I'll be out of your way."

"Oh, okay." She glanced over her shoulder at him. "Don't you need to rewind it first?"

"Yes," Pup said dumbly. "Of course. I need to rewind it."

Abby leaned against the counter and watched as he flipped the camera around in his hands, fiddling with its various parts.

"Need some help?"

Pup looked at her sheepishly and handed her the camera. She took it, wound a tiny crank on one corner of the machine, and snapped open the back.

"No offense," she said, popping out the roll of film and dropping it into the palm of his hand, "but I can kind of see why you're failing art."

"Thanks," said Pup.

"Do you need me to turn off the safety light?"

"The what?"

"The *safety* light. So you don't ruin your film?"

Pup had a vague recollection of Mr. Hughes explaining light sensitivity, but when he tried to remember the details, all he could see was the beautiful, heaven-sent explosion of bat on ball, and Miggy Montero—pinch hitting in a tie game, eighth inning, two outs, bags jammed, a literal dream come true—rounding the bases, and the Flanagan household shaking to the rafters.

"Um . . ." Pup trailed off.

Abby sighed, reached across him, and snapped off the

light switch. The room was plunged into a darkness so total it felt like stones were pressing on Pup's open eyes.

"*That*," he heard Abby's disembodied voice say, "was the safety light."

With his sense of sight temporarily disabled, Pup felt his other senses heighten. He could hear the thump of his own heart, the soft intake of his breath, the reek of chemicals, and beneath that, faintly, Abby Tesfay's scent, like hand lotion and some sort of flower whose name he didn't know. The darkness was so complete that he had to touch his eyes to double-check that they were, in fact, still open. He wondered if this was what it was like down in the abyssopelagic zones of the world's oceans, those unimaginable depths filled with slimy-skinned alien fish that Patrick had once dreamed of exploring.

"Hope you're not afraid of the dark," Pup joked.

"Actually, I love it." He could sense that Abby was standing right in front of him, even though he couldn't see her. Her voice was a round, floating thing in the darkness, like the echo of a bell. "Where I'm from, nighttime is no joke. It gets so dark at night, you can't even see the mountains."

"Aren't you from Chicago?"

"Not originally. I moved here from Eritrea when I was ten years old. It's a tiny country in the Horn of Africa. Ever heard of it?"

"Of course I've heard of it," Pup said. "Just because I forgot to rewind my film doesn't mean I'm a moron."

"Could you find it on a map?"

"Probably not," he admitted. "But don't take it personally. I came in dead last in Mr. Seton's geography bowl last year. I forgot the capital of the United States."

"Seriously?" Her voice in the darkness was flat and amused. "It's Washington, DC."

"Yes, I *know* that, but I just got mixed up for a second. I mean, it *should* be New York. New York's bigger. Anyway. I'm not good under pressure. There's a reason I'm in mostly low-track classes."

She laughed. "You know, for a country that's all about 'everybody is created equal,' American kids are really obsessed with who's in what academic track. Just because you're in low track doesn't mean anything. I bet you're smarter than you think."

Pup considered this. "Okay," he said. "Want to put that theory to the test?"

"Maybe. How?"

"Teach me how to use all this darkroom stuff. If I pick it up fast, then it'll prove you're right. And if I don't, I'll accept my failing art grade and leave you alone."

There was a short silence before Abby's voice floated out of the darkness. "All right. Deal." He felt her fingers brush his palm and grab back the roll from his hand.

"What I'm doing now," she narrated, "is removing the film from its cartridge. Then we have to load it onto the reel. Where are your hands? Wave them around or something so I can find them."

Pup reached out and began wiggling his fingers. He felt a whizzing of air as Abby swept her own hands back and forth to find his. Finally, her fingers caught his wrists, then moved upward so that she could pull his hands over to the reel.

"I'm going to guide your hands to load the film," she said. "If you don't know how to do this part, you won't be able to do the rest."

He felt his fingers, guided by hers, feed the tongue of the film through a round thing.

"Okay," she said, letting go, "now we place it inside the developing tank and screw on the lid."

He heard movement, plastic on plastic, a twisting.

"You can turn the lights on now."

Pup complied, fumbling his large, rangy hands over the walls until he found the switch.

For the rest of the period, Abby explained to him the contents of each of the jugs that floated in the water-filled sink—the developer, the stop bath, the fixer. Eventually her patient explanations poked awake some memories in his brain of the tutorial Mr. Hughes had given in the fall. When Pup had finished pouring and agitating the chemicals, the negatives were ready to hang. On the wall behind the counter was a little clothesline-looking thing, where Abby's negatives already hung drying from little hooks. Pup carefully opened the developing tank, and as he began to hang his negatives beside hers, he saw that the images from Albion Beach, as if by magic, appeared on the glossy little rectangles.

"Thanks for the advice," he said, leaning forward to observe the negative images of the water and the benches and the sandstone columns. "About the composition and the wide-angle lens. These don't actually look terrible."

"It will be easier to tell if you've got anything good once you enlarge them." She pressed in next to him to see his work. "Hey—this is interesting. What is this?"

She was pointing at the final negative, the only one he hadn't taken on the beach, of Luke passed out on the roof.

"Oh, that?" Pup turned his body a little to block the image from her sight line. The last thing he needed was for the girls of photography club to think he came from some crazy dysfunctional family where drunk people slept on roofs and chugged protein shakes to conjure the spirit of their dead brother. "That's nothing. I took that one by accident."

She looked at him like she was going to say something, but the bell rang before she could.

"Hey—thanks again," Pup said as they moved to gather up their stuff.

"Just remember, if you end up not failing art, you owe me one."

With a little wave, she opened the door and stepped out into the blinding light of the hallway, disappearing into the commotion of the passing period.

6

OUTSIDE THE ART ROOM, Izzy stood waiting for Pup, scrolling through her phone in a jean skirt and Vans.

"Hey," she said, sticking her phone in her back pocket when she saw him coming. "Who was *that*?"

"Just this girl I know," Pup said, falling in step beside her as they headed toward the counseling office. "She was helping me with my photography project."

"She's really pretty."

"Oh." He glanced back to where Abby was just turning down toward the cafeteria. "Yeah, I guess she is."

"You should invite her to my house this weekend. I'm having people over."

"Wait. It's Monday and we're already talking about the weekend?"

"You know me, I always get like this when the weather warms up." She twisted her hair into a bun as they walked, and Pup tried not to stare at her bare neck, the hollow of collarbone that disappeared into her T-shirt. "Saturday. My mom said it was fine. It's her turn to host book club, so she and her friends will be too busy chugging wine upstairs to pay attention to what we're doing in the basement. Brody might even be able to sneak in some beer."

"Wait a second." Pup stopped short, and a pair of freshman girls slammed into the back of him. "You're not just trying to get me to chaperone for you again, are you? Because to be honest—"

"Of course not!" Izzy looked at him, offended. "That's why I'm saying you should *invite* somebody. It doesn't have to be the photography girl. It could be anyone! You should try getting out there more, you know? Asking girls to hang out. That way, we could go on double dates!"

Pup blinked. The idea of sitting at Chili's across from Izzy and Brody, watching as they sucked face between bites of their Awesome Blossom, was a nightmare to which he would never subject himself, let alone an innocent bystander like Abby Tesfay.

"We'll see," he said vaguely.

They had arrived at the counseling office. Mrs. Schmidt, phone cradled between chin and shoulder, gave them a familiar wave as they passed her desk and headed back toward the tiny office at the end of the hallway that was framed with blinking holiday lights all year round.

It was here in this office that Pup had first laid eyes on Izzy, on a November afternoon during his freshman year.

His counselor had placed Pup in a group for bereaved students that met once a month during their lunch period. The group was led by Mrs. Barrera, the school social worker. She was the type of educator who spoke in a talk-whisper, spiced up her outfits with festive seasonal scarves, and kept a candy dish on her desk filled with Smarties. Her office walls were hung with photographs of puppies sleeping in flower pots and kittens rolling around in pumpkin patches, and she had boxes of tissues set up all over the place, like a funeral home. There were two springy, worn-in couches lining the office walls, and when Pup walked in with his bagged lunch and his carton of chocolate milk that afternoon, he saw five strangers sprawled across these couches, opening their lunches and avoiding each other's eyes. There was only one couch space left, next to a small, pale girl with frizzy hair tamed into a long braid. Her eyes—they were a pebbly green—flicked to his and then flicked away again as he walked over and sat down next to her. She smelled, pleasantly, like the checkout line at Target: Altoids, dryer sheets, and that round strawberry lip balm all the girls in school carried in their backpacks.

"Okay!" Mrs. Barrera had said, clapping her hands together and perching on a wheelie chair with her cup of Greek yogurt and can of Diet Coke. "Welcome to Bereavement Group, everyone! My goal for this year is to create a safe space to sort through our feelings of loss and to build a community of peers who have been through similar experiences!

Here, we will strive to understand that loss is not something a person should get *over*, but instead, get *through*. I look forward to getting to know each and every one of you so that we can help you get *through* . . . together! With that being said, why don't we start today by going around and introducing ourselves?"

Nobody said anything. After a sufficiently awkward pause during which everyone listened to each other's chewing, Mrs. Barrera soldiered on.

"Okay, then! I'll go first! My name is Lane Barrera. I'm married with two living sons, and I've been a school social worker for ten years! Five years ago, I lost my two-month-old son, Joshua, to Sudden Infant Death Syndrome. But with the help of therapy and time, I've managed to find happiness and joy again, and now I hope to channel my own grief into helping others who are suffering as well!"

Silence.

"Okay!" Mrs. Barrera pressed on, clutching her Diet Coke. Her eyes ranged around the small group of kids slumped around her. "Why don't we begin with you?" She pointed at a kid who'd manspread himself on the couch and had just finished eating a large green apple—core, stem, seeds, and all. He was lunky and black haired, with a faint mustache and a big pair of scuffed, untied high-tops.

"Uh," he said. "What do you want me to say?"

"Well, your name is a good place to start. And maybe tell

us who you've lost. And any other outside interests you might have!"

"Okay." The kid shrugged. "Here goes: Sam. Dad. Suicide."

"Wait," interrupted a trembling girl with about twelve rings on her bitten fingers. "Your outside interest is *suicide*?"

"No," Sam said. "I'm telling you how my dad died."

"Oh!" exclaimed Mrs. Barrera, twirling her spoon through her yogurt. "It's not necessary to explain *how* your loved one—"

But it worked. Sam's deadpan delivery of such a terrible tragedy was so jarring that all six kids, including Sam, burst out laughing. Mrs. Barrera looked horrified for a second, and then relieved. Sam Dad Suicide had broken the ice. Everyone took turns introducing themselves in the same way: and that's how, during that first session of Bereavement Group—or the Pity Party, as they would soon rename themselves—Pup met Kailyn Mom Drugs, Dakota Dad Car Accident, Raheem Mom Breast Cancer, and finally, Izzy Brother Leukemia. The little French-braided girl, it turned out, was the only other person besides Pup who'd also lost a sibling. When it was his turn to speak, he cleared his throat to keep it from cracking. "Pup," he said, looking down at the green squares of linoleum that checkered the counseling office floor. "Brother. Meningitis."

A little later that week, he and Izzy ran into each other in the hallway after last bell.

"Hey!" She smiled at him and lifted a small hand in the air. "Dead-brother high fives!"

Pup, stricken, looked at her hand and didn't move.

"Sorry," she said, her hand falling back to her side. "That was a terrible joke. How long has it been for you?"

"A month," said Pup.

"Oh. God. Sorry. Definitely too soon. The first year is the absolute worst. I'm in year two. It gets easier, I promise."

"I hope so," Pup said.

"We should hang out," Izzy said, looking him up and down in the same way his sister Jeanine often did, as if he were a DIY project she just couldn't wait to start rearranging. "It would be nice to spend time with somebody who *gets* it. People can act so awkward when you have a dead brother. Either they ignore you—"

"Or they act like nothing happened—"

"Or they grab you like this"—she touched his arm for the very first time—"and say, in this urgent whisper, 'How are you *dooo-ing*?'"

"'You're in my thoughts and *pray*-yers, and I am—'" And here, they shouted together, almost joyfully, "'SO SORRY FOR YOUR LOSS!'"

It was at that moment Pup decided he and Izzy were meant to be. They shared a common pain that twisted through their lives, piercing everything it touched. By the end of the semester they were best friends, and Pup never stopped hoping that one day they'd be more than that. At least until Brody Krueger had come along at the beginning of junior year, with his faux California accent and his dirty fingernails, and stolen her away. Pup used to think that his loyalty to Izzy, his willingness to wait for her, showed that he was romantic, patient, true to his heart. Lately, though, he was beginning to feel more like one of those male deep-sea anglerfish Patrick had once studied: a thin, hideous creature, who, once it found its female mate, held on and refused to let go.

"Hey, Kailyn," Dakota Dad Car Accident was saying now as Pup and Izzy walked into Mrs. Barrera's office. "I brought you a *slice* of pizza."

"STOP!" yelled Kailyn Mom Drugs, putting her hands over her ears.

"Come on," Dakota said, holding a wedge of pizza on a Styrofoam plate under her nose. "It's so good. I even got it with your favorite topping: *moist cutlets* of pepperoni!"

"STOP IT!"

"Here," he continued, a look of faux concern on his face. "Take a napkin. I wouldn't want you to get any pizza sauce on your *slacks*."

"I'm literally going to die!" Kailyn wailed. "Mrs. Barrera, make him stop!"

"Okay, okay, Dakota," intervened their teacher, placing a

hand between them. "That's enough."

Dakota grinned at her and took an enormous bite of pizza while Kailyn plucked a Skittle from the bag she'd just opened and threw it at him. Everybody else settled into their seats. Their group had been together for a long time now, and they all knew the routine: once Dakota Dad Car Accident good-naturedly tortured Kailyn Mom Drugs about her word aversions, the session could begin.

"Welcome to springtime, everyone!" Mrs. Barrera clapped her hands together and sat down in her office chair. "May is one of my favorite months of the year—it's a time of rebirth, of renewal, of budding leaves and blooming flowers! But! For those of us who are bereaved, it can be a difficult time as well. All this life growing around us can remind us of what we've lost." She sipped some Diet Coke and consulted her little calendar book. "Kailyn, I'm noticing you had a recent red-alert day. Talk us through your mom's birthday. What were your positives? What were your setbacks? How did you try to strike a balance between honoring her memory and exercising your own self-care?"

Kailyn Mom Drugs was a nervous girl, prone to shrieking and nail-biting. But now that she'd recovered from Dakota's word assault, she seemed uncharacteristically calm.

"Honestly, guys?" She looked around at the group, tossing a yellow Skittle into her mouth. "It was actually a great day."

"How wonderful!" Mrs. Barrera clapped her hands

together again. "Tell us more!"

"Well, when I woke up on the morning of her birthday, it was pouring rain, and it kept raining all day long. But then, just when school was getting out, the weather cleared and the sun came out. So I was walking home, just about to pass my mom's hair salon, and all of a sudden I looked up and there was this gigantic rainbow in the sky. Biggest one I've ever seen. It looked like a *cartoon* rainbow, it was so perfect."

"I remember that!" Sam exclaimed. "Me and my girlfriend were out by the gym dumpsters trying to—never mind, it's not important—but we totally saw that rainbow!"

"Here's the thing," Kailyn explained. "My mom *loved* rainbows. She was obsessed with them. So to see this big fat perfect rainbow at *her* hair salon on *her* birthday . . . I mean, could it *get* any clearer than that? She was reaching out to say hello. To tell me she was okay."

As Pup listened to Kailyn's story, he thought of all the times he had waited and willed and prayed for just such a sign from Patrick. Not a rainbow, of course. But something. He would know it when he saw it. But it had never arrived, and now he didn't believe in signs. He tried to catch Izzy's attention to share an eye-roll, but she didn't look at him. She was listening to Kailyn, rapt.

"That's happened to me before," said Sam, placing his Capri Sun on the floor near his untied shoes. "The sign thing. My dad was the one who introduced me to thrash metal, and last year, I was having a really bad day, and I was waiting at the bus stop feeling like shit when this car pulled up to the red light. All the windows were down, and the driver was blasting 'Black Dawn' by this band called Dethrone. Anybody ever heard of them?"

They all looked at Sam blankly.

"Exactly! They were this insanely obscure Finnish metal band from the eighties. *Nobody's* ever heard of them!" Sam shook his head wonderingly. "Thing is, though, they were my dad's favorite band. I mean, he *learned how to speak conversational Finnish* just so he could understand their lyrics. And here's what's even *crazier*: 'Black Dawn' was his favorite song."

"Whoa," said Dakota.

"Dude, you guys remember that home game we had at the beginning of the year against Lane Tech?" Raheem Mom Breast Cancer was sitting up excitedly, his ham sandwich balanced on his knee. "The one we won twenty-one to three?"

Of course everyone remembered. Raheem Mom Breast Cancer was the celebrity member of the Pity Party, not just because he was a senior but also because he was the star running back of the Lincoln Lions.

"Well, I was standing on the sideline, just before the coin toss. And all of a sudden I get this overpowering smell of *perfume*. And not just any perfume, either." He looked around. "It was Donna Karan Cashmere Mist. *My mom's favorite perfume*. I swear to god, y'all: she was *there*, standing right next to me, on the sidelines that day."

"Didn't you score, like, three touchdowns in that game?" asked Dakota.

"Two," said Raheem. "But I also ran for three hundred yards. Broke the single-game rushing record for ALHS." He clasped his hands together and looked up at the particleboard ceiling. "And don't think I don't know who to thank for that."

Pup put a handful of pretzels in his mouth. His mom had packed them in a plastic baggie and now they kind of tasted like plastic too. He tried to make eyes at Izzy again, but she was opening her mouth to speak.

"I have dreams," she said. "About Teddy. Do you guys have dreams?"

"Totally," said Dakota.

"Absolutely," said Mrs. Barrera.

"All the time," said Kailyn.

"In the dreams where he's sick," she went on, "I wake up and right away I remember that he's gone. But in the dreams where he's still healthy, when I wake up, it's like I'm not alone in the room. I *feel* him. Just as sure as if he's standing there. I can practically hear him breathing."

"Oh, I feel Joshua all the time," said Mrs. Barrera. "Every time I look into the face of a baby, I can practically feel his weight in my arms."

Pup finished his pretzels and reached into his lunch bag

for his peanut butter sandwich. When he saw that his mother had made it on wheat bread, he sighed wearily.

"Pup?"

"Huh?" He looked up from his sandwich to find that everyone in the Pity Party was staring at him.

"Were you saying something?" Mrs. Barrera smiled at him encouragingly. "Has it happened to you, too? Have you even seen a sign?"

"No." He bit into his sandwich.

"None?" Mrs. Barrera's smile wilted just the tiniest bit.

"Nope."

An awkward silence filled the office.

"Don't sweat it, Pup," Raheem finally said. "It's going to happen when you least expect it."

"Yeah. When you most need it."

"When you really start to listen."

"And even if it doesn't," added Mrs. Barrera, "that's perfectly *fine* and perfectly *normal*, too. Everyone's experience of grief and loss is different."

Pup took another bite of his soggy sandwich and said nothing. What he *wanted* to say was that he wished everyone would stop calling it "loss." When you lose something, there's a chance you might find it again. Keys, a missing homework assignment, a few extra pounds. But Pup would never find Patrick. He couldn't feel him anywhere. There was no rainbow, no old familiar song, no ghostly scent floating in the air.

Pup had never even seen his brother in a dream. He finished his peanut butter sandwich in silence, knowing it would hurt everyone's feelings if he just told them the truth: that Patrick wasn't lost. He was just dead.

7

WHEN PUP ARRIVED AT Izzy's party on Saturday night, he walked in through the unlocked back door, as he always did, and came upon a bunch of ladies sitting on high stools around the kitchen island, drinking white wine from glasses that were basically goldfish bowls on stems. Spread before them were a couple of buckets with more wine arranged on ice, plus a tray of cheese cubes, grapes, and an assortment of crackers.

As he pushed the handle and the door squeaked closed behind him, all the ladies' faces swiveled in his direction and Pup cursed himself for forgetting about the book club. If he had only remembered, he could have texted Izzy to let him in through the front door so he could go down to the basement undetected. Pup knew from his experience with his oldest sisters' friends that when groups of forty-something women got together and drank wine, they always wanted to engage him in some weird conversation that was part flirtatious, part mocking, and all around awkward, at least for him.

"Pup!" He barely recognized Izzy's mother, who was wearing a floral-print top, big hoop earrings, and an actual smile. The Mrs. Douglass *he* knew dressed in snappy black power suits, had a mouth permanently zipped shut in a straight line, and had two interests in life: the real estate market and her daughter's grade point average.

"Hi, Mrs. Douglass," he said.

"Ladies," she said, fanning her arms out theatrically as if she were a magician's assistant and Pup was the magic trick, "*this* is the very boy I was just telling you about."

"The chaperone?" A lady in a pink leather jacket up-and-downed him as she raked a Triscuit through a cheese ball.

"Yep." She turned to her friends in that dismissive way adults have of forgetting you're there when they're not directly speaking to you. "Pup's been Izzy's best friend ever since freshman year. They met in a bereavement group at the school. Pup lost a brother too. He caught meningitis when he was away at college. Just terrible. But it's been so wonderful for the two of them to have each other, to have someone who *understands.*"

The ladies all nodded, suddenly very serious. Several of them murmured, "Sorry for your loss."

"And now, poor Pup is the only thing standing in the way between my daughter's virginity and the pawing hands of her fool boyfriend."

"Oh, Caroline." Cheeseball Lady stuffed the Triscuit in

55

her mouth. "Don't you get that if Isabelle really wants to have sex with her fool boyfriend, she's going to find a way, and there's nothing that you, or this adorable ginger right here, can do about it?" She peered at Pup over the rim of her wineglass. "You *are* adorable, you know," she said. "What's your *waist* circumference? You're so—so *lithe*!"

"Kendra, *don't* call him a ginger."

"What's wrong with 'ginger'?"

"It's—well, not racist. That wouldn't be the right word. But it certainly isn't nice."

"I'm sorry, honey," Cheeseball said to Pup. She crossed one tightly jeaned leg over the other and poked his thigh with the toe of her sandal. "Did I hurt your feelings?"

"Uh." Pup looked down at her toe. "No?"

"Good." Her voice had gone all husky, and the other ladies were stifling laughs and winking at each other. "What's your name, anyway?"

"Pup," said Pup.

"Pulp?"

"Pup."

"Pip?"

"*Pup.*"

"Okay. *Pup.* Tell me, Pup, have you ever read a little novel called *Madame Bovary*?"

Pup shook his head. "Can't say that I have."

"Pup's not much of a reader," said Mrs. Douglass, which,

though true, he thought was kind of unnecessary.

"Well, that's all right, honey. I don't think anyone in our book club is either. We were bad little girls"—here, she dragged her toe farther up his leg, prompting more helpless snickering—"and we didn't do our homework. So now, because we can't talk about *Madame Bovary*, we need something else to talk about instead."

"Like Isabelle and Brody," volunteered the lady with the super-long nails.

"Like Isabelle and Brody. So. Don't *you* think, Pup—and I know this is hard for you to hear, Caroline—but don't *you* think that if Isabelle wants to do the horizontal mamba with Brody, she's going to find a way to *do* it?"

"Horizontal mamba!" shrieked one of the ladies, fanning herself with a bar napkin. "Did she just say *horizontal mamba*?"

"You don't need to answer that, Pup," said Mrs. Douglass, giving him a dignified look and placing a protective hand on his arm.

"Kendra's right, though," said another woman, sipping deeply from her glass. "And what's wrong with it, honestly? I mean, I know, Caroline, she's your *daughter*. And she's only sixteen. But jeez, don't you guys remember *passion*?" Her voice had taken on that faraway quality when adults start reminiscing. "The *desperation*? The not being able to wait even one more *second*? You'd do it anywhere, anytime you got the chance! The forest preserve. The beach. The hall closet at some party."

"The laundry room," sighed Long Nails.

"The last shower on the right in our freshman dorm." Cheeseball smiled.

"Mm-hmm. Now it's strictly missionary, under the covers, don't even bother to take your socks off, *if* neither one of you has an early meeting in the morning."

Pup stood there uncomfortably. They had *definitely* forgotten he was there.

"I *do* remember that passion," Mrs. Douglass said, plucking a grape from its stem. "And I get it. But it's like Missy says, this is my *daughter* we're talking about here. And I don't want to leave them alone together for even five minutes."

"Five minutes?" Long Nails said. "Hell, it only takes Larry two!" They all began screeching with laughter then, and Pup, seeing his chance, fled toward the basement.

Padding down the carpeted basement stairs, Pup discovered Izzy and Brody squashed up together on one side of the couch and a very surly looking Julissa Jones on the other. Julissa was Izzy's sort-of friend; they studied together sometimes, but overall Izzy mostly complained about Julissa: how she would quibble with their AP Euro teacher, Mr. Pinski, over half of a percentage point. How she would peek over at your paper to see how you did on tests, and if you did worse than she did, how she would ask you, innocently, what grade you got, just so she could gloat. How she had once stormed out of a study group, declaring, "I can't even *deal* with people who don't understand the underpinnings of the French Revolution." Julissa's signature look was a cool pair of green-framed glasses and a rotating collection of snarky graphic tees. For tonight, she had chosen one that read simply

NOPE

in huge letters across the chest. It was a message that perfectly complemented her scowl and her tightly crossed arms.

Technically, when Izzy had invited Pup over to her house, she hadn't been lying. Technically, four people *was* a party, at least according to his mother's definition. But in reality, it was less a party and more like the double date she'd been threatening to arrange. Which in a way was worse than if she'd come right out and asked Pup to chaperone her hookup sessions with Brody. Izzy was trying to distract Pup, to pawn him off on some other girl. On any girl at all, really, because if she'd thought about it for even one minute, she would have realized that Pup Flanagan and Julissa Jones were the world's most incompatible humans.

Brody, as it turned out, had succeeded in sneaking beer into the basement. Pup was tempted to grab one from the twelve-pack Izzy had hidden underneath their jackets in case Mrs. Douglass came downstairs; after all, everybody else already had a can in hand, and beer, he'd been told, could be very useful at making unbearably awkward situations slightly more bearable. But seeing Luke stumble home with black eyes and ripped shirt collars and puke on his clothes enough times had soured Pup on drinking for good. When Brody offered him a bottle, he waved it away.

"More for me," Brody said. He shrugged, then belched loudly, causing Izzy to dissolve into giggles, which annoyed Pup because up until seven months ago, he'd never seen Izzy giggle in his life, *especially* not at disgusting bodily sounds.

They turned back to the television, some reality dating show whose contestants looked only slightly less miserable than Julissa did. Pup sat down next to her, because it was the only open spot left on the couch, prompting Julissa to scrunch herself up in a protective ball as if Pup really *was* an anglerfish—bulgy eyed, slimy skinned, heinous.

Meanwhile, Izzy and Brody immediately started kissing. Pup pulled out his cracked phone, the crutch he used whenever he wanted to pretend that whatever unpleasant thing that was happening nearby was not happening. But Julissa was a bit more assertive.

"Hey!" She picked up a couch cushion and threw it at the striped blanket they were beginning to pull over themselves. "You perverts need to cool it. There are other people in the room."

"Sorry." Izzy pushed the blanket away and sheepishly began fixing her disheveled clothes. "I forgot." She glanced at Pup, an apology in her eyes. "Do you guys want to play a game or something?"

"Yeah." Julissa took a swig of her beer. "Like what?"

"Well, I think we have Scrabble. Apples to Apples. And maybe Monopoly." She started to get up and go over to the shelf where the Douglasses kept their board games.

"No," Julissa said. "Not a game like *that*. Like, a *party* game."

Brody, who'd been staring with his mouth half open in resting dumb-face, suddenly looked intrigued.

"Yeah," he said slowly, catching Julissa's meaning. "A *party* game."

"What's a party game?" Izzy looked genuinely puzzled.

"You know. Seven Minutes in Heaven. Spin the Bottle. That kind of thing."

"What are we, twelve?"

"Wait, Iz." Brody had encircled Izzy's wrist with his thumb and forefinger. Pup *hated* when he did that. Like Izzy was a little child. Or Brody's property. "I think it could be kind of fun. What do you think, Flanagan? Spin the Bottle? Are you ready for your first kiss or what?"

Pup flamed red. "I've kissed a girl before, asshole."

"When?"

"None of your business." He wasn't lying: He *had* kissed a girl before. Kelley Spear. When he was twelve. Playing Spin the Bottle. But Brody didn't need to know this.

"Well, I think it's a *great* idea," Julissa said. She was already arranging herself cross-legged on the floor, draining her beer so they'd have an empty bottle to spin.

"Me too," Brody said, leaping to the floor in a show of energy he rarely displayed.

"I don't know," said Izzy.

"Yeah," Pup agreed. "We're not in junior high anymore. My vote is for Scrabble."

"Mine too." Izzy shot him a grateful smile.

"Come *on*, you guys," Julissa said. "We'll play one round. And if it gets weird, for anybody, at any time, we'll have a safe word. If you call out the safe word, game's over, no questions asked."

"What's the safe word?" Izzy had gravitated over to Brody and joined the other two on the floor; it was only Pup still holding out on the couch.

"Let's pick something from AP Euro," said Julissa. "AP exams are next week. How about the Defenestration of Prague?"

"The *what*?"

"It was this incident in 1600s central Europe that led to the Thirty Years' War."

Brody and Pup looked at her blankly.

"To defenestrate someone is to throw them out a window."

"Fine," Brody said. "Whatever. 'Defenestrate' is the safe word. I have another ground rule too. As far as same-sex kissing: I'm open-minded and everything, but I am *not* kissing Flanagan. But you two girls, if you land on each other, feel free to go for it." His mouth twisted up into a sleazy grin. Pup noticed a poppy seed wedged between his two front teeth.

Julissa shrugged. "I'm game for whatever."

"I think I need another beer," said Izzy.

Brody volunteered to go first. He placed Julissa's empty beer on the floor and gave it a good spin. It came to a stop pointing directly at Izzy. She smiled and sat up a little straighter.

"Well, this should be easy," Brody said. He leaned across the circle and shoved his tongue down Izzy's throat. Pup closed his eyes until it was over.

"Okay," Julissa said. "My turn." She spun the bottle. When Izzy saw where it landed, the color drained from her cheeks.

"I guess it's your lucky day," Izzy said to Brody. "Two girls in one night."

"Just like the *Today* show feared," said Pup. "A teenage sex party."

"Yeah," Izzy joked, though she wasn't laughing. "And my poor mom is upstairs, drinking wine and discussing *Madame Bovary* like it's all under control down here."

"Pretty sure they're not discussing *Madame Bovary*," Pup said, though no one was paying attention to him.

"Sorry, Iz," Julissa said, without a hint of actual apology in her voice. "I promise it will just be for a quick second."

"It's just part of the game, babe." Brody leaned over to squeeze Izzy's shoulder. "Cool?"

"Fine. I guess." She shook him off and looked away, hugging her knees.

Julissa dropped to all fours and crawled across the circle toward Brody. Pup couldn't see too well because Julissa's butt was in his face, but Izzy, who was sitting next to Brody, had a full view if she chose to look. Instead, she kept her eyes trained on her knees while Julissa put her hands on the carpet in front of Brody's crossed legs, inclined her face, leaned in slowly, and kissed him on the lips. She kept her promise, and only kissed him for a second. But it was a long second.

"That wasn't so bad, babe," Brody was saying now, his mouth glistening with Julissa's lip gloss. "Was it?"

Izzy ignored him and picked up the bottle. "Now it's *my* turn," she said, and gave the bottle a vicious spin as Brody began to chant. "Ju-*liss*-a! Ju-*liss*-a!"

But it didn't land on Julissa, as Brody had hoped.

It landed on Pup.

"Well, we *are* best friends," Izzy said, raising an eyebrow at him and laughing a little nervously. "Not a big deal, right?"

Pup forced himself to laugh, too. "Not at all," he managed to mumble.

So here it was: the moment he had been dreaming of since that November afternoon back in freshman year. But he had never wanted it like this. Being forced into it, with two other laughing sets of eyes watching, as if it were all some elaborate joke.

Izzy took another sip of beer and licked her lips. She paused a moment, setting her jaw. Once, in the cafeteria, Pup had dared her to squirt a whole packet of mayonnaise into her mouth. She had taken the dare, and the look on her face before she squeezed was the same look on her face now.

"Ready?"

Pup nodded. He couldn't speak.

Izzy put her beer down, brushed her hair back from her eyes, and leaned across the circle. She kneeled in front of Pup, put a hand on each of his shoulders, and kissed him, gently, on the lips. It was one second, two seconds, three. It was freshman year sitting next to her for the first time at the Pity Party; it was sophomore year homecoming, her showing up at his house in a yellow dress, pinning a matching bouton-niere to his hand-me-down blazer that had once belonged to Patrick; it was the beginning of junior year just before she'd met Brody and changed and forgotten him; it was her French braids and her freckle-dusted shoulders, her marble-white skin, the mole on the divot of her collarbone, her laughter, the seaweed smell of her hair that summer weekend he'd spent up at her grandpa's cottage on Fox Lake.

She pulled away and sat back on her heels. She looked at his face, in his eyes, and finally saw clearly the thing she had missed for nearly three years. And Pup knew, by the pitying look on her face as this understanding dawned on her, that no matter how much he wished it were different, he and Izzy Douglass would never be anything more than friends.

"Dude," Brody said, bursting into laughter, "your face is so red I think your *zits* are blushing."

"*Defenestrate*," whispered Izzy.

LINE:

a mark made by a pointed object;
a moving point

8

SUNDAYS IN THE FLANAGAN HOUSEHOLD always began and ended in the same way. In the morning, Pup's mom went around the house trying to get somebody to go to mass with her, and everybody made some excuse as to why they couldn't. Exasperated and huffy, Judy Flanagan would eventually give up and go slamming out the door in her white dress flats and matching purse, muttering about the state of her family's souls, with Pup's dad calling after her from the couch: "Pray for us, hun!" An hour or so later she came home in a much better mood, filled with the holy word of god and the neighborhood gossip she'd picked up in the vestibule after the service, and started making sauce.

In the evening, all the siblings came over, along with their spouses and kids, for Sunday dinner. Pup's mother always made the same thing: ten pounds of spaghetti Bolognese, a tossed salad in the gigantic wooden bowl she'd gotten from her great-aunt as a wedding gift, and about twelve loaves of garlic bread. The Flanagans weren't Italian, but pasta was the cheapest food you could get to feed a small army of off-spring. Plus, Pup's mom had learned how to make the sauce from her childhood neighbor, Mrs. Tagliaferri, who'd grown up in the Apennine mountains of northern Italy and, so the story went, had hired Pup's teenage mom one summer to help slaughter chickens in her backyard coop, paying her not with money but with recipes.

The dining room in Pup's house was filled almost wall-to-wall with a giant wooden slab of a table lined with long benches that, if you really crammed, could fit everyone in the family except for a handful of the youngest kids, who ate their dinners in adults' laps or at a card table in the kitchen. It was a tight squeeze, but nobody minded, because the Flanagans were the type of family who believed in togetherness. All twenty-five of the Flanagan children and grandchildren lived within the same pizza delivery zone, a two-mile radius that fanned out around the central point of their house. This meant that in Flanland—which was what Carrie had nicknamed their neighborhood way back when she'd first started dating Luke—you were expected to spend a *lot* of time with your family, whether you wanted to or not. Pup never understood why people got all paranoid about drones and government surveillance. That was his normal life. Dozens of pale blue eyes, all the same shade and sprung from the same gene pool, followed him wherever he went. One time, he'd been walking down the street and sneezed, and his brother-in-law Mike called out "Bless you, Pup!" from a passing car. The first and only time he'd ever tried smoking a cigarette, standing in the alley behind the 7-Eleven with his buddies Robbie and Jeremy and a pack of Kool Milds stolen from Jeremy's aunt, Pup barely had a chance to take his first-ever puff before his sister Mary had whizzed by on her bike and, without even slowing down, reached out and plucked it from his mouth.

Sunday dinners were the cornerstone of Flanland life. Work schedules and vacations were planned around them. Pup's sister Noreen had famously shown up to Sunday dinner one day after giving birth to her third child. These meals were loud, they were chaotic, and they were sacred. If you were going to miss one, you had better have a good reason—and in his almost seventeen years of life, Pup never had. But on the Sunday after Izzy's "party," Luke, without sending out so much as a vague explanatory text, didn't show up.

His absence was noticed by all, but openly discussed by none. It was not brought up except in whispered one-on-one conversations between the siblings and spouses as they helped set the table or corralled their children: *Anybody seen Luke? Somebody call him. Maybe he's studying. He's got the bar exam coming up in, what, six weeks? Yeah, and I'll be glad when it's over. He has been so prickly lately. You can't talk to him about anything. Poor Carrie, having to put up with him for all these years. Hey, somebody text her—she'll know where he is. No, she works at the restaurant on Sundays. Quiet, quiet—here comes Mom.*

Throughout the meal, the family stuck to its favorite feel-good topic: the glorious achievements of Pup's nephew, Declan. Declan was Pup's oldest sister Jeanine's oldest son, and he was actually *older* than Pup by two months and five days. They were in the same grade at Lincoln, though few people ever connected the two of them, and why would they? Declan was effortlessly athletic, smart, handsome, and popular. Not only that, scouts from several prestigious universities were already recruiting Dec to play college basketball. He'd been a starter on Lincoln's varsity team since freshman year, when Pup had warmed the bench for the B team before being cut during sophomore JV tryouts. Declan had received a brand-new car for his sixteenth birthday, while Pup was lucky if his parents let him borrow their boat-length sedan to drive three blocks to the gas station for the occasional Snickers bar. One of Declan's favorite things to do when he saw Pup in the hallways at school was to call out, "Hey, Uncle Pup!" which always got a laugh from his teammates and hot girlfriend, Muriel. It made Pup furious, but there was nothing he could do about it, because he *was* Declan's uncle, ridiculous as it seemed.

That Sunday, Jeanine took the floor as soon as the pasta was doled out. "I hate to brag about my kids," she began, which, as everyone in the family knew, was her standard line before she started bragging about her kids, "but as you know, we've always told Dec that he's a scholar-athlete, and *not* an athlete-scholar. Academics always come first. And clearly, he's been listening."

"Mom," Declan protested weakly, but he knew it was pointless because once Jeanine got going there was no stopping her.

The rest of the family waited politely as she looked around the massive table filled with plates heaped with steaming spaghetti, and made sure everyone was paying attention before she unfurled her news.

"We received a call from Georgetown University on Friday," Jeanine said finally, smiling adoringly at her oldest son. "Dec? Do you want to tell them?"

"*Mom*," Dec said. "Come on." Pup rolled his eyes across the table at Annemarie. She winked back at him. They weren't fooled: Declan liked to play the humility card, but they both knew he was loving this.

"Go on!" chirped Jeanine. "If you can't brag to your family, who *can* you brag to?"

Across the table, Annemarie caught Pup's eye and mouthed, *Everybody.*

"Okay," said Dec at last, now that the suspense had reached peak levels. "I got offered a scholarship. A *full* scholarship." He smiled then, baring his perfectly straight white teeth, which had recently emerged from several years of expensive orthodontics to reveal a megawatt smile just ready and waiting for the ESPN cameras. Pup subtly moved a hand to cover his own overbite. *Damn, Pup*, his brother-in-law Matthew had once observed. *With teeth like those, you could eat a head of lettuce through a tennis racket!*

"It's nothing formal, yet," Dec said after the applause around the table had died down. "The formal offer won't come until senior year. But I've given them my commitment. So I guess it's official: I'm going to be a Georgetown Hoya!"

"Georgetown." Pup's dad rummaged through his pasta in search of a meatball. "Is that a good school?"

"Ted!" Jeanine's husband, Matthew, laughed indulgently. "It's a *great* school. One of the best in the country. Presidents went there. Supreme Court justices went there. Bradley *Cooper* went there." Matthew ruffled his handsome son's hair. "And one day, people are gonna be sitting around dinner tables and saying, 'Declan *Spenser* went there.' We couldn't be prouder."

"It's not a big deal," Declan said, shrugging with fake modesty. "People act like it's so *hard* to get into an elite college, but it's really not, if you put your mind to it, you know?"

"Dick," Pup muttered. Everyone looked at him, because Pup barely ever made a peep during Sunday dinners. Usually, he just wolfed down his food and disappeared out to the alley to shoot free throws, or into the kitchen to hang out with his younger nieces and nephews, who were so much more fun to talk to anyway.

"Pardon me, Pup?" Jeanine was leveling him with her sister-mom stare that indicated she'd heard *exactly* what he'd just said.

"Nothing."

"Hey, Uncle Pup," Dec said, shining his blazing smile in Pup's direction, like an interrogation lamp. "I forgot to ask. How's your art grade?"

A couple dozen pairs of eyes rested on Pup. Even his niece Chloe, who'd been sitting on his lap and happily gumming a piece of garlic bread, stopped what she was doing and swiveled around to train her big blue eyes on his face. He could feel the spaghetti he'd eaten like a brick in his stomach.

"That's right!" Jeanine clapped her hands so that her fat diamond rings clattered together. "I always forget you two are in the same class! Pup, do you have a college plan yet?"

"Not really," Pup said, running a nervous hand over Chloe's mostly bald head. "I mean, I'm only a junior."

"Exactly. You're *already* a junior, and *almost* a senior. You should have started thinking about this months ago. Who's that counselor at school that you like? Mrs. Barbero or something?"

"Mrs. Barrera." Pup leaned over to feed Chloe a tiny chunk of meatball.

"Well, why isn't she talking to you about college? Is she going to write you a letter of recommendation?"

"Maybe? I don't know."

"Well, if she won't even write you a rec letter, what *good* is she?"

"She isn't that kind of counselor," Pup explained, trying to keep his patience. "She's a social worker."

"A *social worker*?" It was now Mary's turn to jump in. "*I* need a social worker. You should've seen the call I was on last night. Neighbors called 911, reported this awful smell. We go into the apartment building, find this poor old guy in the upstairs unit who's been dead on his bathroom floor for two solid weeks. With the radiator on full blast. He'd practically turned into soup!"

"Mary, not while we're eating!"

"Sorry, Mom. I'm just saying—*that* kind of thing can scar a person. But what the heck do *you* need a social worker for, Pup Squeak? When's the last time *you* had to scoop a pile of human stew into a body bag?"

"Not while we're *eating*, for Chrissake!" Pup's dad threw down his fork.

"She's got a point, though," Jeanine said, which was typical, because the sister-moms always had each other's backs. "I thought social workers were there to report the kids in black trench coats before they go shooting up the school! You're not planning on shooting up the school, are you, Pup?"

"Yes, Jeanine." Pup sighed. "I can't wait to get to first period tomorrow so I can detonate my homemade bomb."

"You shouldn't make jokes like that." She pointed her

garlic bread at him. "Not in the climate we're living in these days."

"And *you* shouldn't be so ignorant about what social workers do," interrupted Annemarie. "They help kids with all sorts of issues."

"Right," said Elizabeth, crossing her arms over her massively pregnant belly. "But what's *Pup's* issue?"

"I don't *have* an issue." Pup shrank into his seat while Chloe squirmed on his lap. *"God."*

"See, that's the problem with your generation, Pup. Gen Z or whatever they're calling it." Matthew could never resist an opportunity to blame a given problem on *kids these days.* He never included his own children in these critiques, of course. "Every kid's got an issue. Depression. Anxiety. ADHD. What's the thing that teacher told Pup he had once? Executive functioning disorder? Come *on.* What a load of crap. What Pup needs is a college counselor to talk to him about his applications and to write him a stellar rec letter that makes up for his crappy grades. Not some kumbaya *social worker.*"

"Seriously," agreed Mary. "He's the most well-adjusted kid I know."

"Except that he's failing art," added Declan.

"I'm not *failing* art," said Pup.

"Dammit," said Pup's father. "Judy, I *told* you we forgot to ask him about his grades."

"Pup," Jeanine scolded, "how can you be failing *art*?"

"Hey." Annemarie's voice was sharp; it cut through the din of clinking forks and nosy questions. "Will you guys all shut up already and let the kid eat his dinner? *Jesus*."

Jeanine's face immediately crumpled into a pile of hurt.

"There's no need to be *rude* about it, Annemarie," she said. "I only wanted to *include* Pup in the conversation."

"You're *not* including him. You're prying into his business and talking about him like he's not even there."

"Prying?" Jeanine lifted an offended hand to her heart. "I would never—"

"Judy," Sal, Annemarie's fiancée, interjected, "this Bolognese tastes especially delicious today. You really are an amazing chef, you know that?"

"Oh!" came the squeak of surprise from Pup's mother, her neck and cheeks mottling pink. Judy Flanagan had been feeding her family Sunday dinner for so long that it no longer occurred to anyone to compliment her, or even notice, the prodigious effort it took to make sauce from scratch every week for over two dozen people.

"I actually added some veal this week," she explained. "Just to try something different."

"Well, it's just *wonderful*."

Good old Sal. Annemarie's fiancée had been around long enough to know that changing the subject was usually the best way to defuse a family crisis. The rest of Sunday dinner was enjoyed in a cautious peace. Georgetown was not brought up again. Luke's absence continued to be carefully and thoroughly ignored. Shamed a little by Sal's kindness to their mother, everybody went out of their way to rave about the veal.

Pup didn't even wait for the pineapple upside-down cake to be served before he made his escape out to the alley to shoot free throws. Privacy was a nonexistent commodity in his house, but he at least hoped for maybe five minutes to himself before one of his sisters or nieces or nephews came out and annoyed him some more. And sure enough, he hadn't even made it through his warm-up before he heard the squeak of the chain-link gate and footsteps into the alley.

"Sorry about that in there." Annemarie handed him a slice of cake wrapped in a paper napkin. "The sister-moms can be pretty intense."

"Maybe *I* should start skipping Sunday dinner." Pup rolled the basketball to his sister and took a large bite of cake, wiping the crumbs from his mouth with the back of his hand. "Luke may be on to something."

"Seriously. I love how Mom thinks he's at study group."

Pup blinked. Apparently he wasn't the only one with suspicions.

"You think he's lying?"

"Of course he's lying. When I was in law school, those

study groups always met on Saturdays. Only the most hard-core nerd would be in two study groups a weekend. And that's not Luke. I guarantee he's off somewhere drinking and watching the Cubs. Or just drinking. Either way, he's not studying. But we'll let Mom have her little fantasy." She picked up the ball, bent her knees, and shot from the chalked-in free-throw line. It went straight through the net.

They took turns shooting free throws for a while, lapsing into an uncharacteristic silence that Pup knew could only mean one thing: Annemarie was waiting for him to talk. She was good at that, at waiting him out until he just started confessing. It was why she was such a successful lawyer.

"Can I ask you something?" Pup finally said, shoving the last bit of cake into his mouth and slumping down against the garage.

"Anything, anytime." Annemarie heaved the ball under her arm and sat down next to him. "You know that."

"What was your worst day of high school?"

"Hm. That's a tough question." She laughed. "There are so many to choose from."

"I mean the absolute *worst*."

She thought for a minute, looking up at a squirrel scrambling across the power lines above them.

"Okay," she said at last. "It was the day when someone wrote 'DYKE' across my locker in red Sharpie."

"What?" Pup sat up. "You've never told me that story before."

"Yeah, well, it's not exactly the type of pleasant memory that I like to tell around the campfire."

"Who did it?"

"Well, they never caught anyone, but I've got my own ideas." She began spinning the ball between the tips of her fingers. "Anyway, that wasn't even the worst part of it. The *worst* part was that I'd been all ready to come out to you guys. I was planning on doing it right after I graduated, at Sunday dinner, which was, like, three weeks after it happened. But I figured, if there are kids my *own* age who are still homophobic assholes, then how the hell are my old-school Catholic parents going to take the news? So I ended up waiting *three more years*, until the pretending became so excruciating, I couldn't take it anymore."

"So I was, what, seven, when you told everybody? I don't even remember it."

"Well, that's probably because it was pretty anticlimactic. I don't know why I was so afraid. I should have given Mom and Dad more credit—they were totally fine with it. *Everybody* was fine with it. Even Matthew and Jeanine, who, as you were reminded tonight, can be real pains in the ass."

Pup took the ball from her and started spinning it through his fingers in just the same way Annemarie had. It was a family habit. The cool, nubby surface was comforting to him, like a loved blanket, a tactile memory of his childhood. "When you came out," he said. "What did Patrick say?"

"Patrick?" Annemarie looked at him quickly. "Oh, he just gave me a hug and said he loved me. You know what Patrick was like."

But that was the problem. Sometimes Pup felt like he *didn't* know. Not anymore. Sometimes he felt like he was no closer to getting over it, or getting *through* it, as Mrs. Barrera would say, than he was the moment he walked out of that central Illinois hospital into the darkness and the rain.

"What are you asking me about my worst day of high school for, anyway?" Annemarie asked. "What's going on? Don't tell me this has something to do with Izzy."

Pup looked down at the spinning ball between his hands and nodded.

"Oh no. What happened?"

"Nothing *happened*, exactly. I just realized that I have no chance with her. All this time, I've been kidding myself."

"Oh, Pup." Annemarie reached out to pet his hair, like she'd done when he was a little boy, but she stopped herself in time and her hand fell back to her lap. She knew he hated that gesture, now that he was nearly seventeen.

"I know you're not going to want to hear this," she said, "but I think this is a good thing. Now you know for sure. So now you can let her go."

Just like you did with Pat, he thought, remembering the

day, a few weeks after the funeral, when she and Sal had come over to gather up Patrick's biology textbooks and donate them to a program for underserved high school students. *Patrick would have wanted this*, they'd said, which of course was true. But still.

"Me and Izzy have been through a lot together," Pup said. "And she helps me with my homework sometimes."

"Well, shit. Let's award her the Nobel Peace Prize."

Pup couldn't think of a witty response, so he said nothing.

"Pup, let me ask you something: What do you actually have in *common* with Izzy?"

"Lots of things."

"Name one."

"Um, we're both juniors at Abraham Lincoln High School, for starters. We were born in the same month. We both like sports."

"Izzy does not like sports."

"She does! Remember she came over to our house last year to watch the World Series?"

"The Cubs won the World Series last year for the first time in over a century. Every single person in the city of Chicago watched it, even people who don't know the difference between a home run and a hole in one."

"What's your point, anyway?"

"My point is, if you *really* stop and think about it, if you *really* sat down and listed to yourself the reasons why you think you love Izzy Douglass, you couldn't do it."

"Because love isn't about lists! Jeez, Annemarie, will you stop being a lawyer for five seconds?"

"This has nothing to do with me being a lawyer. Face it, Pup: The only thing you two have in common is that you both have brothers who died. That's it."

"Yeah, well, that's not nothing!"

"I know that! But it's also not *everything*!"

"I'm going inside." Pup scrambled to his feet and tossed her the basketball, a little harder than he meant to.

"Wait!" Annemarie caught the ball and hugged it to her chest. "I'm sorry. I know you think I'm being harsh. But I'm just trying to tell you, Pup. In high school, relationships evolve. And sometimes not for the better. You know, the day after somebody decorated my locker with hate speech, I remember sitting in history class next to my best friend, Andi Trotter. My pen ran out of ink, so I asked her if I could borrow one of hers. When she opened her pencil case, guess what it was full of?"

"Um. Pencils?"

"Red Sharpie markers."

Before Pup could respond, the alley was flooded with white light as a car screeched around the corner and came barreling toward them. It swerved to avoid some recycling bins, and in doing so, caught the corner of the D'Amatos' garbage can, which sent two bags of rancid trash exploding down the alley. Pup and Annemarie scrambled out of the way to avoid being hit just as the car jerked to a stop in front of the garage right beside theirs. The headlights switched off, the driver's-side door swung open, and Luke, with two-day stubble and the beginnings of a black eye, tumbled out of his white Jeep.

Annemarie dropped the basketball and ran down the alley to where her younger brother, swaying on his feet, was standing in front of the neighbors' garage, holding his arm out in front of him with great concentration.

"*Luke!*" Annemarie, the tallest of the five sisters, was the only one with the height to look her brother in the eye, and she was staring him down now with a fierceness that might have scared him if he hadn't been too drunk to notice. "What the hell do you think you're doing?"

"I am *trying*," he said grandly, waving a small black device in the air, "to open the garage *door*, except the stupid thing doesn't seem to be *working*."

Annemarie snatched the opener out of his hand, marched over to where Pup stood, pointed the opener to the Flanagan's garage, and pressed the button. A grinding noise filled the alley, and the garage door began creaking upward.

"Oops." Luke laughed, leaning against his hood as the door yawned open. "Stupid garages all look alike. We need to paint ours different. Stripes. Polka dots. A great big 'F' for Flanagan."

"Or 'Felony DUI.' Give me those fucking keys." She yanked the keys out of his hand, pushed past him and climbed into the driver's seat. "Get out of the way. I'm parking this for you."

"No, you're not." Luke hoisted himself up on the hood and lay sprawled across it, facedown. "I'm staging a sit-in," he called. "Conscientious objector. I will not go gently into that good night. Brother's rights! Justice for Luke!"

"Pup, help me," commanded Annemarie. "Get him off of there."

Pup hesitated. When Luke was this drunk, he was completely unpredictable. He might *seem* fairly harmless at the moment, laughing as he spread-eagled across the hood in mock protest, but it was entirely possible that in another moment he might veer into darkness, even violence. Pup had learned this the hard way. Just a few weeks earlier, Luke had come crashing up the stairs in the middle of the night, kicked his pants off, and starting peeing all over the clean clothes in Pup's laundry basket. When Pup had tried to stop him, tried to steer him in the direction of the bathroom, Luke had looked up at his younger brother with a flat blue lolling gaze and, with pee still splashing all over Pup's clean T-shirts, had taken a lazy, wobbling swing, which had just connected with the corner of Pup's jaw. It hadn't hurt—much—but it hadn't exactly been pleasant, either. After Luke passed out on top of his covers, underwear still tangled around his ankles and bare ass gleaming white in the moonlight, Pup had to spend the rest of the night with a sore jaw, rewashing all of his soaked clothes in the basement so that his mother wouldn't know what had happened.

"*Pup.*" Annemarie was already behind the steering wheel, waiting.

"Okay." He circled the car, squatted down near the front tire so his face was level with Luke's. "Dude. You gotta get off the car. Just let Annemarie park it for you."

"Oh, *do* I." Luke's chin rested on his hands. The boozy smell coming off his pores was enough to make Pup's eyes water.

"Yeah. You do. Please." He stood very still, silently begging Luke. This was the moment, he knew from experience, when it would go one way or the other. Annemarie sat in the front seat and turned the ignition, and the car restarted with a rumble. Luke, with the engine vibrating underneath him, continued to stare at Pup and the moment grew and grew and Pup braced for it and then it snapped and everything relaxed and Luke rolled off the hood, suddenly compliant.

"What did I ever do," he asked, propping himself against the door frame and watching Annemarie ease the Jeep into the empty square of concrete next to their father's Buick, "to deserve not one, not two, but *five* pushy older sisters?"

"Dude, you shouldn't drink and drive."

"The more you know." Luke hummed the jingle from

the PSA, then rummaged around in his pockets and produced a stick of gum. He folded it into his mouth and tossed
the foil wrapper on the ground. As Annemarie climbed out
of the car and slammed the door shut behind her, Pup could
see by the stiff way she walked that she was trying to con-
tain her fury. She cranked her arm behind her head and
threw Luke's keys at him as hard as she could. He tried to
catch them, but they bounced off his chest and clattered to
the asphalt.

"Try to imagine the sound of a two-thousand-pound
vehicle slamming into a human body," she said.

"*Jesus.*" Luke bent down to pick up the keys. "I didn't *hit*
anyone. Except that garbage can just now. Are you gonna file
a wrongful death suit on behalf of the D'Amatos' leftover
chicken bones?"

"Okay, then. Try to imagine how it would feel to have to
explain to Mom and Dad why you weren't allowed to sit for
the bar exam because of your DUI conviction. Are you really
willing to throw away three years of law school because
you're too stupid to call an Uber?"

"I was at Mishka's. It's, like, two blocks away."

"It's nearly two *miles* away, and if I ever see you drinking and driving again, I will call the police on your ass so
fast you'll be in jail before that last shot is even down your
throat."

"I wasn't even *doing* shots."

"Fuck you, Luke."

"Guys." Pup tried to step between them, but, as usual, no one paid attention.

"Good to know you've got my back." Luke smiled contemptuously at her, his swollen face gleaming beneath the streetlights. "You're just like Carrie. Loyal to the end."

"What does Carrie have to do with any of this?"

"Carrie doesn't have anything to do with anything, anymore. But when I find out who she's sleeping with, I'm gonna track down his address and then I'm gonna go to his house and kill him. You gonna report that to the police too?"

"Do you have any idea how crazy you sound right now?"

"Do *you* have any idea how crazy you sound *always*?"

"*Guys.*"

"Everybody's still inside, you know," said Annemarie. "Everybody's going to see what a drunken mess you are right now."

"So? You think I give a shit what everyone thinks?"

But as he staggered toward the back gate, Luke seemed to consider this: the thought of walking into the tail end of Sunday dinner, having to deal with four more angry sisters, and their husbands, and their screaming, demanding children, not to mention his aged, fragile parents. He veered suddenly away from the gate and began lurching down the alley, whirling around once to flip Annemarie off before turning at the street and disappearing into the night.

"Where do you think he's going?" Pup asked.

"Who knows? Who cares?" She glanced over at him. "So Carrie dumped him, huh?"

"Yeah." Pup walked over to the D'Amatos' garage, uprighted their garbage can, and began collecting the scattered trash and placing it back in the bin.

"Well, good for her." Annemarie watched Pup distractedly as he picked up a clot of wilted lettuce and tossed it into the trash. "It's about time that girl wised up."

9

ON MONDAY, Pup had barely flopped into his seat in Studio Art before Mr. Hughes sidled up to his desk, scratching at a frizzy patch of chest hair that stuck out from his unbuttoned collar.

"Flanagan," he said. "Got my project for me?"

"I'm *almost* finished," Pup promised. "The negatives are all done. I just need to enlarge them on the photo paper, and then—"

Mr. Hughes stopped scratching and crossed his arms. "Flanagan, a word at my desk, please?"

Marcus Flood shot Pup a sympathetic look as he followed Mr. Hughes to his desk in the corner of the art studio.

"The thing about deadlines," Mr. Hughes began, settling into the chair behind his desk and lacing his fingers together behind his head, "is that they're not *suggestions*, Flanagan. They're not *recommendations*. They're *imperatives*. If I said the project was due Monday, I meant it was due Monday. Not Tuesday. Not Wednesday. Monday. Which is *today*."

"You're right, Mr. Hughes." Pup trained his eyes on the

grass-stained toes of his Nikes. "It's just that I had kind of a rough weekend."

"Oh, *did* you? Tell me, Flanagan, do *you* have an ex-wife who just served you papers demanding full custody—without visitation rights—of Hershey Kiss, your beloved Cavalier King Charles spaniel?"

"Um. No?"

"Well, then. In *that* case, my weekend was worse than yours. I want that project by the end of the day, or I'm writing a zero, *in pen*, in my grade book, which drops you down to failing. You know that you need a fine-arts credit to graduate, don't you?"

"Yes, Mr. Hughes," mumbled Pup.

"Good. I'll be sitting at this desk after school until three thirty, when I have to leave for my meditation group. If you show up at three thirty-one, tough luck. Now get in that darkroom and get to work!"

Pup fled back to his desk, grabbed his backpack, and hurried out to the hallway and into the darkroom. This time, he walked in as carefully as possible so as not to send photo equipment crashing to the ground again. "Hello?" he called softly, pushing open the door.

In the soft red glow of the safety light, Abby Tesfay, dressed in dark jeans and a plain white T-shirt, was peering down at a proof sheet submerged in a tray of shallow chemicals, sloshing it gently back and forth with a pair of tongs.

"Hey, again," he said.

"Hey." She didn't look up from her work.

"I haven't seen this much of you since fourth period freshman year."

"Were we in a class together?" She glanced up then, surprised. "I don't remember that."

"English. For a little while, anyway." He reached up, unclipped his negatives, and began arranging the photo paper Mr. Hughes had given him onto the enlarger. "It was the low track. I think Ms. Cole moved you up at the semester, though."

"That's *right*," she said. "I *was* in low track. Because I'd moved out of ELL and they didn't really have anywhere else to put me."

"ELL?"

"English Language Learners. I didn't speak a word when I came here."

"Whoa. Really? I'd never guess that. I still remember the speech you gave on Greek Mythology Day. It started like, 'All hail! I'm the goddess with the girdle slung low!' Or something like that. Jack Walters started snickering because you said 'girdle,' which I guess is sort of like underwear, and you stopped your speech and told him to shut up. Do you remember that?"

"Oh, *yeah*!" Abby laughed. "I completely forgot about that! Jack Walters is such a meathead. I was Demeter, goddess of corn and wheat. I wore a cornflakes box as a crown for my presentation. And a homemade necklace made out of Cheerios."

"I remember the cornflakes box!"

"Oh god. I hope nobody else does." Abby used the tongs to fish her photograph out of the chemical bath and clipped it, dripping, to the line. "Okay, so what god were *you*?"

"I was Pan, the god of the forest. Which, like, of *course* I was. Even though we were *supposed* to be assigned at random, all the jocks somehow ended up with the cool gods. Zeus. Aries. Poseidon. And I was a half boy, half goat who prances around the woods playing a flute."

"Oh my god!" Abby had a loud, unselfconscious laugh. It filled the tiny space of the darkroom. "I remember now! I remember your tinfoil ears. And the goat legs! They were these green shaggy things. You told Ms. Cole you made them by cutting up a bath mat!"

"Yeah. The kids with the crafty moms had these crazy good costumes. I had tinfoil ears, a ripped-up old bath mat, and some loose-leaf paper hooves taped to my gym shoes."

"And I wore a box of cornflakes on my damn head."

They giggled, and were silent again, so that all that could be heard between them was the hum of the enlarger machine and the drip of the drying photographs.

After a while Abby asked him, "So what's this final project about, anyway?"

"Well, that's the thing." Pup lifted his paper from the enlarger and submerged it carefully in the stop bath with the long silver tongs. "There *is* no project. Mr. Hughes just wants us to turn in something 'representative of our personal aesthetic,' using any medium we want. But look at me!" He posed for her in his baggy, too-short jeans, his stained Nikes, his Chicago Park District T-shirt, his wiry, untamable hair. "I don't *have* an aesthetic. When I asked him what he actually *meant* by that, he said I should find a way to 'articulate the emergency inside of me.'"

"Oh man. Whenever Mr. Hughes starts quoting Leonard Cohen, you know you're in trouble." Abby leaned forward to scrutinize the photographs he'd enlarged. "What about this one? This is good." She squinted her eyes and peered closer at the image. "Actually—wow. This is *really* good."

She was pointing at the image of Luke, curled up on the roof with the sun lightening behind him and the early morning birds on the power lines, the scattered beer bottles, his unshaven sleeping face so inscrutable, even in sleep.

"*That?* I don't even know why I took that. That's my older brother Luke. He's the kind of guy who threatens to punch you if you look at him for more than, like, a second. He was asleep, though. So I was able to look at him. Maybe that's why I took it. Because it was sort of nice to just stand there and look at my brother."

Immediately, he felt like he had said too much. He braced

himself for what he knew Abby would say next: *Awww*. Izzy was always saying *awww* to Pup, in this high, singsong voice. It was the same expression she reserved for YouTube videos of kittens playing with balls of yarn, and implied how totally adorable he was in a completely nonsexual way. No girl had ever, or would ever, say *awww* about Brody, or Declan, or any other guy who was halfway decent-looking.

But Abby didn't say *awww*. She didn't say anything. Instead, she just stood there in the red light, cocking her head and observing the photograph.

"I'm trying to figure out what's so magnetic about it," she finally said. "I think maybe it's the composition. Your subject looks so—closed off or something. He's a person I want to know more about. Like he has so many things buried inside himself. And the objects. Did you pose those, or are they just arranged like that?"

"You mean the beer bottles?"

"Yeah."

"No, they were just like that."

"And that glass of—what is that, anyway?"

"It's a protein shake."

"See, that's so random. But it works. Mr. Hughes always says that unexpected objects can elevate a photograph."

"Huh," said Pup. "I didn't know that."

"And I love the way the dawn sky contrasts with his dark hair," she went on. "It's such a beautiful way to take advantage of the black-and-white film. Awesome point of view. Awesome juxtaposition and use of negative space. Awesome mood. I mean—I can *tell* how much this person means to you. And I can tell that you were *seeing* him when you made this picture."

"Wow." Pup lifted a hand to his neck. It came away hot. "Thanks."

"Portraiture is kind of my thing, too," she said. "What do you think of this one?"

She inclined her head at the photo that was dripping gently onto the counter. It was a portrait of a woman leaning on a cash register, chin cupped in her palm. She had a thin, calm face, and her deep brown eyes were fringed with thick lashes. Her skin stood dark against the white wall behind her. She was not pretty—*pretty* was a word that was too bubbly and young for what she was—but she was handsome, which was a word Pup's mother used for elegant women whose style she admired. Behind the woman was a refrigerator with clear sliding doors, lined with cans of Fanta, and Styrofoam containers with masking tape labels. Taped on the counter was a little Eritrean flag and a sign that said CASH ONLY.

"Your mom?" Pup asked.

"My *amoui*," Abby said. "My aunt."

"Wow. I can tell you guys are related."

"She's basically raising me. My mom's back in Eritrea."

"Oh."

There was a silence, broken only by the drip of the water.

"It's funny what you said." Abby's voice was quiet. "About everybody's moms making their costumes for Greek Mythology Day. Remember Ali Larson?"

"You mean Persephone? Goddess of spring? With those big yellow wings?"

"Mm-hmm. That shit was *embroidered*. Her mom hand-stitched the whole thing. Pretty sure Ms. Cole gave her an A-plus."

"I don't think she stayed in low track much longer, either."

"But I remember thinking that. About the other kids' costumes. I was so mad about it, you know? Because my mom doesn't even live here, so it didn't seem fair."

"Well, if it makes you feel any better, my mom didn't help me with my costume, either. In case you couldn't tell by the tinfoil and the ripped-up old bath mat."

Abby laughed. "Yeah, I guess I should have figured."

"When was the last time you saw her?"

"My mom? Three years ago."

"Three *years*?"

"Yeah." She reached up to straighten her drying photograph. "But it's okay, because we've got this immigration lawyer helping us, and we've finally straightened out the visa stuff. We find out any day now whether her application is approved. Until then, my life is sort of in suspension, waiting for that moment."

"Oh."

"Hey," she said suddenly. "What kind of name is Pup? Is that like short for something?"

"It's a nickname. When I was a baby, I had real big hands and feet for my size, like a puppy." He held out his hands, spreading his long, spidery fingers. "So Luke started calling me Pup. And even though I hate it, it just kind of stuck."

"If it makes you feel any better," she said, "I hate when people call me Abby. It's not my real name, either."

"It's not?"

"Nope. My real name is Abrihet. It means 'She brings light.'"

"'She brings light,'" Pup repeated. "That's the most perfect name ever for a photographer."

She smiled. "I never thought about it that way, but yeah. It totally is."

"So how come you go by Abby?"

"Because. First period on the first day of freshman year PE, Coach Miller couldn't pronounce my name. She tried a couple times, and then she just put down her attendance book and said, 'You know what? How about I just call you Abby?' I was too afraid to say no to a teacher. And besides, I'd already figured out that here in America, people have trouble meeting you where you are. They have to bend you to become whatever they already know. So I just said to myself, hey, what difference does it make if my PE teacher calls me something that isn't my name? But then the other girls in my gym squad started calling me Abby, too. And then the girls in the other squads. And then the kids in my other classes. And then everyone at our school."

"So, does that mean that outside of school, you're still Abrihet?"

"Yes. Because that's my *name*. When my mom gets here, if she overhears anyone calling me Abby, she's going to laugh her butt off."

"Hey," said Pup. "At least *outside* of school you're still Abrihet. I'm Pup no matter where I go. I mean, what kind of future does a guy named Pup have, anyway? President Pup? Hey, guys, I'd like you to meet the new CEO of our company, Mr. Pup Flanagan. Pup Flanagan, MD. I'll be performing your heart surgery this morning."

She laughed. "Well, what *is* your real name?"

"James."

"James," she repeated, extending a hand. "I like it. Hello, James. It's nice to meet you."

He stuck his sweaty paw into hers and shook. "Hello, Abrihet," he said. "It's really nice to meet you, too."

At the end of the day, just after eighth period, Pup ran to the darkroom and found it empty. He carefully removed his picture of Luke from the drying hooks and placed it, still damp, in a manila folder he had begged off his Spanish teacher.

Then, without even the time to look and see if it turned out decent, he ran into the art room where Mr. Hughes sat, his eyes closed, clouded in the haze of a burning incense stick.

Pup cleared his throat, and Mr. Hughes's eyes fluttered open. He glanced at his watch.

"Three twenty-eight. You like to live dangerously, Flanagan."

Pup pushed the folder across the desk, and Mr. Hughes rested his fingertips on its manila surface. Pup stood there, waiting.

"That's all for now, Flanagan."

"But—aren't you gonna look at it?"

"Of course I am. But not while you're standing here, breathing down my neck. I'll have a grade for you tomorrow. These things take time. Effort. Thought. *I*, unlike *you*, do not take the responsibilities of art *lightly*."

"Come on, Mr. Hughes. It's one picture."

"So was *Guernica*. And yet: it was the greatest anti-war statement of the twentieth century."

Pup arranged his face into an expression of neutrality, and made a mental note to Google *Guernica* as soon as he got home. "Can't you just *glance* at it? So I can go home tonight with an *idea* of whether I'm going to fail art?"

"I could," Mr. Hughes said, leaning back in his chair and ominously removing his glasses. "But I won't. You kept me waiting. Now it's *your* turn to wait."

SPACE:

used to create the illusion of depth

10

YAWNING UNCONTROLLABLY, Pup walked toward the school parking lot on a very early Saturday morning at the beginning of June. The dawn air was heavy and warm and the rising pink sun made the tall, pale brick building that was Abraham Lincoln High School glow softly, like a giant spaceship.

The day after he'd turned in his photograph of Luke, Mr. Hughes had not just given Pup the first A of his entire life, bringing his semester grade up to passing. He'd also informed Pup that he was choosing the photo to represent Lincoln at the Illinois High School Association Art and Design Competition. "I believe in you, Pup," Mr. Hughes had said. But Pup could hardly believe it himself. He'd never been chosen for *anything* before, not even a gym class dodgeball team. Out of all the hundreds of art students at Lincoln, only three others' work had been picked: Abrihet's photo of her *amoui*, a landscape photo by Maya Ulrich, and a blueprint for a skateboarding park designed by none other than Brody Krueger.

When Brody saw Pup coming toward him in the parking lot, he pulled his headphones off his ears and stared.

"Wait, *you're* here?" he demanded. "*You* got picked for this thing?"

"I know," Pup said. "It's almost as shocking as the fact that *you* got picked for this thing."

"At least Brody was in our graphic design elective," Maya said, slurping loudly from a giant iced coffee. "You practically failed Studio One. You're, like, *nobody*."

"Everybody's somebody," retorted Pup, quoting a poster from Mrs. Barrera's office wall.

"Guys, give him a break," Abrihet said. "You should see his photo. It's really beautiful."

"Thanks," Pup said, a smile twitching in the corners of his mouth. Brody and Maya shut up after that, and the four of them stood in an awkward circle in the middle of the empty parking lot until a whining sound pierced the early morning quiet and began to grow steadily louder. Finally, a beat-up sedan in desperate need of a new muffler came barreling into the lot, the rusty front bumper covered with stickers like MAKE ART NOT WAR and TEACH PEACE and I'D RATHER BE A TREE-HUGGER THAN A NEOCONSERVATIVE WARMONGERING CLIMATE-DESTROYING CORPORATE SHILL (the font was pretty small on that particular bumper sticker). Mr. Hughes was at the wheel, wearing aviator sunglasses, his gray-threaded dreadlocks waving like a flag out of his open window.

"You're late, Hughes," Brody called as their teacher stepped out of the car. "How come *we* have to show up at the ass-crack of dawn but *you* get to show up half an hour late?"

Mr. Hughes looked at his watch.

"Krueger, it's not even six yet. I'd say we're still firmly wedged in dawn's ass crack, wouldn't you?"

Brody rolled his eyes and stuffed his headphones back over his ears.

"Flanagan!" Mr. Hughes barked. "You and those goofy long legs of yours better sit shotgun with me. There's less legroom in that backseat than on a coach flight to Kansas on Econo-Air."

"Are you sure, sir?" Pup began to protest. Sure, the extra legroom was tempting, but what kid wants to sit up front with the teacher? "I mean, I really don't mind—"

"Did you just call me 'sir'? What do I look like, an English lord? Now get in front, Pup, and fire up the GPS. We're already running late and I want to get to Champaign before this thing is halfway over."

With an obedient shrug, Pup climbed into the front and watched through the rearview mirror as Brody settled into the back middle seat, spreading his legs so that his knees were touching Abrihet's right and Maya's left. He winked at Pup in the mirror as he buckled his seat belt. Pup entertained a brief fantasy of head-butting Brody, right in the pointy nose that Izzy had once described as "regal," which had prompted Pup to mutter under his breath that he doubted any king in history wore socks as dirty as Brody's.

"Everybody ready to kick some art-show ass?" Mr. Hughes shouted, and Maya responded with a sarcastic whoop.

"Cool. Let's roll." Hughes stuck his coffee in the cup holder, slopping some of it on his hand, and they roared out of the empty parking lot toward the Kennedy Expressway.

11

THE DRIVE WENT BY QUICKLY. Pup kept himself busy by updating Mr. Hughes on what the GPS was saying—though he wasn't sure what was so confusing since all they had to do was drive in a flat, straight, corn-hedged line until they got to the University of Illinois—while eyeing the rearview as Brody chatted it up in the backseat with Maya and Abrihet. While Pup himself was terrible at flirting, he wasn't so clueless as to not be able to tell the difference between innocent conversation and slimy flirtation. And he was *quite* sure that if he were somehow able to secretly record a video of Brody's behavior in the backseat and send it to Izzy, she would be pissed. Probably not pissed enough to dump him, though, which made the whole thing that much more infuriating.

But, in a weird way, Pup was glad to be stuck in the front seat with Mr. Hughes, listening to Brody hit on Abrihet and Maya all the way to Champaign, glad to have this small and manageable and distracting annoyance. The last time he'd been on this road, it had been a different Saturday morning, the harvested fields glistening in the October rain, and he'd been crammed into a car with Luke and Carrie and Sal and Annemarie, with the rest of his siblings caravanning in the cars ahead, each of them staring at their phones, waiting for an update, a text or call with a spark of good news, of hope, that never came.

As soon as they arrived on campus, Mr. Hughes pulled into the nearest illegal parking space he could find and hurried them out of the car.

"Leave your bags in the trunk," he said. "We don't have time to check into the hotel. Hurry *up*, Krueger! You're not walking, you're *sauntering*!"

As Mr. Hughes strode ahead, his messenger bag bouncing on his hip, Maya slowed her own walk to match Brody's saunter and Abrihet fell into step beside Pup.

"So," she said as they headed up a street lined with bars and bookstores that ended in the leafy entrance to the quad. "Have you ever been down to U of I before?"

"Once," Pup answered. "My brother went here."

"Oh, cool. When did he graduate?"

"He didn't finish, actually." Pup changed the subject quickly. "It's a pretty nice place, though, isn't it?"

"It's exactly what I pictured an American university to be like."

Pup knew what she meant. There were these big brick

buildings everywhere that just *looked* like if you went inside, you'd find shelves of dusty, important books and rows of glossy desks lit with green-shaded lamps, where smart kids pored over their studies. The buildings were laid out along a huge rectangular lawn where students basked in the morning sun on blankets, reading books, scrolling lazily on their phones, playing Frisbee, or sitting cross-legged in the grass with steaming paper cups of coffee in their hands. An intellectual-looking dude with neat cornrows read a thick paperback with onionskin pages under the shade of an elm tree. Another kid with pale legs and dark glasses kind of looked like a dork except for the fact that he was jamming on a guitar and people—including a pair of very beautiful spandex-clad young women out for a morning jog—were nodding their heads approvingly as they bounced along the path. As he and Abrihet hurried to catch up with Mr. Hughes, Pup remembered a selfie Patrick had sent him once from somewhere on this huge green lawn. It was morning and the sky was a brilliant blue. In the picture, Pat sported a pair of mirrored sunglasses and his ever-present Cubs hat, soft and faded from years of wear. One of his gigantic biology textbooks was tented over his knees. *#quadgoals*, he had written, with about eight hundred laughing emojis, because Patrick always laughed at his own jokes, even if they weren't funny.

When Patrick had been accepted to the U of I on a full

academic scholarship, the family had celebrated with cheap champagne at Sunday dinner. They could do things like that back then, because Luke still drank like a normal adult. Pup remembered how everybody had been so excited until the moment when Pat announced his major: philosophy.

"But what are you going to *do* with a philosophy major?" Jeanine had demanded. "Go to law school?"

"No." Pat twirled a mouthful of spaghetti around his fork. "Be a philosopher."

"But you can't just *be* a philosopher," Mary had protested.

"Well, Sartre would argue that I can't *be* at all, since being-in-the-world is the same as nothingness. And if I am nothing, who cares what I major in?"

"See, Mom?" Noreen demanded. "See what happens, all because you bought him that black turtleneck for Christmas?"

"I don't know about this, Pat," their father had said. "You gotta think practical. I mean, look at me. I never even *went* to college, but I got in with the union when I was a young man. Got myself set up with good benefits, a nice pension—a salary that provided for eight children. So someone like you? With your brains? There's no *limit* to what you can do. Why can't you ponder the meaning of life in your free time, like everybody else?"

"Dad's right," Jeanine had said, pointing her fork at him. "You have to think about the *real world*, Patrick. Whatever happened to your plans to be a doctor?"

"A doctor in the family *would* be nice, honey," their mother agreed.

"I can get my PhD in philosophy, Ma," Patrick had said, stuffing the forkful of spaghetti into his mouth. "You can still call me 'Doctor' that way."

"Please," snorted Matthew, Jeanine's husband. "I've never seen anyone heal a broken bone with their deep, important thoughts."

"It's *my* scholarship," Pat reminded Matthew through his mouthful of food. "So I can do whatever I want with it. Not my problem if you guys don't get me."

"I get you," Pup had said timidly. Everybody laughed, because Pup was only eleven and therefore he didn't "get" anything. Patrick didn't laugh, though. Instead, he had leaned over to Pup while the pineapple upside-down cake was being passed around and whispered, *"I know you do, Pup Squeak."*

Later that night, shooting hoops in the alley, Pat told Luke, Pup, and Annemarie the rest of his college plans.

"I'm double majoring," he said, dribbling past Pup for an easy bucket. "Philosophy and marine biology. I would have said so, if the sister-moms hadn't jumped down my throat as soon as I opened my mouth."

"Nice," laughed Annemarie. "You realize, they're still sitting around the table as we speak, trying to figure out how to get you to choose something more practical." She shot wide from the post. Pup grabbed the rebound and flipped it back up, missing the easy layup.

"Stop showboating," Luke instructed, chasing down the ball. "You're not using your legs. Low man wins!"

He fired off a quick chest pass that Pup wasn't ready for; he held his arms up too late, and the spinning ball slammed right into his nose. The pain shot through his forehead, and when he tipped his head forward, two streams of blood gushed out. Patrick grabbed his water bottle from the closed lid of the garbage can, sat Pup down in the middle of the alley, leaned his head back and held the cold plastic to the bridge of his nose. "It's all right," he murmured. "It's all right. It's not broken, but you'll probably get two good black eyes that will make you look tough and intriguing to all the girls in school."

Pup nodded as tears filled his eyes. There was nothing he hated more than looking stupid in front of his brothers. To not even be able to catch an easy pass when Declan was already playing travel basketball and setting scoring records at their middle school.

"It's his own fault," Luke called as Pup shuddered with sobs. "When you showboat, you take your head out of the game."

"Will you shut up?" Annemarie yelled. "It isn't enough you have to nail him in the face with a basketball, now you have to make him cry, too?"

"He *isn't* crying," Pat snapped, wiping the tears that streamed from Pup's eyes with the back of his hand. "That's just a physical reaction to the hit he took."

Pup knew that this medical diagnosis was not strictly accurate. He suspected that Patrick knew, too. But if he did, he wasn't going to say anything. He was good that way.

He would have made a great philosopher.

"Nervous, Flanagan?" Mr. Hughes clapped a large hand on Pup's shoulder as they crossed from the sunny quad into the cool dimness of an old building with heavy wooden doors and a sign that read WELCOME TO THE ILLINOIS HIGH SCHOOL ASSOCIATION ART AND DESIGN COMPETITION!

"Why would I be nervous?"

"Maybe because you're sweating like a sinner in church?"

"Oh." Pup wiped his clammy hands on his shorts. "That's just my glands."

"Well, whatever it is, try to relax. All of you." Hughes turned to the four of them. "You aren't expected to do anything—no speeches, no explanations. There's going to be judges who come around and examine the entries. Just stand next to your piece, smile, and let the art speak for itself."

They had entered a huge, hot, high-ceilinged room, with big metal fans whirring in the corners and warped windows where the late-spring light flooded through. A maze of felt-walled displays was set up, where hundreds of photographs, drawings, paintings, and designs were pinned up next to slips of paper containing the name of the artist and the school he or she represented. Along the edges of the room were various dead animals, stuffed and preserved on raised platforms, bolted down in lifelike positions with metal rods.

"We're in the Natural History building," Mr. Hughes explained as he led the group past a giant moose with dull brown fur and a magnificent set of antlers, scored with scars and wider across than if Pup spread his arms out from fingertip to fingertip. The moose's glassy brown eyes stared steadily ahead at a glowing EXIT sign. His nose was surrounded by stiff whiskers but the space around the nostrils looked like it was made of moss or velvet.

While Mr. Hughes went to the teachers' area to help himself to the spread of coffee and pastries, Abrihet, Maya, Brody, and Pup separated into the maze to find their entries. Pup eventually found himself stationed next to a guy whose entry was a black-and-white photo of a bunch of naked headless mannequins piled up in a dumpster in a shopping mall parking lot. It was creepy and weird, but strangely compelling and hard to look away.

"Hi," Pup said to the guy, who was currently peering into the camera of his phone and fiddling with the waxed tips of his little black mustache.

"Hey."

"Cool photo."

The guy put down his phone and glanced over at it, a look of studied boredom playing across his face.

"This isn't even my best work." He sighed. "I'm not sure why they picked it, really. Probably because my other stuff is too provocative."

"Oh," Pup said. He knew that the guy was waiting for him to ask what was provocative about it, but he didn't really feel like giving him the satisfaction. "I'm Pup," he said instead.

"I'm Curt. With a Q."

"Huh?"

"Yeah. Q-U-R-T. I mean, that's not how it's spelled on my birth certificate, of course. But once I turn eighteen and move to Paris, I'm going to get it legally changed."

"Oh."

Qurt tapped through his phone and pushed it across the folding table to Pup.

"This is the entry I *wanted* my teacher to submit," he said. "Instead, it almost got me suspended. Almost got me arrested, as a matter of fact."

Pup held the phone out in front of him and looked at the image, in which a couple of the naked headless mannequins had been propped up against the dumpster so it looked like they were standing. In between them was a skinny, mournful-looking girl with long, stringy hair and an expressionless look on her face. Her hands hung limply by her sides and her shoulders slumped forward. Pup almost mistook her for a mannequin, too, until he saw the pale nipples and the wedge of pubic hair and realized she was a real person who just so happened to be as skinny—and as naked—as the mannequins that surrounded her.

"That's my girlfriend," Qurt drawled. "It was totally consensual and collaborative, but when I tried to hand it in, my teacher freaked. Reported it to the principal. Threatened to charge me with child pornography. Child pornography! When my girlfriend is three months *older* than me. Have you ever heard anything so ridiculous?"

"Um," Pup said.

"But what can you expect from a small-town Illinois art teacher? I was the fool to think he'd ever understand my vision." Qurt glanced at the tag above Pup's picture. *Pup Flanagan. Abraham Lincoln High School.* "Where are you from, anyway?"

"Chicago," Pup said.

"You mean like the actual city, or the suburbs?"

"The city. I mean, I don't live, like, downtown in a high-rise or anything. I live in a regular neighborhood. But in the city, yeah."

"You're so lucky." Qurt sighed.

"I guess," Pup said.

"But wait a minute." Qurt scrutinized Pup's Javier Baez T-shirt that he'd purchased for five bucks from an illegal vendor outside the Harlem blue line station. "You're not really dressed like a city kid. You look more like a bro-dork. I thought city kids were supposed to be cool."

"Well—"

"Oh, *I* get it now," Qurt laughed. "You're into normcore. Cool."

Normcore? Pup had no idea what this meant. He started to explain to Qurt that he was wearing a Baez T-shirt because he was a Cubs superfan, and he was wearing red basketball shorts because his mom had washed them and they'd been sitting at the top of the clean laundry basket, which Luke had managed not to pee all over when he'd stumbled in twenty minutes before Pup's alarm went off at five that morning. But just then, the judges arrived. According to their name tags, they were art professors at the university. Pup stood up straight, smoothing down his wiry hair and wishing he had taken the extra time that morning to locate a pair of pants with an actual zip fly. Real, live college professors! Looking at *his* photograph! He couldn't wait to tell Annemarie.

The judges stood before Qurt and Pup's wall, staring at each photograph for a long time. Finally, one of them spoke.

"What is the name of your piece?"

She looked at both of them over a very professorial-looking pair of tortoiseshell glasses, lips pursed, fingers steepled together. Qurt answered first.

"I call this *Portrait of Nudes in Walmart Parking Lot.*"

"Aha." She jotted something down in the notebook she was carrying. "And you?"

"Um." Pup looked from face to expectant face. He felt his armpits drip. Why had he worn polyester? "This is called . . . um . . . *Luke*."

"*Luke*," repeated Tortoiseshell.

"That's *it*?" Qurt guffawed.

"Yes. I mean, no! See, the *full* title is, of course—" His mind searched in vain for something cool. "*Luke on the Roof*."

Qurt smirked while Tortoiseshell jotted some more in her notebook.

Pup nearly collapsed with relief when the three judges stepped away from the display. They began whispering with their heads leaning together, while Tortoiseshell typed up notes on a little tablet. Then they disappeared back into the felt-walled maze, and Qurt resumed sculpting his mustache in his phone camera.

A little while later, the judges returned. Tortoiseshell smiled first at Qurt, then at Pup. She was holding a stack of pink ribbons in her hand. She walked over to the display and stuck one under the pin that held Qurt's photograph.

"An honorable mention in the category of digital photography is awarded to *Portrait of Nudes in Walmart Parking Lot*," she said, shaking Qurt's hand. Then, she peeled another ribbon from the stack and pinned it next to Pup's photo.

"And an honorable mention in the category of film

photography is awarded to *Luke on the Roof*." She grabbed Pup's dumbfounded hand and shook vigorously, one, two pumps. "Congratulations to you both."

As soon as they walked away, Pup turned to Qurt.

"Wait. We *won*?"

"We didn't win, technically," Qurt sighed, unpinning his ribbon and folding it carefully into his fanny pack. "We *qualified*."

"Qualified? For what?"

"*Regionals.* Don't you know anything? This was a *state* competition. Winning an award here qualifies you for Midwest regionals. They're in Ann Arbor at the end of August."

"Ann Arbor, *Michigan*?" Pup only knew the city because he followed Big Ten basketball.

"No. Ann Arbor, Argentina. *God.* Anyone who qualifies at state gets to present their portfolio at regionals, and if you qualify at *that*, you get to go to nationals in DC and compete for a scholarship to art school. Next thing, you're going to tell me you don't know what a portfolio is."

Pup fiddled with the silky fabric of his ribbon and didn't answer.

"*Oh my god.* A portfolio is a collection of your best images, usually arranged around a theme. Didn't your teacher tell you any of this?"

Pup shook his head. Of course Mr. Hughes hadn't told him! If he had, Pup would never have agreed to submit his photo in the first place. He had just earned himself, along with his pink ribbon, a humongous homework assignment over his summer break, with the very likely possibility that it would all end in his massive humiliation in front of a crowd of intelligent and accomplished Ann Arborians. But he didn't even have the time to freak out about any of this because Abrihet was running toward him, calling his name, and waving her own pink ribbon over her head while Mr. Hughes jogged behind her, smiling so big his gums were showing.

"James!" she yelled. "We won! We won! We won!" Then she was hugging him, and as soon as she let go, leaving Pup in a happy, embarrassed daze, Mr. Hughes reached in for the man-to-man handshake thing, pulling Pup into a half hug and then slapping his back, and he was still smiling in that broad, uncontrollable way, as if he'd completely forgotten, at least for a moment, to be a tortured artist or an overworked teacher. "I *knew* you had it in you, Flanagan," he kept saying. "I just *knew* it."

12

AS SOON AS MAYA ULRICH realized that not only had she not qualified for regionals, but that Pup Flanagan, Studio Art dud and all-around loser, *had*, she burst into tears. On the short drive from the Natural History building back to the hotel, Mr. Hughes made her sit in the front seat so he could give her a soothing pep talk as she blubbered into a tissue. Pup felt sorry for her—sort of—but more than that, he wondered what it was like to be the type of person who actually *expected* to win things.

Once Mr. Hughes checked everyone in, they split up to drop their bags in their rooms and get ready to go out for dinner. Pup was in such a good mood that he didn't even mind having to share a room with Brody for the night, not even when his new roommate sprawled himself across his bed and FaceTimed Izzy, a conversation filled with screen kissing and repeated breathy *I miss you*s, despite the fact that Brody hadn't seemed to be missing her very much when he was flirting with Maya and Abrihet the entire drive down to Champaign.

"Hey, Flanagan!" Brody called. His face was so close to the phone he was practically licking it. "My girlfriend wants to talk to you."

Pup hesitated. He hadn't seen much of Izzy in the two weeks that had passed since their ill-fated game of Spin the Bottle. In fact, he'd gone out of his way to avoid her. Whenever the morning bell rang, he steered clear of the Languages hallway, where he usually caught up with her on her way to Latin class, and instead cut through the weight room to get to first-period English. A few of the varsity football players were always in there, getting huge in the off-season, and they usually heckled his weak physique as he scurried past. Taking the long way also made him late to class, and Mr. Spellman wasn't a fan of Pup even at his most punctual. Still, he'd rather get heckled and lose participation points than face Izzy and the pity he'd seen in her eyes after their kiss. Then again, it wasn't like she'd tried to get in touch with him, either. So maybe she didn't even feel sorry for him. Maybe she didn't think about him at all.

"Flanagan! Are you deaf?" Brody took his phone and tossed it across the room. It dropped onto the hotel carpet with a muffled thud, and Pup, smoothing his hair with a quick sweep of his hand, unwillingly picked it up.

"Hey, stranger!" Izzy's voice was loud, too bright, too falsely casual. She was lounging on her bed, with its mountain of frilly decorative pillows, but she looked nervous. "I hear you won an award!"

"Yeah." Pup took his ribbon from his back pocket and held it up for her to see. "Finally have something to add to the Flanagan family trophy case."

"You know he traded sexual favors for it," called Brody. "It's the only explanation. All he did was take a picture of his drunk-ass brother passed out on the roof of their house. If I'd known it was that easy, I would have taken some snaps at Lily Hubert's graduation party last weekend. You missed it, Flanagan, but it was *sick*. Plenty of drunken photo ops to be had."

"Oh, really?" said Pup. "And I guess you'd know how to compose the shot and expose the film and develop it by hand, too, right?"

"I know how to do plenty of things by hand," Brody retorted. "Just ask Izzy."

"You're such a *per*vert!" Izzy shrieked, craning to look past Pup at Brody in the background, who was smiling to himself and unwinding the cord to his headphones.

"Listen," Pup said, "let me put you back on with Krueger. I have to change my clothes. Mr. Hughes is taking us out to dinner to celebrate."

"No, hang on a second." She sat up on her pyramid of pillows and looked Pup full-on in the camera, focusing her attention entirely, for once, on him. She lowered her voice. "While I've got you on the phone, I actually wanted to talk to you about something."

"Oh." Pup glanced over his shoulder and saw that Brody

had pulled his headphones over his ears, and was blasting his terrible pop country so loud that Pup could hear the auto-tuned twanging from all the way across the room. "What's up?"

"So . . . about what happened at my house. With Spin the Bottle and everything. I just want to say that I'm sorry."

"Okay." Pup could feel the heat rising from the hollow of his throat all the way up through his cheeks and forehead. Did they really have to be video chatting at a time like this? "For what?"

"I don't know." She reached for a pale pink cylindrical pillow that looked like a giant-size version of his dad's cholesterol pills, and held it over her chest. "I just am."

"Well, okay."

"So . . . are we okay?"

"Babe!" Brody lifted a headphone from his ear. "Don't use up all my data!"

"Almost done, babe!" She winced a little, and smiled at Pup. "Sorry."

"It's fine," said Pup. "I really do have to get ready, though."

"Okay. Well. I'll see you at finals week?"

"Sure. Bye, Iz." He ended the call and tossed the phone back onto Brody's bed, not sure if their conversation had left him feeling better or worse.

13

AFTER HE FINISHED GETTING DRESSED, Pup looped his camera around his neck and left Brody, who was busy picking at his neck pimples in the bathroom mirror, to head down to the lobby where they were all supposed to meet before dinner. The girls were already there, Maya stretched on one of the couches with carefully applied makeup over her puffy eyes. She appeared to have recovered from her devastating loss, and was pulling the neckline of her shirt lower as she posed for a selfie to add to her never-ending social media story. Abrihet was standing apart, in a patch of light that poured in through the sliding glass front doors. She had changed into a red dress with flowers all over it and swept her hair into a bun near the top of her head. She looked sort of gorgeous. She wasn't on her phone, or talking to the lady at the desk, or really doing anything but standing there, in a contented kind of solitude, thoughtfully fiddling with one of her earrings. When Pup saw her, a feeling came over him, the same feeling he'd experienced just before he'd taken the picture of Luke on the roof: a need to trap the moment. Before she could turn around and see him coming, he lifted his camera, framed the shot, and snapped her picture.

Mr. Hughes took the group out for dinner at Murphy's, a burger place on campus he used to frequent in his undergrad days. As they ate, he regaled them with stories of his years as a painting major, the campus protests he'd attended against the Gulf War, the life-changing semester he'd spent in Spain. "One cannot claim to have lived a life," he declared between bites of his veggie burger, "until one has stood before *Guernica*."

"Oh, Spain is *such* a spectacular country," Maya said, measuring out a tiny spoonful of fat-free dressing to drip onto her salad. "But when my family vacations there, we spend most of our time on the Costa del Sol. I mean, not that I'm *complaining*, but I told my father the next time we go, we *have* to hit the museums in Madrid."

"Wow," Pup said. "That sounds like some vacation."

"We go to Europe every year," Maya said casually, tossing her long ponytail behind her shoulder. "Sometimes for the beaches, and sometimes for the skiing, depending on the season."

"I've been to Paris." Brody yawned. "It was boring."

"Excuse me." Mr. Hughes dropped his half-eaten veggie burger onto his plate. "Did you just say Paris was *boring*?"

"Yeah." Brody picked up a chili-cheese fry and stuffed it

in his mouth. "And the food was weird."

Mr. Hughes stared for a moment, then put his head in his hands and sighed wearily.

"You guys are so lucky," Abrihet said. "I've never been to Europe in my life."

"At least you grew up somewhere else, though," Pup said, squirting ketchup onto his hamburger bun. "You speak another language and everything. Me? I've never been any-where."

"As of this summer," Mr. Hughes reminded him, "you'll be able to say you went to Ann Arbor."

"I'm sorry," interrupted Maya, "but when you say you've never been anywhere, do you mean you've never been *any-where*?"

Pup shrugged. "There are eight kids in my family. I have thirteen nieces and nephews and another one on the way. We'd have to rent a school bus if we wanted to go on a family vacation."

"But you don't *all* have to go."

"Yes, we do," Pup said. "You don't know my family."

"I totally get that." Abrihet smiled at him. "I have a big family too."

"Are you sure you're not Amish or something?"

"Maya," said Pup, "just because I have seven siblings and a haircut my mom gave me doesn't mean that I'm Amish."

"But that is just so *sad*," said Maya. "I mean—to never have even left *Illinois*."

Pup didn't say anything. Technically, he *had* left Illinois, once. But he didn't feel like talking about the Milwaukee trip, not with Maya Ulrich. It was one of his most treasured memories and he didn't want to risk seeing it diminished in her European beachgoing eyes. Patrick and Luke had taken him to Miller Park for the Cubs-Brewers series as an eighth-grade graduation gift. They took the train from Union Station and bought Pup whatever he wanted that day—two bratwurst and a corn dog, a soft pretzel, a giant Coke, peanuts, a glossy game-day program, even an official MLB-approved Anthony Rizzo jersey that he absolutely loved and that he absolutely couldn't wear now because it just reminded him of that day and made him sad. It had been a June day like this one, perfect baseball weather, cloudless and warm with a light wind, and the Cubs had won 8–2. All of Pup's favorite players had scored: Rizzo, Baez, Bryant. Kyle Schwarber hit a beautiful two-run bomb out to the right center stands, nearly clear out of the park. Toward the end of the game, the Flanagan brothers had even made it onto the Jumbotron. When the Brewers fans had seen them on the screen and began booing them for their Cubbie blue clothing, Luke jumped up and started to bend over. The Jumbotron operator, knowing what was coming, had cut away quickly, but not quickly enough: Luke still managed to moon all forty thousand fans at the ballpark that day. The three of them had laughed the whole way back to the train, and on the ride home to Chicago they decided they'd had so much fun that they hatched a plan to visit all thirty Major League Baseball fields before Pup finished high school. They even made a list: the following summer they could fly to Boston and hit Fenway, then rent a car and drive to Yankee Stadium and Citi Field. Cincinnati, Detroit, the Jake in Cleveland, and even Minneapolis could all be done in longish weekend road trips. Carrie's uncle lived in LA; they could crash with him and see the Padres, the Dodgers, and the Angels in one trip. And they'd already been to the Cell for the Crosstown Classic. Pup would need a passport for Toronto, but that shouldn't be a problem. The plan was to visit their final ballpark—Busch Stadium, because they had to save their most-hated team, the Cardinals, for last—the summer Pup graduated from high school. Yes, they agreed; it was totally doable and it was going to be amazing. They all shook hands to make it official and Pup, sunburned and happier than he'd ever been in just about his whole life, had drifted off to sleep clutching his box score card just as Luke and Patrick were pulling out their phones to consult the next year's schedules.

They had never gone to Fenway, of course. Three months later, Patrick would be gone, and Luke would fold himself away into his law school study groups and his drunken weekends. Pup had once considered asking Luke about Fenway, just to see if he still remembered, but bringing up Fenway meant bringing up Patrick, and you didn't bring up Patrick with Luke, not on opening day, not during October baseball, not during game seven of the Cubs-Indians World Series, not ever.

After dinner, back in their shared hotel room, Brody stuck on his headphones and began jamming, eyes closed, to his awful pop country music while Pup went into the bathroom to take a shower. He brought his pink ribbon with him and placed it lovingly on the toilet lid. He wasn't going to leave his award out there, unattended, with Brody. He didn't trust that guy and his chili-cheese-stained fingers for anything.

He stood under the hot water, eyes closed, mind emptied, for what felt like hours. If he was going to try this portfolio thing, he'd need a collection of great images, like Qurt said, and he'd need a theme. What even *was* a theme, though? It was something they talked about in English class sometimes. The theme was the, like, message, right? The message of a story. But how did you come up with a message when you didn't have a story in the first place? As their conversation at dinner had demonstrated, Pup was a kid who'd never been anywhere, who'd never done anything, who'd never seen anything. What did he have that was worth sharing with the world? He thought of Mr. Hughes's advice: *articulate the emergency inside of you.* As he watched the water swirl between his feet and down the drain, Pup wondered: *What is my emergency?*

By the time he turned off the water, his skin was a boiled pink, tight over his face and bony limbs. He dried off, wrapped himself in a little white hotel towel, and stepped back into the hotel room. Brody, who was digging through his overnight bag, looked up and said, "Forty minutes in the shower, Flanagan? Your right hand must be worn out."

"What? I wasn't—shit!" He jumped backward, nearly dropping the towel and exposing himself to Maya Ulrich, who he only now noticed was standing in the middle of the room.

"How hot was that *water*?" she laughed, checking out Pup's pink naked torso and the prominent ladder of his chest bone. "You look like you just got roasted on a spit!"

Pup hurried past her, clutching his towel. He grabbed his duffel bag and hustled back into the bathroom, shutting the door behind him. He dressed quickly, cursing Brody and wondering how bad his back acne was that day and how much of it Maya had seen, and whether she'd had enough time to take a picture of it and send it to all of her friends.

When he came out again, fully dressed, his ribbon in the back pocket of his jeans, Maya and Brody were sitting together on one of the beds.

"What are you guys doing?" Pup asked. "Where's Abrihet?"

"Where's *who*?"

Pup sighed. "Abby."

"Oh. She's back in our room," Maya said. "Why? Do you like her? I can totally talk to her for you if you want. I'm pretty sure she's single."

"Pup's not interested in Abby," Brody said. "He only has eyes for one woman." He smirked at Pup and leaned back against the headboard. "Don't you, buddy?"

Pup flushed. "I don't know what you're talking about."

"Of course you do."

There was a tense silence. Maya looked nervously back and forth between the two boys. "Am I missing something here?" she asked.

"Not at all." Brody pulled up his Netflix on the shiny new iPad he'd extracted from his bag. "We're gonna watch a movie. As long as it's cool with Flanagan."

"I don't care *what* you guys do," said Pup. "But Mr. Hughes will kill you if he finds out she's in here."

"So? You're no snitch, right?"

Pup didn't answer. He couldn't tell if Brody wanted him to promise not to snitch to Mr. Hughes or to Izzy. After all, Brody and Maya were sitting close enough that their shoulders were touching, and the bottom halves of their bodies were concealed under the covers. *Technically* speaking, Brody wasn't doing anything wrong. But also, technically, Brody was currently in bed with another girl. But even Brody wouldn't dare cheat on Izzy with Maya Ulrich when Pup was right there to witness it. Even *Brody* couldn't be that dumb. Right?

As soon as the movie began and Pup had perched himself awkwardly on his own bed, knowing he wasn't wanted but refusing to get up and leave, Brody slid out from under the covers and announced that he was turning off the lights. Soon the room was nearly as pitch-black as the darkroom at school, except for the flicker from the iPad illuminating Brody and Maya's faces. The screen was too far away for Pup to see it properly; but it didn't matter because he'd seen the movie *Titanic* at least a thousand times. Instead, he opened up his notes app and typed out the title PORTFOLIO IDEAS!!!!

In the time it took for Jack and Rose to meet, fall in love, and have sex in the backseat of a Model T, Pup had only come up with one idea:

FAMILY?

It was at that point that he began to hear a rustling sound coming from Maya and Brody's bed. They were both looking at the screen, but it was clear that neither was actually watching. Pup scrolled more determinedly. The rustling continued and Pup, against his better instincts, glanced over to see where it was coming from. When he saw the movement beneath the blankets he knew, suddenly and certainly, what was going on. He shoved his phone in his pocket and jumped off his bed.

"I'm going out for a walk," he said, grabbing his camera

and heading for the door.

"Cool." Brody didn't even glance away from the screen. "Bring us back some of those mini muffins from the vending machine, would you?"

Pup ignored this shameless request and slammed the door behind him on the way out, hoping it was loud enough for Mr. Hughes to hear.

Outside the hotel, the June air was warm and still. In one direction, green fields of new corn stretched into the darkness. In the other gleamed the lights of the university campus. Pup headed in the direction of the light. Music drifted from the open windows of apartment buildings, but the sidewalks were mostly abandoned—classes were out for the summer, and the town had the lonely feeling of an empty house after a party. He passed by a few quiet bars with neon beer signs hanging in their windows, and cafés where kids were hunched over laptops next to big white mugs of coffee. Walking without a destination, he turned down a dimly lit street lined with tall trees heavy with dark leaves, and he was so preoccupied with all the things rolling around in his mind— his photography portfolio, Brody brazenly receiving a hand job from Maya three feet away from him, Abrihet's red dress and the way the sun had caught the light of her earrings in the hotel lobby—that he probably would have walked right past the house had his eye not caught the two white letters glowing on the dark bricks. But there they were, pale and floating against the dark facade, and it took Pup a moment to remember what they were and what they meant. Two squiggly looking letter *E*s that he'd seen on T-shirts flung on the floor of his bedroom a lifetime ago.

Sigma Sigma.

Patrick's fraternity.

It was a large redbrick mansion with tall stone columns and a big lawn set back from the street. On one end of the sagging front porch, two guys in backward hats were sitting on folding chairs with their feet propped up on the porch rail.

"You lost, man?" one of them called, and Pup realized he'd been standing on the sidewalk staring up at those two letters for an inappropriate amount of time.

"No. Sorry." He pointed. "This is—this is Sig Sig?"

The first guy, small and wiry, with round glasses and a tight gray T-shirt that clung to his stringy muscles, kicked his feet down and nodded. "That's us. Why?"

"My brother was in this house. He lived here."

"Who's your brother?"

"Patrick Flanagan."

"Wait a second," said the other guy, who had a short, dark beard and a half-eaten piece of pizza in his hand. "You mean the guy who . . . ?" He exchanged a look with the kid in the gray T-shirt.

"Yeah," Pup said. "Him."

"Oh. Wow." The smaller of the two, who was olive-skinned and handsome except for the spread of tiny pimples feathering his cheeks, stood up. "I'm Aidan, and this is Travis. Sorry for your loss, man."

"We didn't know him or anything," added Travis. "We're only sophomores. But we know the story, obviously."

Pup looked up at the darkened front windows of the Sigma Sigma house. Everyone had been surprised when Pat announced at the beginning of his sophomore year at U of I that he was joining a fraternity. Pat just wasn't a frat kind of guy. He was too tall, too skinny, too prone to daydreaming, too committed to his dorky biological and philosophical interests. Sure, he liked sports and parties, but not nearly as much as he liked the feeding habits of deep-sea marine life, the symbiotic associations of fungi, or the reproductive processes of plants. Besides, as their sister Noreen had pointed out at Sunday dinner, "You barely even drink!"

"Well," Pat had admitted, "I'm sort of doing it as a favor."

"A *favor.*"

"Yeah. Jack wants to pledge, and they won't let him in unless I join, too. I went with him to rush week, just to see what it was all about, and apparently the guys at Sig Sig found my charms irresistible." He grinned and bit into his garlic bread. "Personally, I can't blame them."

Neither could anybody else at the table. Jack Rinard had grown up with Pat, and even Pup, who was so much younger that all of his siblings' friends seemed impossibly cool, found him obnoxious. He had mossy teeth and dandruff and he never stopped talking. It was perfectly understandable that the Sig Sigs wouldn't want annoying Jack Rinard in their fraternity, and just as understandable that they'd be willing to put up with him if it meant they could get Patrick, too. Patrick had a quality all his own that made people want to be around him; the fact that he never tried to be anyone but himself probably had something to do with it. Or maybe it was simply that he was the nicest guy on the planet.

"Just do me a favor," Annemarie had warned. "Don't turn into some dumb musclehead."

"Too late," Pat said cheerfully. "I mean, yes, the brain is technically an organ and not made of muscle, *but*, some biologists compare its functionality to a muscle, because, like a muscle, the more you use it, the stronger it gets. So, in that sense, I already *am* a musclehead—and the more I learn at college, the more ripped my brain is gonna get."

"Isn't he smart?" their mother said to no one in particular.

"Is that the reason why you wrote those fitness goals?" Luke snickered, but it was an affectionate snicker. "So the rest of your body can catch up with your big-ass brain?"

"What can I say?" Pat had said solemnly, winking across the table at Pup. "My body is a temple."

"Hey," Aidan said. "Do you want a beer or something?"

"No thanks," Pup said. "I should probably head back."

Just then, a third frat brother, baby-faced but mountainous in stature, dressed in khaki shorts and scuffed boat shoes, burst through the front door, a beer in each hand and a family-size bag of potato chips secured under his chin.

"Yo, Meatwagon," said Aidan. "You remember the name Patrick Flanagan?"

Meatwagon looked up at Pup, dropping the bag of chips at his feet.

"Wait—you mean the dead guy?"

Travis winced. "Sorry," he told Pup. "Meatwagon isn't the most politically correct guy in the world."

"*Yeah*, I know the name," Meatwagon continued, cracking open his beer. "I only nearly crapped my pants when those senior assholes made me stay overnight in his bedroom. *Patrick Flanagan*—I'll never forget *that* name! His goddamn ghost will haunt me til the day I die!"

This time, Aidan and Travis both winced.

"Wait," said Pup. "You've been in his bedroom?"

"Meatwagon—"

"During pledge week! I know we're supposed to tell you incoming freshies that we don't haze anymore, but allow me to let you in on a little secret." He dropped his voice to a theatrical whisper. *"It's a lie."*

"Wait," Pup said again. "You saw his *ghost*?"

"Meatwagon—"

"Maybe I didn't *see* it. But I sure as hell *felt* it. Patrick

Flanagan was this guy in our fraternity who apparently died from this weird, rare disease. I want to say scarlet fever?"

"No. Dude—" Travis was now gesturing frantically, but Meatwagon was not to be stopped.

"No! You're right, Trav. It was diphtheria. I don't know. One of those Oregon Trail diseases. *Anyway*, after he died, they had to, like, quarantine the room so the rest of the house wouldn't get infected. They cleared everything out of there, and these guys in hazmat suits came and sprayed the place down and shut the door, and the door *stayed* shut for probably a whole year, until one of the senior guys with a sick sense of humor decided it would be a cool idea to make pledges *sleep overnight in there*, because not only might you get some heinous disease—I want to say it was typhoid fever? Does that sound right to you guys?—but the room was also *haunted*, because this poor dude *died in there*. You want to talk creepy? I'm not a pussy or anything, but *Jesus Christ*, with these old-ass windows rattling in the wind and the lights turned out and this stain on the floor that was maybe *blood*, I was about to shit my—"

"He didn't die in his bedroom," Pup interrupted. "He died in the hospital."

"How do *you* know, freshie?"

"*Meatwagon*—"

"Because he was my brother."

"Your *brother*?" Meatwagon put his hands on his massive

head and looked back and forth between Travis and Aidan, who were slumped in their chairs, glaring at him. "Oh god. Why didn't you guys *say* anything?"

"He died of bacterial meningitis," Pup went on. "There was no blood. You must have imagined that part."

"Dude, I am very, very sorry." Meatwagon placed his beer on the porch railing and stuck out his hand for Pup to shake. "I would like to extend my deepest condolences and express how large of a piece of shit I feel right now."

"You sure we can't get you a beer?" Aidan asked. "Or a piece of pizza? There's some leftover Home Run in the kitchen."

"Or mac and cheese," Travis said eagerly. "We can totally go inside and I'll make you some mac and cheese. I put frozen peas in it and everything, to make it healthy. Please, man. We all feel like shitheads. Let us do something for you."

"Okay," Pup said. "This haunted bedroom. I want to see it."

14

PUP FOLLOWED AIDAN, TRAVIS, AND MEATWAGON through the front door of the fraternity house. Inside was a high-ceilinged foyer unevenly lit by a chandelier with mostly burned-out light bulbs. An Illini flag draped one wall, and the Sigma Sigma flag covered the other. In the air was the faint tang of old beer, sweat, microwavable food—the smell of boys living away from home. A huge front room stood to their left, with a bunch of ripped leather couches encircling a giant television like an altar.

"Usually it's a lot more exciting around here," Travis explained as he led Pup up the wide, winding staircase matted with brown carpet that led to the second floor. "Parties, meetings, that kind of thing. But most of the guys are home for the summer. Our house president checks in on us from time to time, but mostly it's just the three of us until the fall semester begins. Me and Aidan got ourselves a summer gig with the student union, while Meatwagon here makes a living from giving blood and participating in studies with the Psych department."

"Last week, I did a sleep study," said Meatwagon. "I got paid fifty bucks for taking a nap! *College*, man!"

Aidan and Travis laughed while Pup followed behind them in silence, clutching his camera. The second floor was as narrow as the first floor had been wide-open. At the top of the stairs, two cramped hallways led in either direction, lined with fiberglass doors that were all firmly shut for the summer. The walls were white-painted, scuffed in places. There were no windows, just a buzzing line of fluorescent track lighting that gave everything a greenish cast. The scabby brown carpet muted their footsteps as they walked along toward the end of the hallway.

"Well, here it is," Aidan said, stopping at a door near the end of the corridor that looked identical to all the others. "Room twelve."

Pup's heart was pounding and he didn't know why. It was just a door that opened into a room where his brother had once slept, not unlike the door to his own bedroom back home. The Sig Sigs were the ones who had turned it into something sinister. He put his hand on the knob.

"Take all the time you need," said Travis. He and Aidan and Meatwagon were already backing away down the hallway, either from fear or shame, Pup couldn't tell. He turned his back to them and twisted the knob. It squeaked beneath his hand, the door creaked open, and he stepped into room twelve.

The light switch didn't work, but the full white moon that hung in the sky outside the large rectangular window gave off enough light for Pup to see, and to take pictures, if he felt like it. The window was broken, and cracks spiderwebbed out from a huge hole in the middle. A large, smooth rock, about the same size as the hole, lay in the middle of the floor surrounded by shards of glass that glittered in the moonlight. The window had been broken a long time, Pup could tell, because the inside of the room smelled like the outside. Dried leaves had drifted in from the large oak tree outside the window into the corners of the floor and closet, and little scatterings of mouse droppings were piled along the floorboards. The walls were bare, pocked in places with nails where Patrick and his Sig Sig predecessors had hung their flags and pictures and posters. Two twin-size beds stood on either side of the window, stripped down to thin, sweat-stained mattresses on rusting aluminum frames. A wooden desk was pushed against the wall next to the door, bare but for a curved metal reading lamp. Pup flicked on the lamp, and to his surprise it still worked, illuminating a smooth layer of dust across the wood. He opened the desk drawer, and inside all he found was a single bent paperclip. He picked it up and slipped it into his back pocket next to his honorable mention. Then he got up and crossed the narrow room, his shoes crunching the broken glass. He knelt in the doorway of the closet, attached his flash, and began to shoot: the moon-lit broken window; the stained, stripped beds; the glass on the floor; the dust-encased desk. When he was finished, he sat on one mattress, then the other, because he wasn't sure which one had belonged to Pat. He stretched out on the cold plastic that smelled strongly of mold. He closed his eyes and lay very still, waiting for something to happen.

At Pity Party, Sam Dad Suicide had once asked whether you could technically love someone who was dead.

"Of *course* you can," Mrs. Barrera had scolded. "There's no such thing as *technical* love. There's only *love*. It's a word that doesn't need qualifiers. It can stand on the strength of its own four letters. Death is nothing compared to love. Death is a one-time thing. Love never ends." Pup had wanted to believe her, but he was skeptical. Even if what she said was true, it didn't make it feel any less one-sided. Sometimes Pup thought he loved Izzy because loving her felt the same as loving Patrick: a love that went unreturned, unnoticed, a dark wall that absorbed your light but never returned it.

"Are you here?" he whispered.

He was answered, as always, with silence.

15

AFTER HE'D SUCCESSFULLY SNUCK OUT through the back door of the Sigma Sigma house, evading Aidan, Travis, and Meatwagon and sparing himself from having to hear one more time just how sorry they were, Pup went through his self-care checklist. *HALT!* He could visualize the poster on Mrs. Barrera's wall.

Are you:
Hungry?
Angry?
Lonely?
Tired?

Yes, he decided. He *was* hungry—he was already pondering what to buy in the hotel vending machine before heading back to his room—and he was also angry, lonely, and tired. But by the time he arrived back at the hotel, he'd decided that what he'd just learned about the hazing practices of the Sigma Sigma house was really not that big of a deal. First of all, those guys hadn't known Patrick; he could hardly blame them for thinking of him as a ghost and not a real person. And why had Pup even expected to be shown a sign? Had he really been dumb enough to believe Meatwagon's tale about the room being haunted? Besides, if Patrick was going to appear to him, it wouldn't be in that awful abandoned frat-house bedroom. It would be at Wrigley Field, or out in the alley beneath the basketball hoop, or somewhere along the North Branch of the Chicago River, or any of the hundreds of other places they'd been brothers together. There was nothing of Patrick left in that room. So why did he even care?

"Why do I even *care*?" He didn't realize he was speaking the words out loud until the nighttime desk clerk looked up as he passed and stared at him.

"Sorry." He was starting to feeling spinny, and his eyes were beginning to water, which meant that he was either going to barf or cry. He turned around, avoiding the clerk's curious eyes, and walked straight back out the sliding glass doors of the hotel. He followed the curving front driveway around to the back, where a small, totally empty parking lot butted up against wide fields of corn just beginning to tassel. He sat down on a concrete parking block still warm from the daytime sun, rested his elbows on his knees, and pressed the heels of his hands to his eyes. "Sometimes, you just need to breathe," Mrs. Barrera had advised the Pity Party, so he took a deep, shaky breath and exhaled, listening to the silky tassels soughing in the breeze like thousands of wispy mothers shushing their crying children.

"James?"

He jerked his hands away from his eyes to see Abrihet peering down at him. She still had on her red dress with the flowery things all over it, but she had layered it with a zip-up hoodie. "Are you okay?"

"I'm fine." He wiped his eyes quickly and looked away from her. "I think I'm allergic to the corn pollen or something."

She looked at him for a moment as if deciding whether to accept this obvious lie. Then, she gestured at the concrete parking block. "Mind if I join you?"

"Sure." He scooted over to make room, and she sat down next to him in a rustle of clean-smelling cotton.

"I love this," she said, stretching out her bare legs and nodding at the corn. "This kind of quiet."

"Not me." Pup wiped his nose with the back of his hand. "Haven't you ever seen *Children of the Corn*? Out here in the country, nobody can hear you scream."

"So? Back in the city, people can hear you scream, they just don't care. No, I love the silence. It reminds me of home. Makes me feel like myself again."

"That's good." Pup reached into his pocket and took out the paperclip he'd stolen from Pat's bedroom, squeezing it until the sharp end pricked his skin. "I don't feel like myself anywhere."

"You know," Abrihet said, "you don't have to tell me what's bothering you if you don't want. But I know you're not allergic to corn pollen. I don't know if corn even *has* pollen."

"I think it does," Pup said. "I'm not sure, though. My brother would know. He knew literally everything about science. He could tell you all about corn. Or about the tubeworms that live in the hydrothermal vents of the Pacific seafloor. Or the mating habits of scaly-foot gastropods. He would talk about coral for hours if you let him. His specialty was marine biology."

"Scaly-foot gastropods," Abrihet repeated. "Good band name."

"Yeah." Pup managed a laugh, then changed the subject. "So, any word yet on your mom?"

"Actually, yes." He felt her smile in the darkness. "Thanks for asking. We just got word last week that her visa status was approved. She'll be here next month!"

"That's amazing! Now *you* can be the kid in class with the hand-embroidered Greek Mythology Day costume!"

"I know! And even more important, now she can come see me present at regionals! Part of the reason I got into this whole photography thing was for her. To show her that the sacrifice was worth it, sending me away to America. To show her how I've pursued my passions. How I'm being successful. How I'm fulfilling her dreams for me."

"Abrihet, that is awesome. Really." He wiped his nose

again. "I actually think your good news is helping to cure my corn pollen allergy."

She laughed. Then they both went quiet.

"So, your brother," she said after a while. "The one from the picture. Is he the scientist?"

"No, no. Luke's in law school. He doesn't know the difference between a deep-sea anglerfish and a Goldfish cracker. I was talking about my other brother. Patrick."

"Oh. The one who went here, right?"

"Yeah."

"Huh." Abrihet leaned back on the heels of her hands. "I'm looking around at these cornfields and I'm trying to figure out how a person becomes an expert in marine biology at a place like this."

Pup laughed.

"You sound like my dad. He used to say, 'I'll never understand why a city kid like you cares so much about algae.' Patrick just loved it, though. No real reason. He used to take me snorkeling in the Chicago River. We'd go exploring. Pretending like it was a real ocean, since neither one of us had ever actually seen one. Most of the time the only thing we discovered was old diapers and rusty car fenders. But *sometimes*? Sometimes we'd see pouch snails and sunfish and largemouth bass. One time we even saw a coyote running along the bank with a Kit Kat wrapper in its mouth. The thing with Pat was that he always knew how to make regular things seem, I don't know, better." He looked down at the paperclip cupped in his palm. "He's been dead for almost three years now."

His eyes flickered over to Abrihet's face. In the darkness, it was hard to make out her expression. He braced himself for the obligatory murmured condolences, hoping they wouldn't retrigger his corn pollen allergy.

"Wow," she said instead. "He sounds like a classy brother. I can't even get *my* brother to give me a ride to school."

"He *was* classy." Pup was both flummoxed and relieved at her response. "He had a lot of weird talents, too. He could peel a hard-boiled egg in one piece."

"What?" Abrihet sat up. *"Nobody* can do that. I help my auntie out at her restaurant and we peel eggs all the time. We're both top-notch egg peelers, and *we've* never peeled an egg in one piece."

"If I were going to lie about something," Pup said, "would it really be *that?"*

"Good point."

They were both quiet then, looking out into the tasseling corn. A single airplane made its way across the sky above them, like a slow-moving star. When it had disappeared from sight, Abrihet leaned over and took Pup's hand. He was so stunned by the gesture that he couldn't move. He could only sit there, frozen, and feel her fingers, warm and strong around his. She wasn't looking at him. She wasn't moving closer to him. He didn't know what it was, what it meant. It wasn't romantic, exactly. She was only holding his hand, as if to say simply, *I am here.*

After a while, she let go, got to her feet, and brushed off the back of her skirt.

"Listen," she said. "Tomorrow. What are you doing?"

"Tomorrow night?"

"Yeah. My *amoui*—the one from my picture—is having a party at her restaurant, to celebrate the news about my mom. You should come. Have you ever had Eritrean food before?"

Pup shook his head.

"Well, then you *have* to come."

Pup hesitated. Hanging out with Abrihet tomorrow night meant missing Sunday dinner with his family. Pup had never missed a Sunday dinner in his life. But when he thought about his *HALT!* checklist, he realized that, after talking to Abrihet out here behind the hotel, he no longer felt angry or lonely or even tired. He was still hungry, though. And now she was offering to feed him, too. How could he turn that down?

16

"I'M GOING TO GO TAKE A SHIT," Brody announced the next morning as Pup packed his things in his duffel bag.

Pup ignored him, continuing to fold his clothes in silence. It was late when he'd finally returned to his room, taking great care to make as much noise as possible when he stuck the key card in the reader. When he'd walked in, Brody and Maya had both scrambled themselves into poses of staged innocence. But Maya's shirt was on backward, Brody's neck was streaked with lipstick, the sheets of his bed were in complete disarray, and the iPad lay forgotten on the floor. When Maya had hurried out of the room, Pup noticed that her fly was unzipped.

Brody went into the bathroom and slammed the door behind him. He emerged twenty minutes later, walked across the room, and stood directly in front of the ESPN program that Pup was trying to watch on the hotel TV.

"Hey," Brody said. "I just remembered. You forgot to get me my mini muffins last night."

"Are you *serious*?"

"Okay, okay!" Brody laughed, holding up his hands in surrender. "Chill. I'll go get them myself."

A few minutes later he returned from the vending machines with his muffins and a bottle of Gatorade. Pup had finished packing and was sitting on his bed, flicking through his phone.

"Hey, man," Brody said, ripping open the package. "You're not gonna say anything, right?"

"About what?" Pup didn't look up.

"About me and Maya hanging out last night."

"Oh. Is that what you were doing?"

"Yeah. Obviously. We watched a movie. Is that a crime?"

"What movie?"

"You *know* what movie. You were there when we started it. *Titanic.* A nineties classic."

"What happens at the end?"

Brody glared at him. "The boat sinks."

"Nice try." Pup put his phone down. "The boat sinks in the *middle.* At the *end,* Rose drops the necklace off the side of the research vessel. Then she dies and sees Leonardo DiCaprio waiting for her on the stairs up to heaven."

Brody looked at him.

"What is *wrong* with you, man?"

"I have five sisters and seven nieces. And *you're* an asshole."

Brody laughed. "You know what? Go ahead and tell Izzy if you want. It's not like she's going to believe you."

"I've been friends with her since practically the beginning of high school. You've been with her for eight months."

"Not that you're counting or anything." Brody smirked. He was wearing one of those shirts with faded patches and holes along the hem to make it look vintage, when really his mom had probably purchased it for him at an expensive department store. "You think she doesn't know that you're completely obsessed with her?"

"I'm not obsessed with anyone."

"Yes you are. You're obsessed with *my* girlfriend, and everyone knows it, including her. It's so sad. We laugh about it all the time. It's, like, a running joke between us. That time she had to kiss you during Spin the Bottle? She was *disgusted*. As soon as you left the house she ran upstairs and disinfected her mouth with, like, half of a bottle of Listerine. It was one of those big bottles, too. From Costco."

"You're lying," Pup said. "Izzy wouldn't do that. *Nobody* would do that. If you tried to gargle that much Listerine, it would burn your mouth. And besides, she hates the taste of mint. Can't even stand to chew gum. Which you should know, since you're *so* in love with her."

"You think you know her better than I do? Fine. Test it out. Go ahead and tell her I hooked up with Maya. She'll think you're just making it up. She'll think it's just some pathetic attempt at getting her for yourself."

"So you admit it!" Pup leaped off the bed. "You *did* cheat on her!"

"So what if I did? I *dare* you to rat me out! See what happens! She'll laugh in your face!"

Pup's reaction was automatic. He reached out and backhanded the Gatorade from Brody's grip. It flew through the air, spraying an arc of orange liquid all over the cream-colored bedspread.

"You *asshole!*" Brody yelled. "That shit was a dollar fifty!"

"Oh yeah?"

"Yeah!"

"Well, watch *this!*" Pup ripped the bag of mini muffins from Brody's other hand and, in a swift, masterful move he'd learned from Luke, held the bag up in the air and shook its contents—five remaining muffins—into his open mouth.

"You *asshole!*"

"Mm," Pup managed, chewing the enormous mass of preservative-chocked pastry and spraying wet crumbs all over Brody's face. "Delicious!"

Brody lunged, but Pup ducked. A floor lamp crashed to the carpet.

"Boys!" Mr. Hughes was pounding on the door. "What the *hell* is going on in there? Open up!"

"And now you got us in trouble with Mr. Hughes!"

"No, *you* got us in trouble, you *dick!*"

"BOYS!"

Pup opened the door, a wad of muffin going to cud in the side of his mouth.

Mr. Hughes stood in the doorway taking in Pup, Brody, and the orange stain dripping from the bedspread and seeping into the white carpet. "You better hope that's Scotchgarded," he growled. "Now get your crap together and meet me in the lobby. They don't pay me enough for this, I swear!"

Once he'd slammed the door and his footsteps faded in the hallway, Pup turned around slowly to face Brody again.

"You better tell her," he said, swallowing what remained of the muffin cud. "Or I will."

17

BY THE TIME MR. HUGHES dropped Pup back at home after a sufficiently awkward three-hour car ride, it was midafternoon and the house smelled like Sunday: chopped garlic, stewing tomatoes, and the rich scent of pineapple upside-down cake baking in the oven. Pup's mother was standing in the kitchen with the windows open to the summer wind, stirring heavy cream into her big saucepan with a long wooden spoon. When she turned to see who was coming in the back door, it looked a little bit like she'd been crying, but Pup couldn't be sure if that was it, or if her face was simply flushed from standing over the hot stove on a hot day.

"Well, if it isn't my budding Picasso!" She put her spoon down on the Texas-shaped spoon rest Annemarie and Sal had bought for her on a trip to Austin, and came over to give him a hug.

"It's not that big of deal, Mom," he said, speaking into the air over her head. He was so tall now that when his mom hugged him she barely reached his shoulder.

"Of *course* it's a big deal!" She took the ribbon and gasped excitedly, turning it over in her hands. "This color and texture is *exactly* like the nineteenth-century Persian silk rug a gal from Iowa got appraised last night on *Antiques* for thirty thousand dollars!"

"It's not real silk, Ma."

"Still, it's just *lovely*, Pup."

"I have to make a portfolio," he explained. "That's going to be the hard part."

"A portfolio," she repeated. "How *wonderful*. Ted!" she yelled out through the open window. "Come in here! Pup's going to make a *portfolio*!"

Pup's dad hurried in, still wearing his gardening kneepads.

"What's wrong?" he demanded. "Why are you *yelling*?"

She held up the ribbon. "Pup qualified for *regionals*." Ted felt for his reading glasses in his pants pocket, put them on, and examined the ribbon. "Well, isn't that *something*," he said.

"I can't wait to celebrate you tonight at Sunday dinner." His mom's blue eyes were watery as she squeezed his two hands in hers. "Oh, it's so exciting. *Ann Arbor, Michigan!*"

"Um, actually, Mom." Pup looked down at the pair of soft, papery hands that grasped his own. "You don't have to . . . see, this friend of mine. Her aunt owns a restaurant. She won an award yesterday, too, and she invited me to a party. . . ."

"Oh!" She blinked, and her hands slackened in his. "Tonight?"

"It's—well, yeah. I told her I would go. I mean, I promised her. But I can totally come back early. I can be home in time for dessert."

"Of course not!" She smiled tightly while Pup's dad reached out a dirt-encrusted hand and gently squeezed her shoulder. "No, honey. You deserve to go out and have some fun on a beautiful Sunday evening like this."

"Lord knows your brother does," grumbled Pup's dad. "Have you heard from him at all, Pup? Any idea whether he'll be gracing us with his presence tonight?"

"I haven't talked to him," Pup said, which was the truth. Luke had maintained a low profile ever since his argument with Annemarie in the alley. He didn't stay at home much, and when he did, he usually returned in the middle of the night, drunk and not in the mood for conversation. He'd missed three Sunday dinners in a row now.

"I just hope he's been keeping up with his studies," said Pup's mom, reading his thoughts. "He spends more time at Carrie's place than he does in his own bed."

"Yes, well, if it weren't for her influence," his father said, pulling his gardening gloves back on and heading for the door, "god knows what path Luke might go down."

Pup opened his mouth to say something, but thought the better of it. He often wondered, with some unease, where Luke stayed on the nights when he didn't come home, if he wasn't staying with Carrie. But if his parents still didn't know about the breakup, he certainly wasn't going to be the one to tell them.

"Have fun tonight, honey," said his mother. "I'll save a plate for you."

"Are you sure, Mom?"

Pup hovered there in the middle of the stifling, fragrant kitchen, feeling sort of terrible. He'd never been much of a student or an athlete, but at least he'd always been a good son. It was kind of his thing.

His mom put a garlic-perfumed hand on his cheek. "Of course I'm sure," she said gently, but her eyes had grown watery again as she turned her back on him to pick up her spoon and resume stirring her sauce.

18

ABRIHET'S AUNT'S RESTAURANT, Shores of the Red Sea, was sandwiched in a strip mall between a nail salon and an Indian grocery. Pup's father wouldn't let him borrow the Buick to drive all the way across the city to Uptown, so instead it took two different bus transfers to get there on the CTA. By the time he arrived, the party was in full swing and the little restaurant was packed. It was a small square room with a black tile floor, red curtains, and a buffet table against one wall covered in white paper and filled with trays of food. When Abrihet saw Pup walk in, she squeezed through the crowd and met him at the door.

"Jeez," Pup said, looking around. "Your aunt knows how to throw a party."

"Oh." She waved her arm at the groups of people lined up at the buffet, drinking tea and wine at the tables, and crowded around a soccer game on the television above the bar. "These are all just my cousins."

"Whoa. And I thought *I* had a big family."

"Well, most of them aren't *really* my cousins. In our community, we just call each other cousins even if we're not technically related. We grow up with our parents telling us over and over again that us Eritreans in America are like one big family. And then they don't understand that we find it a little creepy when they turn around and expect us to marry the same boys they've been calling our cousins all our lives."

"I hear you," Pup said. "I have seven brothers and sisters, thirteen nieces and nephews—with another one on the way any day now—forty-one first cousins, and over a hundred second cousins. Which basically means I'm at least distantly related to half the people in this city. I'll probably end up marrying one of my cousins by accident, and we'll have a four-headed baby or something."

Abrihet laughed. "Well, I'm not from here, so you can't be related to me. So if *we* ever get married, then you won't have to worry."

Pup swallowed. His palms suddenly felt clammy and he felt a vague jittering in his gut. Was she—? No. Impossible. They were *friends*. He wasn't going to make the same mistake he'd made with Izzy. Besides, no girl had ever flirted with him in his life, and Abrihet Tesfay was far too smart and pretty to be the first. He'd won an honorable mention at a high school art show, after all. Which was cool and everything, but not exactly the type of thing to make girls like Abrihet come running all of a sudden.

"Hey." Pup pointed. "You invited Mr. Hughes."

"Yeah. Do you see that tall skinny guy he's talking to?"

"Yeah."

"That's my dad."

The two men were drinking bottles of beer and laughing together like they were old friends.

"They seem to be getting along, huh?"

"Yeah," said Abrihet. "Which is ridiculous, because I practically had to beg Baba to even let me take AP Studio Art in the first place."

"Really? Why? I thought parents loved it when their kids signed up for AP classes."

"Maybe normal parents do," she said. "But my dad thinks anything that doesn't directly help get me into medical school or dental school is a waste of time. The whole idea of taking a class simply because you enjoy it? That's a very American thing. Baba says he didn't leave his wife and his country and his life behind so that his daughter could spend her school days finger painting. So yeah, I guess you could say this is a little vindicating. Besides, he's in a good mood today." She beamed at him. "We all are. I'm going to see my mom in forty-two days."

"I would totally hug you right now except your dad is looking over here and kind of glaring at me."

Abrihet looked over her shoulder at her father, who was leaning against the wall next to Mr. Hughes and watching the two of them over the rim of his beer bottle. "Yeah," she said, "that's probably a good idea. You already have two strikes against you. One, you're a boy, and two, you're American. My dad doesn't really like me hanging out with American boys."

"Kind of limits your options, this being America and all."

"I think that's the whole idea. Now. Let's go get you some food. It goes pretty quickly. My aunt's cooking is kind of legendary."

She led him to the long buffet table against the wall. It was lined with trays of rich stew and curries and vegetables and these rolled-up tortilla-looking things and it all smelled delicious. Abrihet handed him a plate and began pointing things out: rice and salad, which he recognized, and *tibsi* and *tsebhi*, which he did not.

"This here, *shiro*, with onions and tomatoes, is one of our vegetarian dishes. So are the *hamli* and the *alicha*. Mr. Hughes has already had about three helpings. And you've got to try some of our sweet bread, *himbasha*. *Ooh*, and this." She pointed at a steaming tray filled with chunks of meat and boiled egg swimming in a rich red sauce. "You can't say you've eaten Eritrean food without trying *dorho*. This dish is where Patrick's egg-peeling skills would have come in handy."

Pup stopped short and stared at her.

"What?" She looked at him. "Are you okay?"

"Yeah. Sorry." Pup swallowed, recovering himself. It was just so strange to hear someone bring up Patrick casually in conversation, without tiptoeing around it, without using hushed tones. He leaned over the *dorho* so that she couldn't see his burning face, breathing in the steam and the spices. "This all looks amazing. Where's the silverware?"

"We don't use silverware. What you do is, you take the *injera*—this rolled-up bread here—and you tear off pieces and use it to pick up the food you want. Here, let me show you." She reached over to the stack of spongy bread, tore off a chunk, and, with a graceful sweeping movement of her wrist, picked up a helping of *dorho*, folded it neatly, and popped it in her mouth. Pup knew he would shortly be embarrassing himself with his own attempts at eating Eritrean cuisine, but for the moment, he admired Abrihet for her ability to make forks seem like just another frivolity that Americans thought was necessary even when the rest of the world got along just fine without it, like triple-ply toilet paper or squeeze cheese.

He set about heaping his plate with *injera* and *dorho* while Abrihet went off to work the room. He found an empty chair near the window and began switching off between stuffing his face with food and photographing the party with the film camera that Mr. Hughes had instructed him to bring wherever he went now that he had less than two months to build a portfolio. When he'd gotten through half a roll of film and an entire plate of food, one of Abrihet's older cousins came up to him with a stack of plastic cups and a foamy pitcher of beer.

"Thanks, but I don't really drink," Pup said.

"*James.*" Abrihet had returned to lean over and whisper in his ear. "That's *suwa*. It's a homemade beer made from roasted barley. It would be very rude to decline it. Plus, it's really not even strong. You'd need to drink a *lot* to feel drunk."

"Oh. Well, in that case."

The cousin poured a glass for Pup, Abrihet, and herself. They toasted each other, and even though the smell of beer reminded Pup of his least-favorite memories of Luke, the cool, amber-colored liquid trickling down his throat, mixing with the tastes of spices and onion and stewed meat, was unexpectedly refreshing. He finished his glass, and as Abrihet promised, he didn't feel drunk. He only felt happy, and sort of at ease, which was weird, considering he was at a party where he knew only two people, one of whom was a teacher whose class he had almost failed. But everybody around him was in such a good mood that it was impossible *not* to feel happy right along with them. He thought about how hard it was for his own mother that he was missing one Sunday dinner. Abrihet's mother had missed several years' worth of Sunday dinners, and now she was finally going to be reunited with her family. No wonder everyone was celebrating.

"James," Abrihet said, swallowing the last of her *suwa* and placing her empty glass on the floor next to his chair.

"There's someone I'd like you to meet."

She led him over to a table of women who were drinking tea and talking animatedly in Tigrinya, and who instantly stopped their conversation to stare at him as they approached.

"James," she said, "this is my *amoui.*"

Pup now understood why Abrihet loved to take photographs of her aunt. The woman was tall and striking, much younger than any of his own aunts, and the movements she made lifting and setting back down her teacup were spare and graceful. She had thin gold hoops dangling from her small, roundish ears and thick-lashed eyes sparkling with a glittery bluish shadow across the lids. With a movement of nothing but those eyes, she scrutinized Pup from the uppermost puff of his wiry red hair to the untied laces of his Nikes.

"Nice to meet you, ma'am."

Abrihet's *amoui* inclined her head and said something to her niece in Tigrinya.

"Her English isn't as bad as she pretends," Abrihet explained. "Right, Auntie?" The woman only shrugged, and the rest of the table laughed.

"Well, ma'am," Pup said, sticking his hands in his pockets and then immediately taking them out for fear of appearing too casual, too sloppy, too stereotypically American, "I just want to say, your food is *ridiculous.*"

Abrihet's aunt narrowed her eyes at him while the two

other women at the table glanced at each other and then back at their teacups.

"Ridiculously *good*, I meant," he babbled on. "It's an American saying. Like, meaning, it's so good it's *ridiculous*." He could feel the sweat beginning to accumulate at the back of his neck. Then, remembering the word he'd scrawled into the soft palm of his hand with a borrowed pen on the bus ride across the city, he opened his fingers to read it. The ink was beginning to streak, but it hadn't sweated off yet. "What I mean is, um, *yekeniyely*."

Abrihet looked at Pup in surprise, as did all three of the women at the table.

"Where did you learn that?"

"My sister Annemarie told me I should, you know, learn a couple words of your language before I came tonight. As a sign of respect. So I did some Googling on the bus."

"Did you learn anything besides 'thank you'?"

"Not really," he admitted. "It took me most of the bus ride to figure out how to pronounce it correctly."

Abrihet's aunt ran her fingers across the crisp white paper covering on the table. "My niece will teach you some more," she said in perfect English, without looking at him. Then she turned back to her friends, and they resumed their conversation as if Pup and Abrihet were no longer standing there.

"She likes you, James," Abrihet said as they walked over to check out the dessert trays. "I can tell."

"Really? How?"

"Because she spoke English to you," she said. "And because she sees what I see."

Pup blinked. "What do you see?"

"That for someone who's so different from me, you're really not that different from me."

Pup knew exactly what she meant. Even though Abrihet's family came from a country seven thousand miles from Flanland, even though they spoke a language he couldn't understand and cooked with spices he'd never tasted, big families were the same everywhere: loud and nosy, loyal and prying, bossy and loving, prone to shoveling mountains of food onto their plates before the good stuff ran out. Being at Shores of the Red Sea with Abrihet and her army of cousins felt less strange to Pup than dinner at Izzy's house, with its loud silences and polite questions and clinking silverware.

After he'd wiped his plate clean with a piece of *injera* and drained his second glass of *suwa*, Pup stood up to say his goodbyes. The crowd was beginning to thin, and he figured that if he didn't have to wait too long for the bus, he might be able to make it home in time for his mom's cake.

"I'll walk you out," Abrihet said. "I need some air. And some escape from my relatives. I love them, but they're *so* nosy."

"Tell me about it," said Pup. "I grew up in a house with

eight children and one bathroom. Privacy is a foreign concept to me."

Outside, the sun was setting, making the city glow gold. Pup felt like he was glowing too. Maybe it was the *suwa*, or maybe it was all the delicious food he'd eaten, or maybe it was just the feeling of Abrihet walking next to him, her arm brushing against his, her sandals slapping on the hot pavement.

When they'd reached the bus stop, she pointed across the street to a redbrick building with a little shop on the ground level that sold international phone credit. "That's my apartment. And that one there, down the street a little ways, with the grates on the windows? That's the apartment we lived in when we first immigrated."

Pup looked up at the grated windows, shielding his eyes from the sun.

"That place was so *tiny*," she said, shaking her head at the memory. "And we had to share it with three other families. There wasn't enough room for everybody, so all the kids had to sleep on air mattresses in the kitchen. I could never sleep, though, because the room never got dark enough. There was the microwave clock light. The coffeemaker light. The streetlights shining through the transom. The headlights from cars swooping across the ceiling all night, like a laser show. I'd pull the blankets over my face to drown out the light but even the *blankets* were too bright—they had that

sunny American laundry-detergent smell like fake flowers."
She was quiet for a second. "I remember just lying there,
trying to sleep, except I couldn't because I knew that back
home it was already morning, and I couldn't stop thinking
about my mother. I'd picture her getting out of bed, putting on her tea, standing at the table and pressing designs
into the *himbasha* dough with the end of her fork. I'd picture the sun tipping over the mountains and flooding our
kitchen with light. I'd imagine her closing her eyes, feeling that pink-gold heat on her face, somehow knowing that
somewhere across the world, her daughter was lying awake
on an air mattress and thinking of her." She lifted a hand
to her cheek, as if feeling for the warmth of that faraway
sunlight. "That's why the nights were the worst. Because for
those hours, my mother wasn't even living in the same day
as I was. If it was Friday here, it was already Saturday there.
And I know it sounds weird, but I could feel the absence of
her in my Friday. That's how I became fluent in English so
fast. I'd practice it in my head, lying on that air mattress in
the middle of the night, to make myself stop thinking about
my mother. It was sort of like . . . if I could learn this foreign
language, start thinking in it and dreaming in it, maybe it
would make me feel farther away from her." She squinted
up to where the setting sun had turned her old windows
into brilliant squares of fire. "And it worked, maybe almost
too well. Because now, after all these years of thinking and

speaking and dreaming in English, I feel so far away from her."

"But not for long," said Pup.

"No," Abrihet said quietly. She was still gazing up at the building with the grates all over the windows. "Not for long."

She broke her gaze to turn and look at him. The sun had begun its descent behind the brick apartment buildings and the sky was striated with pink clouds. In this light Pup looked into Abrihet's eyes and wished he was a smarter person with a better vocabulary who could think of the word for the color they actually were. Something deep brown and velvet; newly turned soil in his father's garden, maybe, or tree bark after a heavy rain.

"Hey," said Abrihet. "I'm sorry I said the thing about Patrick before. I shouldn't have just brought him up like that. Like I knew him. Or like I know *you*."

"No!" Pup shook his head. "Don't be sorry. It was just—see, nobody in my family *ever* talks about him. So I was just *surprised*, that's all. In a good way."

"My family can be like that too," said Abrihet. "They'll nag me to death about stupid stuff like a ten-point reading quiz or the way I wear my hair to school, but when it comes to important stuff, like the status of my mom's visa application, I get just this *wall*. If it weren't for my friends, I'd go crazy."

"Yeah, well, I don't really have many friends. I have the Pity Party—that's the bereavement group I'm in at school, but we're not really *friends*. We *can't* be."

"Why not? Isn't that the whole *point* of a support group?"

"Yeah, but . . ." He shaded his eyes with his hands so he could see her more clearly in the setting sunlight. "See, there's a guy in my Pity Party—I can't tell you his name or anything; everything is supposed to be confidential—but he's this big shot on the football team, and that's what everybody knows him as around school. Except *I* know that after his mom died of breast cancer, he got into this habit of sleeping in her favorite purple work blazer every night. And he *knows* that I know that. So he can't wear his normal jock-dude mask around me at school because he knows I know it's bullshit— and therefore, we can't be friends. Make sense?"

"I think so," said Abrihet.

"What I'm trying to say is that I'm *happy* you brought Patrick up to me. Talk about him whenever you want. Ask me anything you want to know. Really."

"That's a promise," said Abrihet. "Because you want to know something, James?"

"What?"

"I really like talking to you."

"You do?"

"Yes."

"Well, I really like talking to you, too." He smiled at her, wishing he had Declan's teeth. She didn't seem to mind, though. She smiled back.

"Your ride is here." She nodded at the bus, which was just

pulling up in a puff of exhaust and a squeaking settling of brakes. Pup fumbled in his pocket for his Ventra card. Stupid bus. It never showed up when you wanted it to, and then, the one time when you wanted to be stuck on a corner for the rest of your life, or at least until you figured out the right words to describe the particular color of a girl's eyes, here it was, right on time.

19

WHEN PUP ARRIVED HOME and crossed through the yard toward the back door, the first thing he saw, silhouetted in the light of the kitchen window, was Luke's profile. The tension that had been building in the pit of his stomach for weeks finally began to ease. After three weeks in a row of playing hooky, the prodigal son had finally returned to Sunday dinner.

But as soon as he climbed the deck stairs and opened the back door, Pup knew immediately that things were not okay. For starters, it was nearly nine o'clock and the drying rack next to the sink was still overflowing with dripping dishes. The Flanagan children always washed up after the Sunday meal, but their mother insisted on putting all the dishes away herself because she claimed that her children couldn't be trusted to remember the correct cabinets to stow the various utensils and pots and serving trays. She always completed this task as soon as the dishes were washed, because after everybody left, she liked to sit down with her weak, milky cup of tea, put her feet up on the shabby tweed ottoman, and binge on *Antiques Roadshow* until it was time for bed. For something to throw her off track, it would have to be major and it would have to be bad.

The kitchen was filled with the familiar Sunday smells of baked garlic bread and slow-simmering meat sauce, but underneath it Pup could smell something cloyingly sweet and acidic, like decaying fruit, or the taste that fills your mouth just before you throw up. The origin of the stench was Luke. He was standing in the middle of the kitchen, his head lolling like a boxer's in a late round, while Pup's parents stood huddled together directly across from him, looking defiant and furious, but far older than he had ever remembered them looking before. It may have been a trick of the light, though, because even Luke looked haggard and haunted; they regarded each other in the middle of that room like the three lone survivors of a shipwreck. Not one of them had even noticed Pup's entrance. Stepping to one corner of the room, he lifted the camera that still hung around his neck from the party and pressed the shutter, then retreated to the breakfast nook, as shaken and disturbed by what he'd captured as an embedded photographer in a foreign war.

"What's *so* important to you?" his mom was demanding. She was making the same mistake that Pup had made in the past, the mistake of trying to reason with Luke when he was past the point of reasoning. "I just don't understand what is *so* important that you haven't been here *three weekends in a row*. And then when you *do* come home, you show up like—" She made a vague gesture with her arm. "Like *this*."

"Like *what*, Ma?" Luke bared his teeth at her in the grotesque approximation of a smile.

"You *know* like what. Like a common stumble bum."

"Mother." Luke leaned against the breakfast nook, his back to Pup, and dug out a cigarette from his pocket. "I will have you know that 'bum' is no longer a politically correct term. How could you be so insensitive to our viaduct-dwelling brethren?"

"Don't you dare light that cigarette in this house." Pup's dad's voice was low and furious. He was wearing his World Series T-shirt with the dribbled bleach stain along the sleeve. "Just when the hell did you start smoking, anyway?"

"I am a man who's full of surprises." Luke stuck the unlit cigarette behind his ear, pushed himself upright from the table and lurched toward the fridge. He swung the door open, bent down, and peered inside, pulling out a foil-covered plate.

"Oh, no, you don't!" his mom said. "I made that plate for Pup!"

"It's okay, Ma," Pup said softly, and every head swiveled toward the place where he was sitting at the breakfast nook, all of them suddenly registering his presence at the same time. "He can have it."

"He certainly may not. If your brother wants to go out drinking all day every Sunday, that's his business. But I'm not going to feed him his dinner if that's how he's going to behave."

"You're not *feeding* me," Luke said, raising his voice to a whiny pitch that was meant to mock their mother's way of speaking, and that made Pup look away in shame. "I'm not sitting in a fuckin' high chair while you spoon some pureed carrots into my mouth. I'm just *eating*." He took the foil-covered plate and stumbled through the open doorway toward the long wooden dining room table. As he passed her, Pup's mom reached up to grab the plate, but Luke, with a crisp, precise movement—sort of impressive for a person who was as drunk as he was—swatted her away with his free hand.

"Hey!" The broken blood vessels squiggling across his father's cheeks surged an angry purple. "Don't you touch your mother like that!"

Luke ignored his father and kept walking. They all followed him out to the dining room but stopped short in the doorway, unsure of what to do next, as he dropped onto the wooden bench, slung the plate onto the table with a clatter, and peeled off the foil.

"Give that back." Pup's mother's voice simmered with choked rage. "I told you. That plate is for Pup."

"*Ma*," Pup pleaded. What was wrong with her? The

woman who avoided conflict at all costs was now suddenly ready to go toe to toe with a whiskey-drunk Luke? Didn't she know yet that the only way to handle him in these situations was not to engage with him at all? "I *ate* already. He can have it."

"See?" Luke smiled again, that hideous baring of teeth. "Permission granted."

He ducked his head toward the plate, scooped up a hunk of pasta with his bare hand, and shoveled it into his mouth.

"That is *enough*!" She was yelling now. Pup had not heard her yell at anyone—not even at the television when a poppet doll had gotten completely lowballed by the eighteenth-century toys expert on *Antiques Roadshow*—since before Patrick died. In a way, it was sort of nice: proof that the fiery woman who had raised eight children was still inside of her somewhere. She reached across the table and grabbed the plate from beneath Luke's hands. He was on his feet in an instant, still chewing, the pasta hanging out of his mouth like strings of intestines. With another precise, brutal movement, he whirled around and yanked the plate back. Pup and his father stood paralyzed as his petite mother, still dressed in her purple skirt from Sunday mass, and his drunk, hulking, brother, whose belly had gone slack with alcohol but whose shoulders were still humped with muscle, grappled for a long second with the plate of Bolognese. And then Luke's hand was grasping her shoulder, his thumb digging into her collarbone, shoving her away from him with all the violence and contempt the darkest part of himself could muster. She flew backward and the plate was in the air. It turned once and then hit the hardwood, cracking down the middle like a half-moon, the sauce exploding against the faded floral wallpaper like blood spatter, while Pup's mother landed heavily on top of the plate with a painful thud.

"Mom!" Pup dropped to the floor, his knees squelching in cold pasta, as she struggled to catch her breath. Beside him, Luke was deflating like a balloon. His rage, choked off from its source of oxygen, had collapsed. He only looked small and mean and so terrified at what he had just done it had nearly sobered him up.

"Ma," Luke whispered. Their mother gasped and floundered on the floor like a caught fish, her legs churning in the red mess, meat sauce caking in her hair. If it wasn't so awful, so humiliating and violent and *awful*, it almost would have been funny. She flailed her arms, and then her breath finally caught, first one huge gulp of air and then another. Then, she was still, breathing evenly and moaning softly, her cheek pressed into the wet floor.

"Oh, god," said Luke. "Ma. I didn't mean to." He fell to his knees, on the other side of her body from Pup. He prostrated himself on the floor next to her so that his face was inches from hers on the hardwood. "Please," he said. "Ma. I didn't mean to."

"Get out," their father said quietly, putting his foot between his wife's face and his son's. "You no longer live here. Get your things and get out of this house."

"Mom." Luke was only speaking to her. He was only seeing her.

"*Out!*" roared their father.

"Pup." Luke looked up from where he was lying next to their mother. His voice was pleading again; the same voice he'd used on the roof the night Pup had taken his photograph. "Tell them."

"Tell them what?" Pup hated himself for beginning to cry.

"You leave Pup out of this!" shouted their father. "Whatever it is, I don't want to hear it!"

"Dad—" said Pup.

"No!" Their father held Pup back with a shaking forearm. "Just get the hell out of here!"

"I'm sorry," Luke whispered. He rose slowly to his feet. The front of his jeans and shirt were stained red, as if he'd just committed a brutal murder. "I'm sorry." He looked around wildly, at his father, at Pup, at his mother who was huddled, breathing softly, on the floor. In three strides he was in the kitchen and kicking open the back door, so hard the top hinge sprung away.

"*I'm sorry!*" He was howling now, and in his voice was a grief so overwhelming, an anguish so dark that even Pup, who thought he knew a thing or two about pain, could not even recognize its bottom. *"I'm sorry!"* Luke wailed again, doubled over with it, and then with a wild shove that ripped the door off its other hinge and sent it clattering onto the deck, Luke ran out through the street-lit yard and disappeared down the alley.

FORM:

objects that are three-dimensional

and can be viewed from many sides

20

THE NEXT DAY, FINALS WEEK BEGAN. Two exam periods per day for four excruciating days, as if the school administration enjoyed prolonging the torture for as long as possible. The day was blue-skied and beautiful, but Pup walked to school cotton-brained and filled with dread. He'd stayed awake practically all night listening, half in hope and half in fear, for Luke's lurching footsteps on the stairs. He didn't remember falling asleep. He dreamed of nothing, as always. In the morning, he came downstairs to find his mom puttering around the kitchen like nothing was wrong, except that every time she turned or leaned down to pick something up, she grimaced in pain.

"Mom." He reached up to the cabinet to get her instant oatmeal. "Are you all right?"

"I'm fine, dear," she said, breathing shallowly. She took the box from him and moved gingerly toward the stove. "I just slept on my arm funny last night."

"Mom." Pup looked at her. "Are you serious? You know I was *there*, right?"

She turned her back on him and began shaking the oat-meal into a saucepan. "I just don't want any more trouble," she said quietly.

"Are you hurt?"

"I'll be fine. And I don't want you telling Annemarie or any of your other sisters about this." She poured water into the pan and turned on the stove. Then she covered her face with her hands. "I just don't want any more *trouble*."

"Okay, Mom. *Okay*." Pup went over to hug her, but as soon as he put his arms around her, she cried out in pain.

"Please," she said, backing away. "Just tell them, if they ask, that I tripped on Adalyn's teething giraffe, okay?"

He agreed quickly, without hesitation. He was so used to covering for Luke, it no longer really even felt like lying.

It occurred to Pup, as he joined the stream of kids heading through the school's main entrance before the first exam period, that he hadn't so much as cracked open a book to study for finals. Which seemed, at this point, like the least of his problems. He took his usual shortcut through the locker room and had to sprint the rest of the way toward his Spanish classroom because Señora Perez had a policy of locking the door on late test-takers. He'd left the house in such a daze that he'd forgotten everything but his camera, and he had to borrow a pencil from the very unimpressed girl who sat in front of him. He sweated his way through sixty brutal minutes of vocabulary, conjugation, and translation, before Señora Perez had to nudge him awake, not gently, during the audio portion at the end. Finally, mercifully, the bell rang, and as Pup walked out of the classroom stupefied and brain-scrambled, he almost walked straight past Izzy, who was waiting for him in the hallway.

"There he is!" She threw an arm around his shoulder. "State art show winner *and* ladies' man."

"Huh?" He looked at her in confusion. Had she heard somehow that he'd gone to a party with Abrihet and the rumor mill had taken it from there?

"Yeah! Brody told me all about you and Maya."

"Wait. Me and *Maya*? *Me* and Maya?"

"To be honest, Pup, I'm so happy for you." She clapped her hands together, the way Mrs. Barrera did whenever someone in Pity Party had a breakthrough. "So, are you two, like, dating now? Are you going to call her? Or was it just a random hookup?"

Pup carefully placed his pencil, which he'd forgotten to return, behind his ear.

"Izzy," he said. "I didn't hook up with Maya Ulrich."

"You didn't?"

"No. *Brody* did."

Izzy took a step back, the smile fading from her face.

"But he told me . . ."

"I'm sorry," he said quickly. "I would have called you last

night to tell you. But I wanted to give him the chance to do the right thing and tell you himself. And I got sort of preoccupied last night. My brother—"

"But that can't be."

"I was right *there*. When they were . . . doing stuff. I mean, when she was doing stuff to him. I left the room after that. I'm really sorry, Iz. He's such an asshole."

"Pup." Her eyes were suddenly brimful of tears. "I can't believe you."

"Wait. What?"

"I know you never liked me and Brody together, and that's fine. I can live with that. But to sit here and *lie* to me? To try to *sabotage* it?"

"Izzy," he said. "I'm not lying. Why would I lie?"

"You *know* why."

Her voice was rising. A crowd of sophomore girls began circling nearer to gorge on the drama like vultures.

"Brody wouldn't cheat on me. And he definitely wouldn't *lie* to me."

"*Yes, he would. He did.* Because he's a total—"

"Stop." She held up a hand. "Just *stop*. What, you want to be the hero? Save me from my horrible boyfriend so I can run into your arms instead? I know how you feel about him. And I know how you feel about *me*."

"Izzy, you *know* me. I would never—"

"Yeah, I do know you, Pup. Ever since freshman year

you've been tagging along after me like some sad, abandoned puppy dog. You've never been able to stop *worshipping* me for a minute to just be my *friend*. It's pathetic."

"*Wait* a minute, Izzy." He reached out his hand to her, but she ducked away.

"Don't touch me. And don't call me anymore either, okay?"

At that moment, Brody came ambling around the corner. He was gnawing on a churro stick from the cafeteria breakfast menu and his upper lip was furred in sugar. Izzy ran to him, crumpling into his arms. The sophomore vultures, seeing that the drama was over, scattered away down the hallway, and Brody locked eyes with Pup over Izzy's heaving shoulder.

He was positively grinning.

21

PUP MUDDLED THROUGH HIS ENGLISH EXAM as best he could and fled school the moment the final bell rang. The last thing in the world he felt like doing was wedding cake tasting with Annemarie and Sal, but he'd promised them weeks ago he would go, and if he suddenly turned down the opportunity to eat free pastries, they'd know something was up.

He arrived at the bakery a few minutes before they pulled up, which gave him time to window-shop the neat trays of éclairs, the rows of fat red strawberries dipped in white chocolate, mini crème brûlée crusted over with golden sugar, and cream-filled cannoli dusted with bright green pistachios. His stomach growled. He wasn't the type of person who lost his appetite when he was sad.

"I have to *go*, Jeanine," Annemarie was saying as she climbed out of the driver's side while Sal followed behind her with a cup of coffee, winking at Pup and making a yapping signal with his free hand. "Yes . . . I will ask him. . . .

Yes. . . . I'll call you later. . . . I don't know what time. *Later.*"
Annemarie hung up, and dropped her phone back in her
purse.

"God, am I glad to see you." She gave Pup a quick hug.
"What. The hell. Is going. *On?*"

"What do you mean?" Pup's palms were already sweating.

"Well, I spent the morning with Mom and Dad at the
ER. Apparently, Mom has a dislocated shoulder. What do
you know about this?"

"I guess she tripped and fell over baby Adalyn's teething
giraffe." *Pup Flanagan,* he thought. *Ever the obedient son.*

"That's what she *claims,*" Annemarie said. "But what I
want to know is: What *really* happened?"

"I wasn't home last night, remember?" He stuck his sweaty
hands in his pockets. "But, I mean, if she said that's what happened, then I guess that's what happened."

"So when you got home—had she already fallen?"

"Y-yes."

"Did you see her?"

"Uh, no. She was already asleep."

"Then how do you know she'd already fallen?"

"Because I saw her this morning at breakfast, and she told
me! Jesus, I thought I came here to eat cake, not get the third
degree!"

"Was Luke there when you got home last night?" Sal
asked. "Sorry to pry, Pup. But—was he?"

"Luke?" Pup looked back and forth between Sal and his sister. "No," he said, guessing, hoping it matched with whatever his mother was telling everyone.

"Have you talked to him?"

"I texted him this morning," said Pup. "But I didn't hear back." It was the first truthful statement he'd made since the beginning of their inquisition. He'd written: **I don't want to talk to you. Just write back so I know you're alive.** He hadn't gotten a response.

The server arrived at their table with a pot of tea and a large silver tray of cake slices, each labeled with its own little card: *Vanilla buttercream. Flourless chocolate with fresh raspberry coulis. Salted caramel with crushed pretzel crust. Banana walnut. Red velvet rum.*

"This all looks delicious," Sal said, smiling up at him.

"Oh, it *is*." He gave them a little bow. "Enjoy, everybody!"

"Thank you!" they all called brightly, smiling at each other stupidly as he folded the tray and turned away.

"Her arm is in a goddamn sling," Annemarie said, her smile dropping as soon as the server had disappeared through the swinging kitchen doors. Sal picked up a fork, carved out a piece of the flourless chocolate, and held it out to her. "Come on, honey," she said. "We're supposed to be having fun here."

Annemarie relented and accepted the bite. "Mm," she said. "That's *good*."

Pup dove into the vanilla buttercream, hoping his interrogation was over. But Annemarie had her lawyer pants on now and she was not about to let him off easy.

"I just want to know one thing," she said after they'd polished off the banana walnut. "Does Mom's injury have anything to do with the fact that Luke got kicked out of the house last night?"

Pup paused. "Where'd you hear he got kicked out?"

"He showed up at Noreen's last night at three in the morning. Drunk out of his mind, of course. Clothes covered in some unidentifiable orange substance. He banged on the door until he woke up all the kids, including Adalyn, who they *just* got sleeping through the night."

"He was crying," Sal continued. "He was kind of incoherent, but Noreen managed to get out of him that he'd had a big fight with your mom and dad, and that they'd kicked him out of the house. Dylan wouldn't let him in, but Noreen felt bad, so she gave him a sleeping bag and unlocked the garage for him, told him he could crash there."

"The *garage*?"

"That was my reaction, too," said Sal. "I mean . . . drunk or not, he's still *family*."

"You know what?" Annemarie scraped some frosting off a slice of coconut cake and tasted it. "I don't blame them. First of all, it's not like it's winter. And second of all, the *last* time they let Luke crash on their couch, he got up in the middle of the night and pissed all over the kids' Legos."

Pup thought of the laundry basket incident from a couple weeks ago but decided it was best not to say anything.

"So where is he now?" He was trying to keep his voice casual. If he sounded too concerned, he might give away just how bad things had been last night.

"Who knows? Noreen went out there in the morning to bring him a cup of coffee. He was gone, and the sleeping bag was neatly rolled up and put away on a shelf. She doesn't even know if he ended up sleeping there at all."

"What about everybody else? Elizabeth? Jeanine? Mary?"

"Trust me, I've been fielding phone calls from the sister-moms all day. Nobody's seen him other than Noreen last night."

"So if nobody knows where he is . . . does that mean he's missing?"

"He's not missing. You act like you've never seen Luke on a bender. He might not show his face for three, four more days."

"Yeah, but this time he was worse than he's ever been. I mean," he said, catching himself as Annemarie's stare intensified, "it *sounds* like he was worse, anyway. If he's not at Noreen's, and he's not at Carrie's, and nobody's heard from him, then where is he? Don't you want to know where he *is*?"

"I want to know that he's getting his shit together,"

Annemarie said. "And until that happens, I don't care where he lays his head at night. He's got plenty of friends he can lean on. Me, I don't want to see him. And neither should you. Or did I not just tell you that our sixty-five-year-old mother is walking around with her arm in a sling?"

"I told you," Pup mumbled. "She slipped on Adalyn's teething monkey."

"Aha! I thought you said it was a giraffe."

"Monkey, giraffe, what's the difference? Sorry that I don't pay close attention to the animal species of my nieces' teething toys!"

Annemarie looked at him for a long moment.

"Man," she said. "I wish I could get five minutes with you on the witness stand. No offense, Pup Squeak, but I'd tear you apart."

"Pup," Sal said gently, placing her fork on her empty plate, "when you texted him today—did you get a delivered receipt?"

Pup took his phone from his pocket and pulled up the text.

"Yeah. So?"

"So that mean's he's still reading your messages and charging his phone. He's around here somewhere."

"That only means that his phone hasn't run out of battery yet. He could be lying somewhere, dead, and his phone could still be on."

"Pup." Annemarie folded her hands on the table. "Listen to me. Now, I don't know what happened—trust me, I'll find out, though—but I think it's better for you, for Mom and Dad, even for Luke, that he's out of the house. He's not some dumb kid who doesn't know how to make it on his own. He's a grown-ass man. Just take a deep breath, okay? I'm sure he's fine."

"That's what you said last time."

"What?"

"With Pat." He looked at her steadily. "When Jack Rinard called, and Mom and Dad ran out of the house and drove straight to Champaign as soon as they hung up with him. The first thing I did was call you. And you said, 'Just take a deep breath. I'm sure he's fine.' So I did. And he wasn't."

"Well, folks!" The server had materialized beside the table and all three of them jumped. "Decisions, decisions, right?"

"Yes," Sal said, smiling at him tightly. "I'm sorry, but I think we're going to need a minute to make up our minds."

"Take all the time you need!" He looked around at their faces, his smile twitching a little, then hurried away into the kitchen.

"You're right." The color had drained from Annemarie's face. She put a hand to her forehead, as if to ward off a headache. "You're right. I did say that. I'm so sorry, Pup. I'm sorry. But this is different. The situation is different. The people involved are different. The—"

"I have to go." Pup pushed his chair back and it scraped loudly across the hardwood.

"Wait, Pup. Please."

But he was already running for the bus stop, the bells of the bakery door tinkling merrily behind him.

22

PUP SAT WITH HIS CAMERA and phone on his lap as the bus made its tedious progress through the afternoon traffic.

Write back, he'd just written. **Please. I just want to know you're okay.**

No response.

He jiggled his knees impatiently, until he could take it no more and decided he could probably get there faster if he ran. He yanked the cord, grabbed his backpack, and got off at the next stop, still a couple miles away from his destination. But as soon as he began to run, he felt better. He loped down Lawrence Avenue, the sun at his back, scooting past the Pelatas vendor and the used-rug salesmen, the pair of sisters selling oranges and watermelon from the bed of their pickup truck, moms pushing strollers, mustached men arguing with each other in Urdu, skateboarders, bicyclists, a zonked-out drug addict begging for change outside the Admiral strip club. By the time he'd reached Marylou's Pizza and stepped into the dim bar at the front of the restaurant, he was breathing hard and pouring sweat. He took a moment to collect himself, hands on his knees, then walked over and sat down in his usual seat at the first red booth. Ronaldo, who was stretching pizza dough behind a glass partition just to his left, gave him a nod, then spun the dough expertly into the air, his face obscured by a cloud of flour.

Carrie was leaning on the counter, order pad in hand. Her thick dark hair was pushed back with a bandanna and on her feet were the pink Nike high-tops Luke had bought for her that Christmas. Seeing her shoes gave Pup a stab of hope: She couldn't hate Luke *that* much if she still wore the shoes he'd bought her, right? Maybe they'd even gotten back together at some point, and Luke had neglected to tell him—which would be a very Luke thing to do—and maybe Luke was sleeping off his hangover at Carrie's place right that very minute. If Pup could just confirm that Luke was safe, then he could be free to hate him, without having to deal with the awful strain of worry that now squeezed at his heart.

Carrie had been working at Marylou's for as long as Pup had known her. It was how she'd bought the dress she wore to Luke's senior prom, how she paid her way through college, and, now, how she supplemented her preschool teacher's salary over the summers. In all those years, she'd never let Pup pay for a meal. Her back was turned to him now, and she was chatting with the bartender, Bernice, who was the only seventy-something-year-old lady Pup knew who still wore fake eyelashes and miniskirts. As soon as Bernice saw Pup slide into the booth, she whispered something to Carrie, who stiffened, but didn't turn around. Pup made a point of taking some money out of his wallet and laying it in front of him on the table, so they knew he wasn't expecting anything for free.

A short while later, Carrie appeared at his side and set a tall glass of Sprite with grenadine on a cardboard coaster in front of him.

"Put your money away," she said.

"No. I don't want you to think that's why I'm here."

"I know that's not why you're here." She handed him a straw. "But I still don't want your money. You want your usual?"

"You don't have to do that," Pup said. "I just had a bunch of cake."

"I already put the order in. Should I tell Ronaldo to cancel it?"

"Oh," said Pup. "I mean, I guess if you already put the order in."

"Good. It's not like you to turn down food. I'll be back in a minute."

She walked away to tend to the lone other table in her section, and Pup stuck his straw into his Shirley Temple and took a long sip. He could feel Bernice watching him, so he took out his phone and pretended to be doing something important.

A few minutes later, Carrie appeared with a paper container of six mozzarella sticks, well done, and an extra cup of marinara sauce. She placed it on the table and then slid into the booth across from him.

"I have to ask," she said. "How's your brother?"

"That's actually why I'm here," Pup said. "I thought maybe *you'd* know." He bit into a cheese stick, and a stream of hot grease gushed down his chin.

"Me?" She handed him a napkin. "I haven't talked to him since we broke up last month."

"Not at all?"

"Not one call, not one message, not one word. I mean, I know *I* broke up with *him*, so he's totally within his rights not to ever talk to me again. But I guess I just thought that after eight years together, he might try to fight for me. Or beg me to reconsider. Or promise to change. Instead he just let me go." She looked out the window at the traffic on Lawrence Avenue. "He almost seemed . . . I don't know. Relieved."

"So you don't know where he's staying?"

"He's not staying at your house anymore?"

Pup shook his head.

"Why?" He could feel her eyes boring into him, but he couldn't look up to meet them. Pup had always had an innocent crush on Carrie. She was warm and kind and patient, and had golden, lit-from-within skin. She wore her nails long and painted with glittery colors and she always smelled good, even after a twelve-hour shift running tables at a pizza place. "Pup," she said gently. "What happened?"

He dunked his cheese stick into his cup of marinara. "He had a fight with my parents. Kind of a big fight. He ended up—my mom ended up getting hurt."

"*What?*"

"So they kicked him out of the house."

"When?"

"Last night. I know he's probably fine, but he won't respond to any of our messages. Not from Annemarie, not from me, and *definitely* not from the sister-moms."

"When you say your mom got hurt. Did Luke—"

"It was an accident," Pup said quickly.

Carrie made a soft sound from the back of her throat. She rested her head in her hands for a moment and her dark hair spilled across the wooden table. When she looked up, her eyes were wet. "He was drunk," she said. "Wasn't he?"

"Yes."

"Of course he was. He always is."

"Well. Not *always.*"

Carrie crossed her arms and leveled him with her cut-the-bullshit look. Pup concentrated on his bitten nails.

"Sometimes when he says he's going to study group," he said, "I think he's lying. I think he just goes to Mishka's. I don't think he's even studying for the bar anymore."

"Well, no." She picked up a napkin and folded it absently

between her fingers. "Why would he be?"

Pup just looked at her. The question was snagged in his chest.

"Oh, Pup." The napkin fluttered from Carrie's fingers onto the table. "You don't know."

"Know what?" His cheese stick suddenly felt gelatinous and gross in his mouth. He forced himself to swallow.

"Pup, Luke failed out of law school last year. He's got thousands of dollars in loan money that he's been drinking away at the bar instead. How could you not have—I mean, how could *he* not have . . . How did he hide that from you?"

"But that can't be." Pup shook his head. "He got up with me every Tuesday and Thursday morning this whole semester. He'd give me a ride to school, and then he'd drive down to DePaul for his Wills and Trusts class."

Carrie smiled ruefully. "Every Tuesday and Thursday, Luke was too busy drinking at Mishka's Tap to be worrying about wills and trusts."

"At eight in the morning?"

"Sure. Why not, if you don't have anywhere to be and you've got piles of loan money that you don't have to spend on tuition anymore? He didn't seem to be too concerned about what he was going to do when the loan companies started expecting him to pay all that money back—with interest. It was one of the subjects of our many, many arguments."

"God." Pup ran his finger over the divots and bumps in the tabletop, the names and dates and carved messages of love. "I feel so stupid."

"Pup." Carrie reached across the table and put a warm palm on the top of his hand. "You're not stupid. I'm so sorry. I love your whole family, you know that. And I loved Luke. I still love him." Her voice broke. "But his drinking—it's gotten so bad. *So* bad. And your family . . . you were all so determined not to really see it. But I just couldn't watch him destroy himself anymore. Maybe I'm not strong enough. Maybe I'm not loyal enough. I knew Patrick. I loved Patrick. But he wasn't my brother. I don't know what Luke felt—what any of you felt—" She looked at him and the tears that had gathered in her eyes spilled in two wet tracks down her face. "But it's like he's so filled with rage and he's so angry and he's put himself in a place that I can't reach. He's just gone from me. So what choice did I have? I hated myself for leaving. For giving up on him. But I just couldn't do it anymore."

"It wasn't an accident, with my mom's shoulder," Pup said softly. He ran his finger along a heart stabbed through with an arrow. "Not really, anyway."

Carrie shook her head. "Even *I* never thought it would get that bad. Bad enough that he would hurt someone he loved like that. His own *mom*. So maybe I was just as blind as everybody else."

"Carrie, you've got to help me find him. I just need to know he's okay."

She shrugged. "Finding him's the easy part. Where else would he be but Mishka's?"

23

PUP HAD NEVER BEEN INSIDE Mishka's Tap before, even though it had stood on the same corner at the outskirts of Flanland for as long as he could remember. It was a huddled brick building decorated with a blue-striped awning that had been bleached gray by years of sunlight, and it didn't even have a sign, just a neon Old Style logo that blinked in the front window. As Pup opened the dinged-up metal door and stepped inside for the first time, he wondered whether Mishka's was even its actual name, or just a nickname like his own that the bar had been given long ago and never been able to shake.

When his eyes adjusted to the relative darkness of the room, he could make out a long, polished wood counter with rows of liquor bottles on one side of it and guys about his dad's age on the other, drinking beer from glass mugs. The walls were decorated with faded photos of dead Chicago luminaries, and the jukebox was one of those old ones, where you hit a big metal button and a thick plastic page flips behind the glass. A sticky brown carpet covered the floor, curling up at the edges where the staples had come loose, and the whole place reeked of stale smoke and wet dog. The source of one of those smells was a mangy-looking mutt with a mottled, patchy coat stretched out beneath the jukebox, who barely lifted his lumpy head to glance at Pup as he stepped carefully past it.

The woman behind the bar was slow-moving and jiggly armed, with bottle-red hair and a low-cut T-shirt that revealed sun-spotted cleavage and said QUEEN OF FUCKING EVERYTHING across the front. When she saw Pup approach the counter, she put down the bottle of vanilla-flavored vodka she was wiping down with a dingy rag and shook her head emphatically.

"Oh, no you don't," she said. "Turn your skinny ass around and walk right back out that door. We don't serve twelve-year-olds here."

A few of the guys sitting at the bar swiveled in their stools to laugh at Pup and his skinny ass.

"I'm just looking for my brother," he said.

"Yeah? Who's your brother?"

"Luke Flanagan."

A low whistle from one of the patrons, a snicker from another. The bartender set her bottle down on the counter, her face looking suddenly pinched.

"Well, you won't find him here."

"Are you sure?" Pup asked. "Because I know he's been hanging out here a lot—"

"*Used* to hang out here a lot. Not anymore. He is no longer welcome in this establishment, if you must know the truth."

"Fighting," explained the gravel-voiced old man at the end of the counter, whose neck hung down to his collar in two grayish loops of skin.

"Oh," said Pup.

The bartender replaced the vanilla vodka on the shelf and picked up another bottle, this one bubblegum flavored. "When you find him," she said, twisting the rag along the neck of the bottle, "you tell him he owes me three hundred bucks for the mirror he busted in the men's bathroom."

As Pup stepped out of the old-ashtray stench of the bar and back into the freshness of the evening, he looked down at his hands and saw that they were shaking. Luke was missing. Luke was lost. He imagined it happening all over again: standing next to a coffin, with eyes that stung and shoes that pinched as the endless line snaked past. Men shaking his hand, women hugging him, some looking him dead in the eye, some looking away, but all of them saying the same thing: *Sorry for your loss. Sorry for your loss. Sorry for your loss.* He couldn't bear to go through it again, to watch his family go through it again. To be the only son left. Rush hour was beginning to set in as he stood in the middle of the sidewalk and pulled his phone from his pocket. Professionally dressed people, freed from work for the day, moved past him, absorbed in their own phones, their own lives.

I just need a yes or a no, he wrote. **Please. Are you alive?**

He reached the bus stop just as his phone buzzed in his pocket.

YES

The wave of relief washed through his body, overwhelming him. He sagged against the bus shelter and wrote back, his fingers shaking.

Where are you

No response. He tried again:

Are you okay

Nothing.

Suddenly he was angry at himself for even following up. He'd made contact, hadn't he? That was all he had wanted. To know that Luke was alive. He didn't care if Luke was okay. Luke *wasn't* okay. That much was obvious. He had attacked his own mother, had wrenched bone from joint, had knocked the air from her lungs.

He could have killed her.

Alcohol didn't do that to everybody. Whiskey made his father sleepy. Wine made his sisters giggly. Beer made Izzy and Brody horny. It never made any of them violent. It never made them smash bar mirrors or pee all over floors or take swings at their siblings or fail out of law school. Pup thought about how his mother had looked lying there in the mess on the dining room floor, clawing the air to pull it back into her lungs. How when she'd fallen, her skirt had flipped up and he'd seen the crackles of thin purple veins across her bare thighs. The way she had struggled to get up, her hair falling out of its bun, the twisted pain in her face and the odd angle of her drooping shoulder. And Luke's suffering cry, how it had set Pup's hair standing on end, and made him love his brother the most he had ever loved him at the exact moment he was hating him more than he'd ever hated anyone.

Forget him.

He could come crawling back when he was ready to stop being a drunk asshole, when he was ready to ask their mother for forgiveness. When he was ready to set things right. And if that day never came, so be it. Pup didn't need Luke: he still had five siblings left.

He turned off his phone and dropped it back into his pocket.

24

PUP LIMPED THE REST OF the way through his finals, scurrying from exam to exam down the most obscure corridors of the school, and this was how he successfully managed to make it to the last bell of his junior year without running into Izzy or Brody. He spent the first week of summer break looking at the world from behind his camera lens. Day and night he roamed Flanland, shooting roll after roll, shooting obsessively, relentlessly, throwing himself into his portfolio project with a single-mindedness that would have impressed even the most type-A Honors kid. His family didn't know what to make of it. They weren't exactly comfortable with the way he would suddenly appear, his stealthy entrance announced with the click of a shutter button, but they were so pleased and surprised that he had an interest other than Cubs baseball that they put up with it. Even when he wasn't taking photographs, he was thinking about photography. He was reading about photography. He was talking about photography with Abrihet, in late-night marathon phone calls that were so long and intense and wonderful that for a while he could forget about the humiliating conclusion to his relationship with Izzy and the fear that gnawed at him whenever he let himself wonder for too long where Luke was staying and what Luke was doing. All of a sudden, art had become necessary: making it, studying it, thinking about it. Every press of the shutter release felt like a tiny refusal to accept that his life wasn't completely out of his control, that at least part of his story was his to tell.

Mr. Hughes had gotten special permission from the principal to allow Pup and Abrihet access to the darkroom over the summer to work on their portfolios. They had plans to meet there on a Saturday morning in the second week of break, and Pup couldn't wait to stand beside her in that tiny space, working in absolute darkness in the belly of their summer-emptied high school, to drop their photo paper in the developing bath, agitating the liquid, creating soft ripples and watching together as their images began to come alive. Each chemical reaction felt like a miracle: With his own hands, he could turn a blank sheet of paper into a tiny mirror, a translation of life into pictures. It was the closest he'd ever come to saying a prayer and feeling like someone was actually listening.

That Saturday morning, Pup arrived at school as planned, camera and film rolls weighing down his backpack, eager to get to work and forget everything that was happening in his real life. He waved to Anthony, the security guard, who glanced up from his *Us Weekly* magazine to wave back, and headed down the basement stairwell, down the long, empty art corridor toward the darkroom.

But as soon as he opened the door and saw Abrihet working in the soft red glow of the safety light, he knew something was wrong. She agitated her photo paper through the developing chemicals listlessly, her head slightly turned, her gaze fixed on some faraway point. She didn't even turn around when she heard him come in.

"Abrihet?" Pup hovered near the door, unsure if he should even come in.

"Hey."

"Are you all right?"

There was a silence, amplified by their great solitude in the massive building.

"My mom's not coming." Her voice was barely audible.

"Oh no." Pup closed the door softly behind him. "Why not?"

She didn't answer him. She just held the tongs and dragged the photo back and forth in the bath.

"Was it something with the visa?"

She shook her head. "I thought it was my dad. I thought it was his fault. I started screaming at him—I've never screamed at my father—and I was screaming at him and my auntie came in and she told me it wasn't his fault at all. She said it wasn't my dad and it wasn't money and it wasn't even the government or the documents or the application. It was *her.*" She turned to him suddenly, tears standing in her eyes. "The only reason she's not here is because she doesn't *want* to be here. She doesn't *want* to come. She says that some people are meant to go while others are meant to stay. She says she knows I'm in good hands, and that I should come visit her every year, and that she doesn't want to leave her home, and her country, and all the family we have left there, and her mountains. Her *mountains*, James! Who wants to be with a mountain more than they want to be with their own daughter?"

Pup just stood there. He didn't know what to say. All he wanted to do was take the two steps across the room and put his arms around her. But he was held back by the memory of Izzy in the hallway after his Spanish exam. She had shrunk away from his touch with such complete disgust. *Don't touch me.*

"I don't even know why I came here today," Abrihet said, flicking away a tear as it skidded down her cheek. "I'm not going to regionals."

"What? But that's crazy. Why *not?*"

"I wanted to show her how well I've done for myself in this country. How hard I've worked, how much I've learned. How much the sacrifice was worth it." She dropped the tongs and reached for her backpack. "But now that she won't be here to see all that, it doesn't matter."

"But that's bullshit!"

Abrihet froze, her backpack halfway to her shoulder.

"Ex*cuse* me?"

"It's *bull*shit, Abrihet! You think *I'm* not going through some shit right now? My brother just . . . my family won't . . . Izzy doesn't . . . ."

"*Izzy?* You're talking about that girl *Izzy* right now? This isn't some silly little high school drama, James. This is my *life*. My *mother*."

"That's not what I . . . I *know* it is." He ran a hand through the tangle of his hair. "What about what Mr. Hughes says? About using art to articulate the emergency inside of you?"

"We can't all be Leonard Cohen, James. I don't feel like *articulating* anything. I just feel like crying, okay?" She slid the strap of her backpack onto her shoulder, pushed past him, and opened the door.

"So you're just going to quit? Do you really think that's going to make it better?"

"You know what, James?" She turned to look at him, but the light from the hallway was flooding in all around her and he couldn't make out the features of her face. "You have no idea what this feels like. You still *have* a mom in your life, okay?"

"And you still have a brother in yours. You think I don't

know what it feels like to miss someone?"

"I think," she said quietly, "that you don't even know me, or my family, or my life. I was stupid to believe that you ever could."

She stepped out into the hall and the door slammed behind her. Pup was alone again in the weak red glow of the safety light. He looked down at Abrihet's photo paper, where it floated like a dying leaf on the rippling surface of the chemical bath. It was a picture she'd taken at the bus stop where they'd waited together the night of her aunt's party. Across the street, centered in the frame, was the redbrick apartment building with its rows of grated windows that had been her first home in this country, where she had tossed and turned on her kitchen air mattress, reciting her English words in the strange American brightness, teaching herself to build a wall of language between herself and her mother. Pup picked up the tongs and lifted out the photograph, trying to salvage it, but it was too late. It had been so overexposed, it had returned to the white blankness from where it had started.

TEXTURE:
the feeling of an actual surface

25

SEEING TEACHERS OUTSIDE OF SCHOOL always felt a little weird. At the beginning of his freshman year, Pup had run into his English teacher, Ms. Cole, at the public pool, wearing a bikini and running after one of her kids. For the rest of the school year, she'd be standing at the front of the room in one of her pink cardigan sets, talking about Edgar Allan Poe or whatever, and Pup would think about how awkward it was that he knew what her belly button looked like. But with Mr. Hughes, it was different, mainly because he didn't really dress or act like a teacher even when he was *in* school, so you didn't really expect him to dress or act like one outside of school. Which is why Pup was relatively unfazed when he went to meet his art teacher for coffee one afternoon in the middle of June and saw him leaning against the condiments bar looking like he'd just disembarked from a cruise ship: straw hat, Hawaiian shirt with big green macaws all over it, denim shorts, and a pair of sandals that looked like they were made out of rope.

"Flanagan," Mr. Hughes said, putting down his newspaper

to shake Pup's hand. "What are you drinking?"

Pup looked up at the menu behind his teacher's head. Americano? Mocha? Steamer? He panicked, scanning the board for an item he actually recognized.

"Hot chocolate!" he read. "I'll do one of those."

"Really? It's ninety degrees, Flanagan."

"Oh. Right. What are you drinking?"

"Iced coffee."

"Huh. Okay, I'll have an iced hot chocolate."

Mr. Hughes stared at him, a smile twitching at the corners of his mouth. "You're an odd duck, Flanagan," he said. "I like it. One iced hot chocolate, coming right up."

Drinks procured, they chose a table near the front window and sat down. Mr. Hughes looked at his watch.

"I guess we'll wait a few more minutes for Abby to show up before we start," he said. "It's not like her to be late."

"I don't think she's coming." Pup stuck his straw between the fast-melting ice cubes in his drink.

"Not coming? Why not?"

"She didn't tell you?"

Mr. Hughes crossed his arms. Two bright-green macaws stared at Pup from the sides of his sleeves. "Tell me *what*?"

"She's not coming to regionals."

"What? Why the hell not?"

"Well, she's going through some . . . personal problems."

"*Personal problems?*" Mr. Hughes laughed. "What's that

supposed to mean? Life *itself* is one long personal problem!"

"I agree." Pup slurped his drink.

"Well, did you try to change her mind?"

"Yeah. When we were in the darkroom, we had a big argument about it and everything. But then she just kind of left."

"She *left*? Well, why didn't you run after her?"

"Because she didn't want to talk to me!"

"Well, have you tried *calling* her? Or, I'm sorry, I forgot you kids today don't call each other. Have you tried *texting* her?"

"Yes." Pup peered into his drink.

"Well? Did you get a response?"

"No. And for the record, I also *did* call her. Four times, to be exact."

"And?"

"She didn't answer."

"Well did you leave her a voice mail?"

"No."

"Why not?"

"Because voice mails are for old people!"

Mr. Hughes ripped his glasses off and pinched the bridge of his nose. Then he stuffed them back on his face. The way he treated his glasses, it was a wonder he didn't go through twenty pairs a year. "Okay," he said. "Okay. Let me think about this. We'll talk about this later. For now, let me see what you got."

Pup took out the folder from his backpack and pushed it across the table. Mr. Hughes opened to the first page, tore off and replaced his glasses a few more times, and began to look through the stack of images. Pup sat across from him, drank his iced hot chocolate, and waited. Mr. Hughes took his time scrutinizing each shot. Sometimes he leaned back, other times he leaned forward, his face contorting into a series of squints, smirks, and scowls. At one point, he even reached into his teacher-satchel-man-purse thing and pulled out a magnifying glass to scrutinize the images even closer. Finally, when Pup was slurping up the last remaining granules of chocolate powder from the bottom of his cup, Mr. Hughes closed the folder and looked up.

"Well," he said, tearing off his glasses with a sense of finality.

"Well," Pup said.

"I'm curious, Flanagan. What do *you* think about this portfolio?"

Pup hated this teacher trick, when they turned the tables on you, asking how you'd grade yourself if it was up to you. But since it *wasn't* up to you, the only reason they asked was so that you would insult yourself, saving them the trouble.

"Well, uh, I mean, I'm not an expert, so I don't know," he answered. "But I thought some of the pictures came out pretty cool."

"Pretty cool," Mr. Hughes repeated, skeptically rubbing his chin.

"I guess."

"Well. *I* didn't think they were cool at all."

"Oh, totally." Pup spoke quickly, to cover for his sinking heart. "I get it."

"I thought they were remarkable."

"Sorry?" Pup, who'd been staring down at the boomerang pattern that danced across their linoleum table, looked up to meet his teacher in the eye.

"Your attention to detail, your ability to trap a moment in time. Your mastery over lighting, over composition, over tension! And framing! And texture! Your point of *view*. The way you *see* people." He was shaking his head, but not in the way Pup's teachers usually shook their heads at him. It didn't look like disappointment. It looked almost like . . . admiration?

"Everyone in these photos, they're people who are close to you, right?"

"Yeah. Mostly."

"It's like, you have found a way to honor them. All of them. To make the unremarkable extraordinary. This one, for example." He pushed a photo of Pup's mother across the table, the one he'd taken of her sitting in the kitchen after the dishes had finally been finished for the night and the counter wiped down with Windex. Her head was bowed, her gray hair was pulled back into a little bun at the nape of her neck, her colored pencils were lined up neatly on the table, and she was shading in the scales of a fish from the coloring book he'd bought her at the U of I campus bookstore. "I mean, my god, has the loneliness of motherhood ever been captured so well?"

Loneliness of motherhood? Pup was fairly certain that his mom hadn't been alone for more than ten minutes in at least forty years, if ever. How could she ever be lonely? He didn't know what Mr. Hughes meant, but he certainly wasn't going to argue the point. Besides, he loved that picture too, though he couldn't have explained why.

"And this one." He tapped his finger on the corner of the shot of Luke and his parents at the beginning of that terrible fight. "This has so much emotional intimacy that it's almost painful to look at."

Mr. Hughes shuffled through the rest of the pictures and then closed the folder.

"You're part of a big family, that right?"

"Youngest of eight."

"Used to listening more than you talk?"

Pup smiled. "I figured out a long time ago that in my family, if I try to talk, no one listens anyway."

"Well, that silence, that watching, that listening—it's taught you to see like an artist. I've been trying to teach kids that kind of seeing for years."

He pushed the portfolio across the table.

"I want you to hang on to this, Pup. Even after regionals are over. You'll need it when you're applying to art programs next year."

"Art programs?"

"Yes, Pup. There are these things called universities. At them, you can choose to major in art."

James Flanagan, undergraduate. James Flanagan, bachelor of fine arts. He bit the inside of his cheek to control the stupid grin spreading across his face.

"But don't look too pleased with yourself, young man," Mr. Hughes said, waggling his finger at Pup. "You've still got one more important job to do."

"I do?"

"Yes. Convince Abby to change her mind."

26

PUP RETURNED FROM HIS MEETING with Mr. Hughes, his portfolio under his arm and his face in his phone, composing messages to Abrihet without actually sending them. He had never been good with words—which was part of the reason why he loved photography—and every time he thought he had something good to say, something that would get her to change her mind, he second-guessed himself and deleted the unsent message. He was so preoccupied with this task that as he climbed the front steps to his house, he nearly tripped over the girl who was slumped, hugging her knees, on the top step.

"Izzy?" Pup stumbled backward and caught his balance on the iron railing.

"Sorry." She looked up at him. Her eyes were red and mascara leaked across her temples. "I should have called first."

"How long have you been sitting there?"

"A while." She held up an empty glass. "Your mom brought me some lemonade."

"Oh."

She drummed her fingers on the empty space next to her on the step.

"Sit with me a minute?"

Pup hesitated. The way she'd humiliated him in the hallway after his Spanish exam still stung. It was going to sting, he thought, for a long time.

"I'll totally get it," she said, "if you don't want to talk to me. And if you tell me to get the hell off your stoop I'll totally understand. I just came to tell you that I broke up with Brody." She burst into tears then, and buried her face between her knees. Seeing her cry like that dissolved Pup's will. He sat down next to her, his portfolio balanced across his lap.

"I'm sorry, Iz."

"No, you're not," she said, and sniffled. "You never liked Brody. I'm not blaming you. But you never liked him."

"What are you talking about?" Pup objected. "I *adore* him. He has so many great qualities: He's lazy. And pervy. And a liar with gross fingernails and corn-chip breath. I could go on."

"He does *not* have gross breath and nails!"

"Can you honestly look me in the eye," Pup said, "and tell me that he didn't taste like Cool Ranch every time you kissed him?"

The corner of Izzy's mouth twitched into an almost-smile.

"Okay, he did. Sometimes. Stop trying to make me laugh."

She hugged her knees tighter. "Anyway, it doesn't matter. It's over. He cheated on me. We were at a party at Cory Meier's house, and he disappeared for a while. I went to pee, and just as I was about to flush, I heard this, like, fumbling, on the other side of the shower curtain. I throw open the curtain and who's there? *My* boyfriend tangled up in a bath mat with Maya Ulrich. Who, by the way, was topless."

"Wow," said Pup. "Classy."

Izzy nodded miserably. Across the street, the Nicholsons' automatic sprinklers switched on. The late-afternoon sun slanted through the arches of water, making little rainbows all across their lawn. "Hey, look!" Pup pointed. "It's the ghost of Kailyn's mom."

"Don't make fun of Kailyn's rainbows, Pup." Izzy looked across the street at the sprinklers. "It's like Mrs. Barrera says. We all have different ways of dealing with our grief."

"True. She sees rainbows, you pick terrible boyfriends."

"Well, he *was* a good distraction," she said. "I'll give him that. I didn't even have time to be sad on the anniversary of Teddy's death, because I was so busy caring for Brody and his infected tongue piercing that day."

"He numbed it with a blue raspberry freeze pop and stabbed it through with a thumbtack," Pup recalled. "What could possibly go wrong?"

Izzy laughed and then was quiet.

"I should have believed you." She twisted her hands in her

lap. "After all we've been through together, I should have known you'd never lie to me."

"Yeah, Iz. You probably should have."

A longer, somewhat painful silence followed.

"So what's in the folder, anyway?"

"Oh." Pup ran his hand over the plain cover. "It's some photographs for this competition I'm in."

"The art thing you were doing down in Champaign?"

"Yeah."

"That's great, Pup. Really. Not to sound like my mom, but it's great to see you having *interests*. Can I see them?"

"I don't know," he said. "They're kind of . . . personal."

"Personal?" She blinked up at him with her wet green eyes. "But you just said you're entering them in a competition. Aren't people going to see them then?"

"Yes, but . . ." He trailed off. He didn't know how to explain it to her. Mr. Hughes had been the first to see his portfolio, and no one but Abrihet— who had been there with him the whole time, had worked alongside him, had taught him and critiqued him and helped him—could be the second. "Sorry, Iz. I just can't."

Her smile fell a little at the corners. "Not even a quick peek?"

"Nope. Sorry."

"Okay." She fished a tissue from the back pocket of her denim shorts and wiped away the smears of mascara around her eyes. "I guess I deserve that."

"Nobody deserves anything," Pup said. "We only get what we get."

"One of Mrs. Barrera's famous nuggets of wisdom." She stood up and put the tissue back in her pocket. "Anyway. I just came to tell you about Brody. And to say I'm sorry. And I hope you win your photography thing."

"Thanks, Iz."

"So . . . friends?"

"Friends."

She stuck out her hand. Pup took it, and her warm fingers wrapped around his. But he didn't feel anything at her touch except a kind of distant affection, a bittersweet sadness. He understood that next year, senior year, his relationship with Izzy would be no different than his relationships with the other members of the Pity Party: hallway friends and nothing more. They would never be close again. And that was okay with him.

She gave him a little wave before descending his front steps and crossing the street. As she passed the Nicholsons' front lawn, she leaned out of the heat and into the sprinkler. The water cascaded against her body, breaking up the rainbows into sparkling fractals of light. It would have made a great photograph, if Pup had been looking. But instead he had opened his folder to the shot he'd taken of Abrihet in the university hotel. *Sepia*, he was thinking. A warm brown color, best known for its uses in digital photography. He and Patrick had once had a conversation about sepia, a conversation that Pup had forgotten completely and now, for some reason, remembered perfectly. Before it became a color in its own right, Patrick had explained, it was the name of a dye first produced by the ancient Greeks from the ink of the cuttlefish and popular for centuries among artists for writing and painting. Leonardo himself had used sepia to create his famous drawings of the human body.

"And don't be fooled by the name," Pat's lecture had concluded. "A cuttlefish is not actually a fish at all. It's a mollusk."

"Wait," Pup had said. "Are you talking about Leonardo the Teenage Mutant Ninja Turtle? Or somebody else?"

Patrick had laughed and slung his arm around his little brother. "Oh, Pup," he'd said. "I still have so much to teach you."

Sepia. Pup closed the folder and looked up. Izzy was gone, and he knew what to do, now that he'd finally found a name for the color of Abrihet's eyes.

27

TWO BUS RIDES LATER, Pup was in Uptown, walking down Broadway and nervously chomping on a breath mint. Abrihet had told him that she sometimes helped out at Shores of the Red Sea in the summer, when the small back patio opened up and doubled the number of tables in the restaurant. Showing up there unannounced had seemed like a great idea when he'd first boarded the Lawrence Avenue bus, but now that he had actually arrived and was standing on the sidewalk looking through the front window at Abrihet's aunt, who was pouring tea for two old people at the only occupied table in the whole place, his confidence dried up. Abrihet had said that her *amoui* liked Pup, but her father was a different story. He remembered, with a nervous shiver, the scowl on Mr. Tesfay's face a few weeks earlier when he'd watched Pup laughing with his daughter across the room. Before her aunt could turn around and see him, Pup ducked away from the window to reconsider. Hiding himself in the narrow gangway between the restaurant and the chain-link fence that separated it from the alley, he took out his phone and dialed Annemarie's number. She would know what to do, and she would give it to him straight: if this was a terrible plan, she would say so. The phone rang once, twice, three times. Four times. Then, her voice mail picked up. Pup couldn't believe it. It was the first time in their long history that she hadn't answered his call.

In a meeting, the text buzzed immediately in his hand. **Sorry. Give me ten minutes?**

Okay

Pup stood in the narrow passageway and waited. The wall was westward facing, and as the late-afternoon sun began to sink in the sky, the bricks behind him practically glowed with heat. He chewed another breath mint and wiped his face with the hem of his T-shirt. A minute passed. Then two. Then five. At the eight-minute mark, he heard, around the corner, the front door of the restaurant open and close, and footsteps heading in his direction. Panicked, he considered running, or even scaling the fence and disappearing stealthily down the alley, but before he could even get his first ungainly foot into a toehold in the chain link, Abrihet's *amoui* was standing at the entrance of the gangway.

"Well?" she said. "Are you coming inside?"

As his phone began to ring in his pocket—Annemarie must have finished her meeting—he followed Abrihet's aunt inside, stumbling a little over the red patterned rug at the entrance, through the mostly empty restaurant, and up to the counter. The elderly couple had looked up from their lunches to sip their tea and stare at him.

"Are you here to eat?" She pointed at the plastic-covered menus that were stacked in a neat pile next to the cash register.

"No, thanks, ma'am. I'm actually here to . . . uh . . . is Abrihet here?"

"In the kitchen." She indicated the swinging metal door behind her with a small movement of her head.

"Can I talk to her? It will just be a quick second."

"No."

"No? Okay." Pup backed away from the counter, feeling equal parts disappointed and relieved. "Thanks, anyway. I'll just—"

"Wait."

She stepped from behind the counter and plucked at a handful of napkins from the dispenser on the empty table next to him. Then, clucking her tongue in disapproval, she began dabbing at his forehead and cheeks. "Why do you sweat so much?" she demanded. "You can't talk to my niece looking like this." Pup was too surprised to answer her. He just stood there, perfectly still, as the napkin was pressed to the wetness beading his upper lip.

"*Now,*" she said, satisfied, tossing the damp napkins into the garbage can next to the counter. "*Now* you may go."

On the other side of the swinging door, the kitchen was small, cramped, and stiflingly hot. The shelves were crammed with sacks of rice, lentils, flour, coffee beans, and big clear plastic jars of red and brown and yellow spices. The two small windows along the back wall were pushed open and a big box fan whirred in one corner, blowing the soupy air around. In the middle of the space was a six-burner stovetop. Abrihet stood before it, stirring something in a large metal pot, her face shining with sweat, her hair pulled back into a hairnet.

"James?" She looked up when he walked in, and the long wooden spoon bobbed in the pot. "What are you doing here?"

"Abrihet, I need to talk to you."

She fished out her spoon and her eyes returned to her cooking. "About what?"

"Is that *dorho* you're making?"

"Yeah. You want a taste?"

"Obviously."

He stepped closer. She dipped a piece of *injera* into the pot and handed it to him. He folded it into his mouth, swallowing heat; flavor; rich, slow-cooked chicken; and tomatoes and *berbere*. A rivulet of sweat jettisoned down his back.

"That is so freaking good."

"Thanks." She cleared her throat. "So. What's up?"

"I'm here," Pup said, looking her in the eyes, "because I have a confession."

"A confession?" Abrihet placed the spoon carefully on the counter. "About what?"

"Well, I—I lied to you."

A hand moved to her hip. "About *what*?"

"About my Greek Mythology Day project."

"*What?*"

"Remember that time we were in the darkroom together and I told you that I made my goat legs for my Pan costume from an old bath mat?"

"Um. Yes?"

"Well, I was lying. Half lying, anyway."

She stared at him, waiting for him to continue.

"It wasn't an old bath mat, like I told you. It was brand-new. I found it in the linen closet with the T.J. Maxx tag still on it."

"Wow, James." Abrihet sighed and picked up her spoon again. "If that's the worst thing you've ever lied about, then you're an even nicer person than I thought."

"Let me explain," he said. "Okay?"

She picked up a jar of *berbere* and shook some into the pot, tasting the results with the back of her spoon. "Okay."

"See, there were a bunch of old towels and stuff in that closet. I could have used any of them. But I took the brand-new one on purpose because I wanted my mom to notice it was missing. I wanted her to get mad at me for taking it. Like, I wanted her to get *pissed*. To really yell at me, you know?

Make me ride my bike all the way to T.J. Maxx right then and there and buy her a new one with my own money."

Abrihet picked up the salt, shook some into the pot, tasted. She didn't say anything, but he could tell by the stiff way she held her shoulders as she cooked that she was listening.

"See, my brother had been dead for two months, and my mom was disappearing right before my eyes. She, like, *shrunk*, Abrihet. She didn't just lose weight. She lost *height*. Even her voice got softer. She stopped watching *Dateline: To Catch a Predator* with me on Saturday nights. She stopped bowling. She stopped grocery shopping and dyeing her hair and cooking. My sisters had to take over making Sunday dinner. She stopped doing pretty much *anything*. And in my family, you can't just ask somebody if they're okay. You can't just talk to them. In Flanland, what you have to do is steal a brand-new green bath mat from the linen closet and hope that it provokes a fight. And then hope the fight will start a, like, real conversation."

"Did it?" Abrihet's voice was quiet. She stirred and tasted. "Provoke a conversation, I mean?"

Pup looked down at his Nikes. "She never even noticed it was gone."

He glanced toward the swinging kitchen door, hoping Abrihet's *amoui* wouldn't come through before he finished saying what he needed to say. He went on, the words coming out in a rush. "You were right, Abrihet. What you said the other day. I *don't* know you that well. I don't know your life. And I don't know your family. But I know your *work*. I know your *talent*. And I know what it's like to feel invisible. Unnoticed. Sometimes even by my own mom. And even if photography can't fix that feeling, it's still the best thing that's happened to me since Patrick died. It taught me to speak. And it led me to you."

Abrihet looked up at him. The only sound in the kitchen was the gentle simmering of the *dorho*.

"I guess what I'm trying to say is that we should be doing this together. I don't care about winning. I don't care if I come in last place. I just want to do this one thing with you. I want it to be us. I want . . . sorry. Hang on." She watched him as he shrugged off his bag, unzipped it, and pulled out the plain manila folder. He slid it across the counter to her. She wiped her hands on her denim shorts, picked it up, and opened it to the first image, the one he had placed at the top for her to see. It was the portrait he'd taken of her, standing before the glass doors of the hotel lobby in Champaign. Pup watched her eyes move over and then linger on that photograph. He saw her see herself as he saw her. Abrihet. *She who brings light*. More precious than any mountain. She gazed at the photo for a long time before she finally looked up and into his eyes.

"I never even knew you took this," she whispered. "It's beautiful." She placed the picture back into the folder, holding it carefully by its edges so as not to leave any finger-prints. "Do you really mean it?"

"Mean what?" The air was thick and fragrant with heat from the stovetop burners and the steaming pot of *dorho*, but Pup realized that he was no longer sweating. Instead, his nervousness had concentrated in the center of his chest and his heart began to jump and skitter. "I didn't say anything."

"Yes, James." She reached up and pulled off her hairnet. Black waves tumbled around her shoulders. "Yes, you did."

Her hand was against his cheek, first one, then the other, and she was cupping his face in the palms of her hands. She was reaching up and he was reaching down, to the soft curve where her waist flowed into her hips, and when she touched his lips with hers it was nothing like Spin the Bottle in Izzy's basement. That kiss, Pup knew now, had been nothing at all. But this: this was something totally different. When Abrihet kissed him, the jumping and skittering in his chest calmed, then stilled. Afterward, he could not remember how long it had lasted. It could have been a minute. It could have been an hour. His heart had become water, and she had found her way inside of it, running her fingers through its soft, sandy bottom, shining her light on all the buried things no one before had ever been able to reach.

28

"YOU'D BETTER GO," SHE SAID GENTLY, pulling away
to put her hands on his shoulders. "If my auntie walks in on
us, I'm dead."

"When will I see you again?" He leaned his head to the
side, resting it on her hand.

"Remember when I said if I helped you pass art, you owed
me one? Well, I think it's time to cash in on that."

Pup, leaning in to kiss her one last time, was more than
happy to agree.

They spent the following week together in the belly of
their empty high school, developing Abrihet's film, making it into prints, sorting the prints into piles, narrowing
the piles into smaller stacks of her strongest images. They
worked together in an intimate and easy silence, bodies close,
fingers grazing against waists and shoulders grazing against
shoulders, never kissing but always close enough to kiss,
unworried, knowing they would have many more chances for
that when their work was finally finished.

For her portfolio, Abrihet was doing a series on her

Uptown community, a neighborhood that was home to many Eritrean immigrants, but also other new arrivals from Ethiopia and India and Pakistan, Ghana and Nigeria, Vietnam and Cambodia. She had walked around her neighborhood, capturing street festivals, church picnics, kebab vendors, beachfront barbecues at Juneway Terrace, hipsters lining up for a show outside the Aragon Ballroom, old women with raw and peeling hands riding the red line home from their nighttime office-cleaning jobs. Her work was vibrant and kinetic and beautiful, crowded and overflowing with life. The hardest part of the whole process was narrowing it down to just twelve shots.

Working together feverishly, they got it done just in time, and at the end of the week Mr. Hughes met with them in the school art studio to review Abrihet's portfolio and get the two of them registered for regionals. Breaking out his magnifying glass, their teacher squinted and grimaced his way through her folder while she and Pup sat together across from him, fingers intertwined beneath his desk.

"What can I say, Abby?" Mr. Hughes finally said, tearing off his glasses and then jamming them back onto his face. "This is brilliant. If you two don't get sent to nationals, there is no justice in this world." He slapped her folder shut. "But don't take that as a guarantee or anything, because in case y'all haven't figured it out yet, there *is* no justice in the world."

"Don't worry, Mr. Hughes," said Abrihet. "You happen to be talking to two kids who've already learned that lesson."

"Well, good." They watched as their teacher's eyes wandered to the picture of the weird-looking dog Scotch-taped to the front of his grade book. "Better to learn young, I guess," he added bitterly.

"Mr. Hughes," Abrihet said gently. "Did you lose custody of Hershey Kiss?"

"My ex doesn't even know how to groom him properly!" he yelled, ripping off his glasses and tossing them on the desk. "She never does his undercoat right! And then it gets so tangled that it irritates his skin!"

"What's an undercoat?" asked Pup.

"Mr. Hughes, you're an amazing person," Abrihet said fiercely, "and if your ex can't see that, she doesn't deserve you anyway."

"Thank you, Abby." Mr. Hughes cleared his throat. "I appreciate that."

Pup sat there, confused. He'd thought they'd been talking about a dog. He had, he realized, much to learn about love. He gripped Abrihet's fingers under the table as Mr. Hughes turned to the laptop on his desk. "But enough about my personal woes. The important thing is that in a couple weeks' time, if luck is on our side, I'll be cheering you two on when your names are called for nationals. The only thing left to do now is register." He clicked over to the art show's website. "Abby, what's the name of your submission?"

"I'm calling it *Uptown*."

"Can't go wrong with a one-word title." They watched as he pecked out the word into the registration database with his two pointer fingers. "Like *Guernica*. Simple. Minimalistic. Powerful. What about you, Flanagan?"

Pup blinked. He was so bad at titles. He needed a word.

"Um—how about *Flanland*?"

"What the hell is 'Flanland'?"

"It's my neighborhood," Pup explained. "Well, like, the neighborhood *within* my neighborhood. All twenty-seven of my immediate family members live there. So that's what we call it."

Mr. Hughes wrapped his finger around one of his dreads, considering this. "But your pictures aren't really *about* your neighborhood. Not the way Abby's are, anyway. She's got streetscapes. El platforms. Jazz clubs. Restaurants. Specific physical spaces. Your portfolio is mostly portraiture."

"Well, it's still about my family, though, isn't it?"

"It is and it isn't. I mean, if it's about your family, then why include the picture of this abandoned dorm room here? Or, for that matter, this picture of Abby? You need to think about *cohesion*, Pup. *Thematics*. If you want to make it to nationals, it all has to tie together. It has to be greater than the sum of its parts. It's not just about the individual shots."

"I see what you're saying." Pup flipped through the twelve pictures in his portfolio. "But if it's not about Flanland, then what's it *about*?"

"What are you asking *me* for?" Mr. Hughes's hands hovered impatiently over the keyboard. "It's *your* project, Flanagan!"

Pup didn't know what to say. He crossed his leg to scratch a mosquito bite on his ankle.

"I've always thought . . ." Abrihet glanced over at him, then trailed off.

"What?" Pup looked at her.

"Nothing," she said quickly.

"Spit it out, Tesfay," said Mr. Hughes. "We're on a deadline here."

"Well . . ." Her eyes slid to his. "I guess I always thought it was about Patrick."

As soon as she said it, Pup saw immediately that she was right. His entire portfolio was about Patrick. About his dying, about his absence. It was there in the sag of Pup's father's shoulders as he knelt in the back garden pulling dandelions. It was in Annemarie's faraway smile as she leaned into Sal's arms on the deck after Sunday dinner. It was in the grip of his sister Elizabeth as she lay on the front room couch with her brand-new son, Oliver, curled to her chest, clinging to him as if she'd already begun calculating the chances that she might lose him one day. It was in Luke's face, drunk and twisted with rage just before he knocked their mother to the ground, or closed and inscrutable as he lay sleeping off his hangover on the roof. The negative space of Patrick—it was everywhere. It was even in the self-portrait Pup had taken late one afternoon beneath the basketball hoop in his alley. He remembered developing that shot, alone in the darkroom on the day Abrihet had walked out. He'd stood over the chemical bath as if it were a mirror, watching the contours of his own face deepening on the photo paper. And when it was finished, he'd jumped back, stunned, thinking for a wild moment that maybe his sign, his ghost, had finally appeared.

But no. It was not a ghost. It was only that Luke had been right: the older Pup got, the more he looked like Patrick.

VALUE:

degrees of lightness and darkness

29

PUP ARRIVED HOME FROM the meeting with Mr. Hughes to find his mother sitting on the front room couch dressed in a white pantsuit with the jacket draped over her shoulders and her slinged arm pressed against her floral blouse. Her hair was set in gray waves, and she'd swirled makeup onto her cheeks and lips. She was sitting very straight with her purse in her lap, watching the door and dabbing at her eyes with a tissue.

"Mom?" Pup looked anxiously around the empty room. "Are you waiting for someone?"

"I bought this suit last month for Luke's graduation." She smoothed the creamy fabric with her free hand. Pup could smell her perfume—the spicy, orange scent from the dusty, beveled glass bottle on her dresser that she used so sparingly it had lasted her for years. "It starts in an hour. We can still make it if he comes home in the next ten or fifteen minutes." She looked out the front picture window where Pup's dad was looping chicken wire around his tomato plants. "Your father thinks I've gone goofy." She picked an invisible piece of lint

251

off of her lapel. "Maybe I have."

"You're not goofy, Ma," Pup said, although the strange bright look in her eyes, the angry slashes of makeup on her cheeks, made him say the words without much conviction.

"It's just that I know he would never skip his graduation. And he'd never go without us. I figure he's going to come walking through this door any minute now. And when he does, I've got his suit upstairs hanging in plastic, pressed and ready to go."

"Mom." Pup sat down on the couch and took her free hand. It was cold and trembling, despite the heat of the summer afternoon. "I have to tell you something."

Behind him, he heard a floorboard creak. He turned around and saw his oldest sister, Jeanine, standing in the doorway between the dining room and the front room, holding two glasses of iced tea and listening intently to their conversation. "Sorry," she said. "Am I interrupting?"

"Yes," said Pup.

"No," his mother said at the exact same time. They looked at each other for a moment before she continued. "Pup was just saying he has something to tell me. And I think I know what it is." She ran her carefully painted fingernails along the wooden handle of her purse. "Jeanine just told me this morning. Carrie broke up with Luke. Apparently, Jeanine, you're the only one of my children who feels I have the right to *know* anything."

"Did *you* know about this?" Jeanine was shooting Pup her best sister-mom stare.

"Yeah."

"Since when?"

"I don't know," he said. "A month, maybe?"

"A *month*? And you never told anybody?"

"I told Annemarie."

"You and Annemarie." She shook her head disapprovingly. "Thick as thieves."

"Did Annemarie tell *you*?"

"Are you kidding? Of course not. I'm only her *sister*. Why would she tell *me* anything? No, Mary ran into Carrie's mother in the cheese locker at Costco yesterday afternoon. Had to pretend like she already knew. She said she felt like an *idiot*."

"Well, it doesn't even matter," said Pup, "because that's not what I had to tell you anyway, Mom."

"Oh." Judy Flanagan's red-rimmed eyes flashed with fear. But she pushed it away with a determined blink. "Well? Go ahead, dear."

"Luke's not going to his graduation because Luke isn't graduating. He failed out of law school last year."

His mother made a small noise. Her purse fell into her lap and her hands went to her face.

"I *knew* it!" Jeanine banged the glasses on the coffee table, sloshing some iced tea all over the new issue of *Better Homes and Gardens.* "I *knew* something wasn't adding up. Who told you about this?"

"Carrie."

"*Jesus.* You *talked* to her? I bet *she* gave you an earful. God, I could *kill* him. All his brains. All his opportunities. All his *potential.* Squandered. Gone!"

From behind their mother's hands came a ragged sob.

"*God*, Jeanine! Will you stop?" Pup put his arm very carefully around his mother, taking great care not to touch her injured shoulder. "You're not being, like, helpful right now."

"Not being *helpful?* Don't talk to *me* about helpful, Pup! I've got my own family to take care of, in addition to this one, in case everyone's forgotten. Do you even understand the logistical *feats* I had to undertake this morning to juggle the kids' summer sports camps with getting Mom to her PT appointment?"

"Well, it looks like you got her there and back." He dabbed at the spilled iced tea with the edge of his thumb. "So maybe you should, like, leave now."

"You want me to *leave?*" Jeanine gawked at him, her face twisted with both hurt and surprise. She and Pup were the bookend children of the Flanagan family. They were separated by six siblings and twenty-seven years; they had never even lived under the same roof. Pup loved Jeanine, of course, but not in the way he loved Luke or Annemarie or Patrick. She felt less like a sister to him and more like a distant aunt, and not the nice kind who overfeeds you and spends way too much money on your birthday present. Jeanine stood there for a moment, waiting for Pup to apologize, or at least to change his mind. When he didn't, she picked up her glass from the table, wiped her eyes with a tissue she'd extracted from the tiny waist pocket of her yoga pants, and quietly left the room. As soon as they heard the back door shut, Pup's mom turned to him and clutched his hand.

"All this time, I thought he was staying with Carrie. I never would have let your father kick him out if I knew he had no place to go. *Never.*"

"But Mom. You had to do *something*. I mean—look at your shoulder."

"My shoulder will heal," she said sharply. "But Luke . . . there's something broken inside of that boy. And when your child is broken, you don't turn them out. When your child is broken, that's when they need you the most." She pressed a tissue to her face and when she brought it away again there were little crescents of black makeup beneath her eyes. She looked at him accusingly. "You should have told me, Pup."

"I don't like to upset you, Ma. You *know* that."

"I'm not a Ming vase from *Antiques Roadshow*, honey! I raised eight children, didn't I? And watched one be buried, didn't I?"

Pup jumped to his feet. He was suddenly furious. "Yeah, and as soon as you came home from the funeral you took down his picture and replaced it with a fat angel with dead eyes and weird nipples, and you never spoke of him again!"

"That 'fat angel,' young man," she shouted, "is a religious picture all the way from Italy! It was a gift from Father Gambera to bring me comfort in my time of suffering and, if you must know, it was blessed by Pope Francis himself!"

"Who *cares*? Will you stop erasing him, Mom? *Patrick's* face is the only one that belongs on the seventh step. That was his name. That was his *name*! Patrick! And you won't even say it out loud!"

"I don't need to say it out loud! That name lives in my heart every minute of my life, so I don't *need* to say it!"

They were alone together in the front room, staring at each other as if from across a great distance. Any other time Pup had tried to bring up Patrick to his mother, her tears had broken his heart, had made him relent, had sent him scurrying back into their agreed-upon silence. But not today. Today, after all that had happened and all that he'd learned, her tears just made him angrier.

"You know what, Ma? Maybe *I* need you to say it! Did you ever think about that? Did you ever think about what it's been like for *me*, to be stuck in a family where nobody ever talks about anything? Where everything that hurts gets shoved down inside to just, like, *rot*?"

"Fine, Pup!" His mother threw her purse to the floor. She was crying hard now, but Pup still didn't feel guilty. He felt great, actually. Finally, at last, she was fighting with him. "You win! I'll say his name. Patrick! Patrick! Patrick, Patrick, Patrick! Patrick Michael Flanagan, my son, who's been dead for nine hundred and eighty days and"—she looked at her watch—"six and a half hours. There! I said it. *Now* are you happy?"

"Yes," he said quietly. And it was true. There was still life in her, after all. He watched her as she squinted out the window at her husband's tomato plants, letting the tears fall.

"And now I've turned my other son out into the street, and I've lost him, too."

Pup sat back down next to her, sinking into the worn cushions. "Luke's not lost, Mom."

"Well, then where is he? Nobody's heard from him in over three *weeks*, Pup. Where *is* he?"

"I don't know. But I know he's somewhere. I still text him every day, and even though he doesn't answer, I always get a delivered receipt."

"I don't even know what that means," she said miserably.

"It means he's around. It means he's charging his phone. It means he's not lost. Not the way Patrick is lost, anyway."

"Well, if he's not," she whispered, leveling Pup with her blue, watery eyes, "then go and find him."

30

PUP CLIMBED THE STAIRS SLOWLY, sticking his middle finger up at the angel on the seventh step with extra viciousness. The air in the second-floor bedroom was muggy and hot. It made him feel anxious and claustrophobic, so he shoved open the crescent window in his bedroom and stepped out onto the roof. The sun was setting, one of those spectacular, sky-on-fire sunsets that photographers dream about, but Pup barely noticed. He took his phone from his pocket and composed the text message.

What you did was really bad, he wrote. **It was probably the worst thing you ever did. But I still love you and so does everybody else so just come home already. Please.**

He took a deep breath and tapped send.

The automated response came back immediately:

Not deliverable.

Pup felt the world go quiet as he stared into the phone in his palm at those two words on the screen. A familiar terror was building inside of him, a terror just like the last time he'd been blindsided by two little words.

Bacterial meningitis.

When he'd first heard those two words, as he rushed to stuff his bag into the trunk of Annemarie's car on that rainy afternoon two Octobers ago, he'd figured it was a kind of flu. Maybe a bad flu, but nothing that modern science couldn't fix. But then, as their three-car caravan of family members sped down I-57, rain pelting the windshield and the dead corn lying hacked down in the fields on either side of the road, he'd Googled it. *An acute infection of the brain and spine. . . . Complications can be severe. . . . Mortality rate without immediate intervention high . . .* Medical explanations of fluid and membranes and strains of bacteria had been interspersed with the stark language of sad poetry: *grave. Profound. Catastrophic.*

All they knew, as Annemarie jerked her car to a stop and she, Pup, Sal, Luke, and Carrie ran through the hospital parking lot, huddled together against the rain, was what Patrick's roommate had reported to their mother: that he hadn't been feeling well, that he'd gone up to bed to take a nap, and that when they'd gone upstairs to check on him, hours later, they were unable to wake him up.

It was only after they checked in at the front desk, were redirected up to the ICU, and met their glazed-eyed father in a long, white-walled hallway that they learned Patrick was in a coma. *A coma?* he remembered asking nobody in particular.

But that doesn't happen to real people. That only happens in soap operas.

And, in a way, he was right: It was nothing like a soap opera. If it was, Patrick, in that faraway, underwater state he was in, swimming in the abyssopelagic depths of his own brain, would have been called back up to the surface by their voices, by their pleading voices that gathered around his bed to whisper and bargain and pray for him to wake up. Their words would have pierced the darkness and he would have swum back up to them. It would have happened slowly, beautifully, the climactic tear-jerking scene: first, the miraculous wiggling of the fingers. Then, the faintest flutter of an eyelid. And then suddenly, the heavy lids would flick open, revealing those clear blue eyes, awake, alert, alive. "Where am I?" he'd mumble, and the hospital room would become the corner of Clark and Addison at the moment Michael Martinez's grounder landed in Rizzo's glove during the tenth inning in game seven of the World Series, times a thousand. Times a million.

But this wasn't a soap opera and it wasn't playoff baseball, and Patrick would never open his eyes again. As soon as Pup saw his brother lying there in the bed, his face an expressionless mask, his chest as pale as carved marble and pocked by wires and tubes, he understood this. Everybody did, even his mother, even if it took her two more days before she could agree to turn off the machines.

☁ ☁ ☁

Pup slipped his phone back into his pocket and climbed through the window back into the bedroom. He went into the closet and rummaged into its farthest reaches, past the clutter where Luke had discovered Patrick's protein powder, to a little nail all the way in the back, on which hung his brother's stained and faded Cubs hat. He lifted it from its nail with his fingertips, then crawled beneath the hanging clothes and out of the closet. Still holding the hat with the edges of his fingers, he folded himself through the small front window and climbed out to the roof. Then he lay down on his back and dropped the hat gently over his face, so that the sunset coming through was filtered into a muted, warm gray-blue, the color of the sea.

Pup breathed.

He'd done this before, just once or twice. Only on the very worst days. He couldn't do it regularly, he knew, because if he did, he would destroy it. The hat still possessed the faint-est, faintest scent of Patrick—shampoo, deodorant spray, and that other, ineffable Patrickness that could never be re-created and that would never again exist anywhere in the world except in the fibers of this hat. Like a rare sea scroll or a lost page of an ancient text, Pup knew that if he touched it too much, he would soil it, and the very thing that made the hat so precious would disintegrate.

Once he'd arranged the hat over his face, he didn't try to

speak to Patrick. He'd tried too many times, and too many times he'd been answered with silence. So instead he just breathed, and after a few moments the memory came stealing along, settling down around him as gently as a cool sheet on a hot night.

August. Two weeks before Pup started high school. Two months before Patrick died. It was the first in a three-game Cubs-Pirates series and their seats were terrible, partially obstructed in the upper reaches of Terrace Reserved, but at least they were free: Noreen's friend had been called out of town at the last minute and couldn't use them. The game was just as terrible as the seats; eight scoreless innings, followed by an Andrew McCutchen solo shot in the ninth, and the Cubs lost. Still, it was summer, and it was Chicago, and it was Wrigley Field, and Pup had spent the day in his obstructed seat eating nachos and filling in box scores with his two brothers, and that meant it was still a very good day. When the game was over, Luke wanted to burn off his beer buzz before they made it home for Sunday dinner. He suggested that they walk the three miles to the Addison blue line and take the El the rest of the way home. "Why not?" Patrick had shrugged, and they'd set off, walking west across the city.

They were a couple blocks from the station when they passed a bar. It was a dumpy old place with grimy windows, a brick facade in major need of a power washing, and fossilized gum all over the sidewalk. In the doorway, an old man in a filthy winter coat and duct-taped gym shoes stood begging for change. As soon as he saw them coming, he stepped out into the middle of the sidewalk and blocked their way.

"Let me guess," he slurred. "Brothers?"

"Yeah, man." Patrick smiled at him. "How'd you know?"

"The eyes. You all got the same eyes."

He stepped closer to them, peering, turn by turn, into each of their eyes. There was something mesmerizing about him, so that even Luke stood passively and allowed the man to peer up at him, close enough to touch. Pup could see now that he wasn't old, as he'd first appeared. He was maybe a couple years older than Annemarie, not quite thirty. But booze and drugs had done something to his skin, putting cracks into everything. His hands were shaking so hard it looked like he was dancing.

"Help a guy out, will ya?" He held out a battered Dunkin' Donuts cup, and the change rattled itself.

"Sorry, man," said Luke. "I spent all my cash at the game."

He tried to keep walking but the man caught a handful of Luke's jersey from behind.

"Hey!" Luke yanked his shirt from the homeless man's grip and shoved him backward. "Keep your hands off me."

"Why should I?" the man shouted. His coat had fallen open, revealing a bare, yellowish chest and a belly as distended as a pregnant woman's. There were two small purple circles—bruises, lesions, cigarette burn scars, maybe—just beneath his ribs. "Why *should* I?" he yelled again. "You got your family. You got your two brothers here. I got nothin'! No family. No brothers. *Nothing.* And you're standin' here, tellin' me you spent all your cash at the *game*?"

"Here, man." Patrick leafed quickly through his wallet and pressed a wad of cash into the man's hands. "Go get yourself something to eat, okay?"

The man took the money and stuffed it into his coat pocket. Giving Luke one last vicious glare, he retreated back to the doorway and into the bar, the screen door slamming behind him.

"Saint Patrick." Luke brushed off his jersey and rolled his eyes. "You really think he's going to go buy himself a sandwich with that money?"

"It's his business what he does with it," Patrick said quietly. Through the shadow of the screen they could see the man approaching the bartender, ordering something brown in a short glass. "It was mostly singles, anyway."

Just like that, the day was spoiled. The three brothers walked the rest of the way to the train in a moody silence. They rode home in silence, and they walked from the station back to Flanland in silence. It was only just before they went in the house that someone finally spoke.

"Hey, Luke," Patrick had said. "I'm not trying to be, like, preachy. But next time you see a homeless guy like that who wants some money, just try to remember what Mom always says."

Pup knew immediately what Patrick meant. *There but for the grace of God go I* was a favorite phrase of their mother's. Luke must have known, too, because he rolled his eyes and went inside, letting the screen door bang behind him right in Patrick's face.

Pup sat up with a start and tore off the Cubs hat. The sun was sinking behind the apartment buildings just west of Flanland, and his shadow had grown long.

He knew, at last, where to find his missing brother.

31

THE CICADAS HAD COME EARLY this year. Usually it wasn't until later in the summer that their collective chirping reached this crescendo, a relentless blood-beat thrumming that began just around sunset, drowning out all other sounds. As Pup got off the train and stepped out into the twilit city, the insects' molted shells lay scattered all over the sidewalk, gleaming in the streetlight like broken glass. They crunched under his Nikes like dead leaves. Luke had been gone for just over three weeks now, and as Pup approached the doorway of Mayor's Packaged Liquors and Tap on shaking legs, he knew in his bones that if Luke wasn't here, then Luke was gone forever.

The bar stood between a bankrupt sandwich chain and a for-rent former insurance office. If Pup hadn't seen the place so clearly in his memory, he might have walked right past it. It was exactly the kind of place that was meant to go unnoticed until it caused a problem, like the hardy, scuttling cockroaches that had lived in the cabinets of Sal and Annemarie's first apartment. And, like cockroaches, who were rumored to be the only creatures equipped to survive a nuclear holocaust, Mayor's Packaged Liquors would keep surviving long after the trendier, flashier places that surrounded it came and went, an ugly but necessary part of the urban ecosystem.

It was hard to tell whether the place was open or closed, since Pup could hear no music or noise coming from inside, and the windows had been soaped up to prevent anyone from seeing in or out. But before he could even put his hand on the front door handle to find out, a white, familiar shape in the alley beside the sandwich shop caught his eye. There, parked in front of a locked dumpster, its windshield bristling with orange parking tickets, was Luke's white Jeep.

Pup approached the car cautiously, just as a huge gray rat with sleek, oily fur lumbered out from underneath it, so close he could hear the hiss of its tail as it dragged across the sidewalk. He jumped back as the rat scuttled past, his heart pounding, the cicadas screaming. He approached the driver's-side window. He'd seen enough *Dateline* to know that when you find a missing person's car, there's a good chance your missing person is very close by. The only question is whether they're dead or alive when you find them. Well, whatever was in that car, he was going to have to look. He might be the only son left in his family, and he owed that much to his mother. But as he peered inside the driver's-side window, holding his breath, all he saw was a pile of empty gum wrappers on the passenger seat. The seats were not covered in bloodstains. There was no bloated body with wide, dead eyes staring back at him. There was no overpowering smell of a corpse rotting in the trunk. Pup let his breath go and jiggled the door handle. It was locked. Okay. He was getting close. He could do this. With a renewed sense of purpose, he strode out of the alley, braced himself, and threw open the door to Mayor's Packaged Liquors, hoping, praying, that Luke would be crouched over the bar counter, drunk as hell, maybe, but alive.

His hopes were dashed as soon as he walked inside. Luke was not sitting at the bar counter because there *was* no bar counter. Pup's memory must have been wrong. Mayor's Packaged Liquors wasn't a bar at all; it was a down-on-its-luck liquor store, nothing more than a maze of cluttered aisles lined with grimy-looking bottles of booze, a lotto machine, and a bowl at the cash register filled with shriveled, brown-spotted limes.

An enormous woman with skin the color of an uncooked turkey was perched on a stool behind the bulletproof glass of the cash register, fast asleep and snoring shallowly. When Pup cleared his throat, she didn't even stir.

"Excuse me," he said.

Snore.

"Pardon me."

Snort.

He brought his hand down gingerly on the little silver bell next to the bowl of limes and she startled awake, coughing phlegmily. In the next instant Pup found himself staring straight into the neat black hole of a cocked handgun. His intestines rearranged themselves into liquid form while he waited for the woman to take in his dorky backpack and his skinny praying-mantis legs and realize that he was no threat to her.

"Sorry about that," she said, stashing the gun back under the counter. "May I help you?"

"Yes, ma'am." Pup glanced down at his shorts to make sure he hadn't peed his pants. "I'm—uh—looking for someone."

"In the tippling lounge?"

"The what?"

"The tippling lounge."

"Oh." He looked at the woman. She didn't exactly seem in the mood for questions. "Um. Yes?"

"Well, you know the basics, right?" The woman adjusted herself on her stool like a roosting hen. "You get fifteen minutes for each dollar you spend. Bathroom key is a flat rate of five bucks. Cash only, of course."

"Of course." Pup nodded vigorously, to make up for the look of total mystification that was surely plastered across his face. He reached into his wallet and peeled off a dollar from the small stack of singles he'd collected mowing his uncle Mitch's lawn. "I guess fifteen minutes is enough?" He pushed the bill across the counter. The woman glared at it, then at him.

"Boy, what you think I sell in this place for one solitary buck? The cheapest hooch in this store is still gonna run you five bucks, minimum. And I *don't* sell loose cans anymore, so don't even think about asking."

"Um . . ." Pup looked around the liquor store, half expecting to see a list of rules nailed to the moldy wall. Instead, all he saw was a faded Budweiser ad from the 1996 Super Bowl, so ancient that all the Clydesdale horses majestically prancing around that poster had probably long since been turned into glue. "Ma'am," he finally said. "This is my first time here—"

"You don't say."

"—and so I don't really know, like, the rules."

The woman opened her mouth, produced a prodigious yawn that exposed all the pink ridges of her throat, and heaved herself off her stool. She was so small and round that her chin barely reached the counter. "The rules are as follows," she began, counting off on her stubby fingers. "One. For every dollar you spend in my store, you get fifteen minutes in my tippling lounge. So, for example: Buy yourself a twelve-dollar bottle of Jack Sprat Brandy, you get three hours in the lounge. Four dollars an hour, see? Treat yourself to a fifteen-dollar bottle of Captain Havana's Fine Imported Rum, you get three hours and forty-five minutes. Get it?"

Pup nodded, trusting her figures. Math had never been his strong suit.

"Two. You want a key to my bathroom, it's a five-dollar flat fee. And if you can't afford it, that don't mean you can go defecating in my alley. We got a rat problem back there already, in case you haven't noticed. Three. As far as beds, those are first come, first served. I wash the sheets pretty regular, but regular don't mean daily—I'm a busy woman. Bed bugs and the like is a risk you take. This is Mayor's Tippling Lounge. It ain't the Four Seasons. Okay?"

"Okay," Pup said woodenly.

"Four." She leaned forward, her bosom straining against the puff-painted leopard that leaped across the front of her T-shirt. "And listen carefully because this is the most important rule. Rule number four is that I don't bother you, and you don't bother me. I ain't asking you questions, because I ain't want to know. You can laugh back there, you can cry back there, you can dance around naked and play 'The Star-Spangled Banner' on the kazoo for all I care. What you do in the tippling lounge is your business. But!" She held up a finger like a teacher driving home a particularly important point. "Just remember it's your business *alone*—as in, no guests are allowed unless they get approval from *me*. This is a tippling lounge and not a brothel, understood?"

"Okay," Pup repeated.

"Good. Now. You seem like a nice boy: sweet, scrubbed

behind the ears, trusting if a bit dull. So I don't think we'll have any problems. But if you *do* decide to cause any trouble for me—fighting, fornicating, overdosing—I reserve the right to ban you for life. In other words: You die back there? I'll kill ya." She began hiccuping violently, and Pup was beginning to think she might need the Heimlich maneuver when he realized that was just how she laughed. "Now," she said, wiping away the tears that were collecting in the pouches beneath her eyes. "What can I get for you?"

"How much are the limes?" Pup indicated the sad-looking bowl perched on the edge of the counter.

"What? I don't know. Nobody comes to Mayor's to buy *produce*. Only reason I still stock 'em is out of habit. Guy we all called Marbles—he had a turned eye that rolled around in his head just like a marble—he used to like to squeeze a lime over his tequila. But he dropped dead last year—massive coronary—and here I am, still stocking his damn limes."

"How about I give you a dollar for this one?" Pup chose a lime from the bowl, the least shriveled-looking one, which still had patches of green between its puckered swaths of brown skin. "That buys me fifteen minutes, right?"

The cashier scowled at him and snatched the dollar off the counter. "You're a cheap little bastard, you know that?" She lifted an egg timer from a row of several that were lined up along the top of the cash register. "Now go on back there and get to work doing whatever perverted business you've got planned with that piece of fruit. You've got fifteen minutes and not a moment longer." She cranked the egg timer so that it began to purr along with the faint chorus of the others. "Time starts now."

32

THE TIPPLING LOUNGE WAS LOCATED through a metal door at the back of the liquor store and down an impossibly long flight of concrete stairs, as if they led to an ancient catacomb and not a standard Chicago basement storage room. As Pup made his way down the darkened stairwell, the air seemed to grow both muggier and colder at the same time, and the walls on either side of him grew slick with green lichen. He heard a faint skittering of rodent claws across stone, felt the drip of condensing water from an overhead pipe slide down the back of his neck. Down, down, down he went, using the flashlight app on his phone when it became too dark to see, until he reached a bumpy stone floor with crevices that were filled with shallow puddles of dark water. A wooden door stood directly at the bottom of the stairs, and a very faint light was coming through on the other side of it. Pup thought about knocking, but decided against it. He'd already bought his fifteen minutes. Like it or not, he had every right to be here.

☁ ☁ ☁

The lounge itself was as damp as the stairwell, the walls furry with moss. Someone had made a half-assed attempt to make the place more homey by putting down a large, square Oriental rug that was matted and stained in places with tar-like marks that Pup couldn't identify as dried blood or bile or something worse. In the middle of this rug was a long, low, glass-topped coffee table with a centerpiece made of an upturned fedora hat filled with stubbed-out cigarette butts. The smell of sewage seeped from the half-open bathroom door, where a single toilet stood under a naked light bulb, as if it were being interrogated. In one corner, two mattresses were pushed up against the wall, each occupied by a human-shaped lump buried beneath a pile of thin, worn blankets so that all Pup could see were the bottoms of bare feet—large, calloused, filthy. In the other corner, sitting on a sagging futon with his hands resting on his thick thighs, his eyes half open, was Luke Flanagan.

He was neither awake nor asleep. A mostly empty whiskey bottle lay at his feet. If he heard the sound of the door opening and Pup's muffled footsteps on the rug, he gave no indication. If he saw Pup standing before him with a phone in one hand and a sad-looking lime in the other, he did not react. Pup circled Luke for a moment, like a diver approaching a new and dangerous species. He didn't want to loom, didn't want to startle. He squatted on his haunches, level with Luke's knees, so that if his brother woke up suddenly and took a swing, he would catch air.

"Hey," Pup said in a low voice. "Luke."

The eyes fluttered for a moment, but Luke did not answer.

"Luke." Pup reached out and shook a knee. His brother's jeans were slippery with grease and cold to the touch.

The eyes fluttered again, and creaked open. They rested on Pup without seeming to see him.

"Luke," Pup said. "It's me."

He opened his mouth. His lips, dry and cracked and whitish with dead skin, pulled apart so that he could speak.

"Leave," he croaked.

Then he closed his eyes.

Pup jiggled a knee again, without any response. But he hadn't shared a bedroom with Luke his whole life for nothing. He knew by the consciously unmoving way Luke held his body that he was awake now, and that he was only pretending not to be.

"I'm not leaving unless you come with me," Pup said.

No response.

"I'll carry you out of here over my shoulder if I have to."

That did the trick—Luke's dry white lips cracked themselves into a half smile at the idea of his skinny, noodle-armed little brother heaving two hundred and twenty pounds of booze-soddened limbs up that massive flight of stairs.

"So this is where you've been staying," Pup said.

Luke smiled again. His eyes were still closed. "Nice digs, huh?"

"Luke, just come with me. Please. Just come home."

"Home?" Luke leaned down slowly, like a very old man. "Home is here, at least until I finish this whiskey. Or until my egg timer dings and I have to buy another. Ms. Mayor up there." He reached around for his bottle, and Pup quietly pushed it out of his arm's reach with his toe. "She runs a tight ship."

"Mom's not even mad anymore," said Pup. "I swear. You were barely out the door before she'd forgiven you."

"*Leave.*" Luke's eyes had snapped open suddenly, and they were blazing blue, feverish, but strangely clear. They weren't so much the eyes of a drunk as the eyes of a person who'd been crushed by some unspeakable sadness.

"No."

"Yes."

"*No.* Not without you." He tossed the lime into Luke's splayed lap. "There's about twelve hours' worth of limes up there rotting in the bowl at the cash register and I'm gonna buy all of them, one by one, if that's how long it takes to convince you to come home with me."

"Fine." Luke got to his feet slowly, the lime rolling off his lap and settling into some dingy corner. "Then *I'll* leave." He fumbled around in his pockets and pulled out his car keys.

"Don't you dare," Pup said. His voice was rising. One of

the sleeping drunks on the far bed had awoken, rolled over, and was watching the two brothers from the mattress, his eyes gleaming like an animal's. "Don't you even dare. You'll kill someone."

"Good," said Luke. His eyes were yellow-cast, bloodshot, and very, very far away. "Maybe it'll be me."

He lurched toward the door.

Pup grabbed him by the shirtsleeve, twisting it up into his fist. "You leave, I'll call the cops. I'll report you."

"I bet you'd like that." Luke's face was very close to Pup's, the bottom half of it obscured by the thick black growth of a beard, and his unbrushed teeth were filmed over with yellowish gunk. "You. Mom. Dad. Our sisters. Carrie. Everybody. Not one of you even knows the worst things I've done. Not one of you. But still you'd love to see me locked up, wouldn't you?"

"You're goddamn right I would!" Pup yanked Luke closer by his shirt, twisting it around his fist so tightly his knuckles went white. He didn't even care that he was crying. "I'd lock you up forever before I let you die!"

Luke tried to shake him off, something he could have done easily under normal circumstances, but Pup's grip was strengthened by sheer fury, and Luke's had been weakened by his bender. They stood there for a moment, grappling with each other, as Pup reached again and again for the keys. Luke got a foot between Pup's legs, taking advantage of his little brother's innate clumsiness, and in an instant Pup was tripping forward, still clinging to Luke's shirt. He heard a terrific rip as the fabric tore down the front and then Pup was falling, holding nothing but a torn strip of cloth, and as he went down his face caught the sharp glass corner of the coffee table. A sudden avalanche of pain rocketed through his head, and he felt a hot spill of blood ooze from the torn skin at his temple. He tried to pull himself to his feet, feeling gummy and light-headed, but it was too late. He heard the slam of a door, the dull, uneven thud of drunken steps up the concrete stairs. He staggered forward, wiping the blood from his eyes, and threw open the door. With the pain whooping and contracting in his skull, running up the stairs was like trying to run up an undulating rope bridge; he had to keep stopping to catch his balance, and by the time he'd made it to the top and run through the maze of bottles in the liquor store and passed the enormous woman with the gun and the raw-turkey skin and made it outside onto the sidewalk and into the alley, Luke was already gunning the engine. Pup could only watch as Luke jerked the Jeep into reverse, slamming into the dumpster behind him as a river of startled rats darted out in all directions. Then he veered crazily into the street and turned around the corner and out of sight.

Standing in the middle of the alley, Pup took a shaky breath, wiped the blood from his eyes again, and pulled out his phone. His finger smeared red across his screen as he tapped in the number with trembling fingers.

"911," the operator said. "What is your emergency?"

By the time he'd reached the bus stop, he could already hear the sirens.

33

PUP WAS TOO AGITATED AND AFRAID to stand still and wait for the bus, so he found himself half jogging, half sprinting the two miles to Sal and Annemarie's apartment. By the time he arrived he was dripping with sweat, his hair looking like he'd stuck his finger in an electric socket. The two women were waiting for him on the front steps.

"I'm so glad you called me," Annemarie said, meeting him on the sidewalk to grab him in a fierce hug. "You did the right thing."

Inside, Sal dabbed at his gash with a warm cloth, then covered it with a square of gauze and a Band-Aid while Annemarie made him a ham sandwich and poured him a tall glass of iced tea. Then they sat with him at the kitchen table and watched him eat. When he was finished, pressing the crumbs with his finger, he told them about his day: Judy Flanagan in her pantsuit waiting for Luke to come home for his graduation. Pup's journey into the bowels of Mayor's Packaged Liquors and Tap. The empty whiskey bottle, the fight, the 911 call.

He didn't tell them how he had known where to find Luke, though. He didn't tell them about breathing Patrick's hat over his face, how it had triggered a memory-dream. That part was too private, and anyway, logical, practical Annemarie would probably never have believed it.

"You did the right thing," Annemarie repeated.

"What you did took real guts, Pup," Sal added. "You should feel proud."

"I don't feel proud," Pup said. "I feel like shit."

"Most hard decisions in your life leave you feeling like shit in one way or another."

"Now what do we do?"

"We wait," said Annemarie. "Someone's going to have to bail him out. He's not going to call any of the oldest sisters. He's not going to call Mom and Dad. He's not going to call Carrie, and he's not going to call you." She tapped a finger on her phone screen. "All that leaves is me."

"But how do we even know he got arrested? Those sirens might not have been the police. They could have been an ambulance. What if he . . ." Pup couldn't bring himself to speak the thought that had been mushrooming in his head during his run to Annemarie's place. A fender bender had become a T-bone crash had become a crumple of hot metal against a brick wall. Massive internal injuries. *Grave, profound, catastrophic* injuries.

"If it will make you feel better," said Annemarie, "I'll call

Mary. She's working the ambulance tonight. She can tell us if something came over the radio."

"Why don't I call her?" Sal said gently. "You two stay here and talk."

Annemarie nodded as Sal picked the phone up off the table, squeezed Pup's shoulder, and went into the bedroom to make the call.

"He failed out of law school," Pup said as soon as Sal shut the door behind her. "Last year. He's only been pretending to go to his classes and his study groups. He's mostly just been drinking. Did you know that?"

"No," Annemarie said. She picked up Pup's empty plate and brought it to the sink. "I didn't. But now I know why Jeanine's been blowing up my phone all day."

"Patrick died a month after Luke started law school. He still managed to survive that year, and with an A average, too. So what changed? What *happened*?"

"I don't know if anything happened, necessarily." Annemarie ran the plate under hot water and stared out the window into the neighbors' kitchen across the courtyard. "Grief isn't the same for everyone, Pup. Some people just can't move on."

"And some people can't move on fast enough." His voice was neutral, but as soon as the words came out of his mouth she whirled around, dropping his plate in the sink with a clatter.

"What's *that* supposed to mean?"

Pup shrugged. "Nothing."

"Oh, no. You don't get to 'nothing' *me*, kid. You're gonna make an accusation, you better be prepared to back it up with evidence."

"Fine. You want evidence? How about the time you and Sal gave away all of Patrick's stuff when he was barely dead in the ground?"

"We didn't give away his *stuff*. We *donated* his *textbooks* to an organization that needed them. Hoping that some tiny shred of good might come out of something that was so irredeemably horrible."

"You could have waited."

"For what, Pup? For him to come back to life and finish out his degree?"

"See?" Pup shouted. "Even now, you're being, like, sarcastic. But you're just as bad as Mom and Dad. You never even talk about him. Never! And you hate Luke for being an alcoholic . . . but you know what? At least the fact that he's turned into a drunk lunatic proves that *someone* in this family is as messed up as I am about Patrick. It proves that someone else cares!"

"You think I don't care?" Annemarie looked at him, her voice breaking. "You think I'm not messed up about it? How could I not be, Pup? Patrick was my little brother, and I . . ." She stepped toward him, raising her hand. For a moment he thought she was going to hit him. Instead, she slid her fingers down her own face, brushing against the tiny purplish lines that squiggled along her cheeks.

"Do you know what these are?"

"They're broken blood vessels," he said. "Dad has them too."

"Dad has them because he's old. You know why *I* have them?" Tears were standing in Annemarie's eyes. She let her fingers fall away from her face. "I got these from hurting myself. Slapping myself, to be specific. So hard and so much that I burst the blood vessels beneath my skin."

Pup sat at the table and gaped. He felt sick.

"After Patrick died, I was in such darkness, Pup. I started to get this feeling that I was dead too, that I was stuck in some in-between place that wasn't quite hell but that also wasn't— that *couldn't* be—my real life. So I'd go into the bathroom and I'd stand before the mirror and I'd smack myself, over and over, until I felt like I'd woken the fuck up, until I'd hurt myself so much I'd convinced myself that I was still alive, that it *was* my real life. That Patrick was dead and he was never coming back, so now I had two choices: either give in to the darkness, or gather every ounce of strength I had and move the *fuck* on. And guess which one I chose?"

They regarded each other there in the kitchen, neither of them moving, neither of them breathing. The tears that stood in Annemarie's eyes began to streak down her face.

"Guys?" The door creaked open. Annemarie turned away

toward the sink, hiding her face as Sal poked her head out into the kitchen. "I've got Mary on the line. Police pulled him over maybe half an hour ago. Arrested him without incident."

Pup felt his knees buckling with relief.

"She wants to talk to you, Pup. She's going nuts. Wants to know what the hell's going on."

Annemarie turned back to face them. She'd wiped her tears away. She took the phone from Sal's outstretched hand. "I'll handle this," she said. "Pup, you just relax. Finish your iced tea. Have a shower if you want. The bed's all made up for you in the guest room. After I get off with Mary, I'll call Mom. I'll let her know you're staying here tonight. Okay?"

"What are you going to tell her about Luke?"

"I don't know." She went into the bedroom and put her hand on the door.

"Annemarie?"

"Yeah?"

"Tell her the truth."

She nodded, once, then closed the door softly behind her.

Sal put a plate of cookies in front of him, refilled his iced tea, and disappeared out the sliding glass balcony doors to give him some privacy. She was good like that—it was one of the reasons she got along with Annemarie so well. Pup ate the cookies and finished his tea. Then, too tired to wash the stink of Mayor's Tippling Lounge off his body, he went into the guest room, peeled off his sweat-streaked clothes, and climbed beneath the covers. Touching the tender place at the side of his head, he took out his phone and placed it beside him on the pillow.

Abrihet, he wrote.

A minute later, she responded:

James.

His mind rushed with words, with all the things he wanted to tell her about Luke, about what had happened that day, about what had been happening for years even though they'd all tried so hard not to see it. But he was too exhausted. Too exhausted and too sad.

Good night, he finally wrote.

And only when she wrote back a few minutes later: **Good night,** could he allow the exhaustion to wash over him into another night of dreamless, fitful sleep.

34

MANY HOURS LATER, Pup awoke to a soft knocking on his bedroom door.

"Yeah," he mumbled. His mouth was dry and his forehead thrummed with a dull headache. He lifted his fingers to the Band-Aid at the side of his head and felt the flaking crust of dried blood.

"Good morning," Sal called from the other side of the door. "Eggs?"

Pup pulled on the clothes he'd tossed to the side of the bed the night before and stepped out into the kitchen. Sal had opened the glass balcony doors to let in the warm air of the morning and the room was bright and clean and sunny. Pup sat down at the kitchen table as she placed a glass of orange juice and two aspirin in front of him, and now she bustled around the kitchen busily, frying eggs and turning slices of organic bacon with a silver pair of tongs.

"Is Annemarie at work?"

"No." Sal slid the eggs and bacon in front of him, then sat

across from him with her mug of coffee. "She went to go deal with your brother. He called her just before dawn."

"What happened?"

"Well, they charged him with aggravated DUI, and he's got a court date next week. She bonded him out and took him to the emergency room. They're there now. When you're done eating, I can drive you home, and then I'll go meet them there."

"The emergency room," Pup repeated.

"Don't panic. He's going to be fine. He's just been pretty hard on his body the last few weeks, and Annemarie wants him to get checked out. Assuming he gets the all-clear, she'll bring him back here, make him eat something, put him to bed. And tomorrow? That's when we start having the tough conversations that your family—no offense—is so good at avoiding."

"Does he hate me?" Pup squinted down into his eggs, bracing himself for her answer. Sal wasn't a Flanagan, and he knew she would give it to him straight. She had grown up in a normal, modern family, with a golden retriever, high-speed internet, and a socially acceptable number of siblings. A family where people didn't deal with the bad stuff by pretending it didn't exist.

"No, Pup. He doesn't hate you." Sal's voice faltered for just a moment as she reached across the table to grab his hand. "If anything, he loves you best of all."

35

WHEN PUP GOT HOME, his mother was waiting for him in the same place on the couch where he'd left her the day before. She had changed out of her pantsuit and washed the makeup off her face. The curls she'd set in hot rollers for Luke's graduation were starting to wilt around her shoulders.

"You found him, Pup." She pushed herself to her feet using her good arm. "I knew you would. I knew that only you could."

Pup nodded. "I guess Annemarie told you where he was."

"Yes. She told me everything."

"Good."

"Come here, dear. Let me look at you."

Pup crossed the faded blue Oriental rug to meet her where she stood. She reached up and brushed her fingers along the cut on his forehead. "Are you all right? Did you put some Neosporin on it?"

"I'll be fine, Mom."

"Dad and I are headed over to the hospital to meet the rest

of your sisters." She picked away a piece of his hair that had stuck to his face with dried blood. "Do you want to come?"

"No, Mom." He shook his head. "I'm really tired. I think I might just go upstairs and lie down."

"Okay." Her eyes grew momentarily brighter, the only outward sign that he'd hurt her feelings. "Can I bring you anything?"

"No, thanks. I just want to sleep."

He climbed the stairs slowly, like an old man. He was too tired to even remember to give the seventh-stair angel the finger.

When he got to his room, he yanked the shades down and slept sweatily through the afternoon. He was awoken at one point by the sound of the key twisting in the front door lock, followed by the murmuring of conversation. He could make out the voices of his parents, at least two of his sisters, and some nieces and nephews—Adrienne and Charlie and maybe Tara, and the joyful babbling of eleven-month-old Chloe. Pup usually loved seeing his nieces and nephews, but right now the thought of dealing with all of them overwhelmed him. He rolled over, pulled a pillow over his head, and went back to sleep.

Later still, the voices had dwindled to just two—his mom and his dad—and he smelled hot dogs cooking on the grill in the yard, and also possibly the little yellow onions that his dad grew in the garden and liked to cook in aluminum foil drizzled with olive oil. His stomach growled. He hadn't eaten anything since the breakfast Sal had made for him hours ago. But even the promise of hot dogs with grilled onions and, most likely, homemade potato salad, could not flush Pup out of his room. Every time he thought of Luke in that place, the smell that had come off him as they had grappled over his keys, the yellow film over his unbrushed teeth, the cracked lips, the suffering in his eyes, Pup felt sick. He just didn't know how he would handle it if his family started asking him a million questions, or worse, if they didn't ask him anything at all.

It was only after he heard the slow creak of his mother's footsteps up the stairs; after he felt her silently listening outside his door, knuckles poised but unable to bring herself to actually knock; after the slow retreat of her steps back down the stairs again; only after he heard the click of the television and the muted excitement of the appraisers on *Antiques Roadshow*, after the house grew quiet and enough time had passed that he knew his parents would both be asleep on the couch, that he tiptoed downstairs. With a pang of sadness, the first thing he saw on the kitchen counter was the plastic-wrapped plate containing two hot dogs with grilled onions and potato salad that his mother had made up for him. In the stillness of the house that always seemed to be speaking to him in a volume just below what he was capable of hearing, Pup stood on the moonlit kitchen tiles and ate his dinner cold. When he was finished, he brushed the crumbs into the sink, washed his plate, and, closing the screen door very softly behind him, went outside to shoot free throws.

He'd just finished his warm-up and was getting ready to start his drills at the post when he saw the figure shambling down the alley, hands deep in pockets, shrouded in a hoodie despite the warm night.

"Hey." His face was freshly shaven, and without the black beard it looked pale and tender, like if you poked it with your finger it might leave a lasting indentation. "Annemarie told me I'd probably find you out here."

"Well." Pup dribbled the ball once, twice, visualized the rim. "Here I am."

"I have a court date in a couple weeks. Annemarie's going to try to get my charge downgraded from a felony to a misdemeanor. We'll see. Either way, it's not good."

"You looking for an apology or something?" Pup released the ball into the air. It banked off the backboard and Luke caught it.

"I'm not looking for an apology."

"Well, then why are you here?"

"To talk to you about something."

"About what? Give me the ball."

"No." Luke leaned against the garage and slid down to sitting, holding the ball in his lap. "Just sit with me for a second."

"Why? Why should I listen to anything you have to say?"

"You shouldn't. But I need you to listen anyway." Luke swallowed, and the tender, scraped skin of his neck moved up and down. "Please."

Pup sighed. He sat down next to his brother.

"I have to tell you something that I never told anyone before."

"I already know. Carrie told me. You've only been pretending to go to law school."

"Yes. I have. But it's not that."

"Oh."

"It's about Patrick."

Pup flicked his eyes in Luke's direction, but his brother was staring at the asphalt.

"I was the last person to ever talk to him."

Pup blinked. "When? The day he—the last day?"

"Yes. He called me that morning. He said he felt like crap. Headache, body ache, stiff neck, puking. I said, 'Well, were you out last night?' And he said yeah, he'd been at a party for his fraternity. And I said . . ." Luke paused to swallow again, as if there was too much saliva welling in his throat. "I said, 'Well, idiot, you're hungover. Go get some Taco Bell and call me later.' And he said, 'No, Luke, like I feel *really* crappy.' And I said, 'How much did you drink?' He said one beer. He asked, 'Could I be hungover from one beer?' And I started laughing. I said—" Luke leaned his head down and pressed it against the cool nubs of the basketball. He closed his eyes and breathed into the rubber. "I said, 'Well, Pat, what can I say? You're a fuckin' lightweight.'" He looked up at Pup, his blue eyes hollowed out by the darker blue bags that hung beneath them. "I told him to go to the gas station, buy a Vitaminwater, take a couple aspirin, and go take a nap. So that's what he did. He took my advice. And then—a few hours after I hung up with him—that's when Rinard called Mom, saying they couldn't wake him up. But by that time it was already too late. And if I had just listened—if I hadn't been such a dick, if I hadn't brushed him off—he'd still be— he'd still be—" Luke couldn't go on. His pressed his face into the curve of the basketball.

Pup sat frozen beside him. He remembered when Jack Rinard had called the house. He'd been sitting at the kitchen table doing his Spanish homework, conjugating verbs. His mother had answered the phone, listened for a moment, then buckled against the counter, dropping the kitchen sponge she'd been holding. He could still remember the wet sound it made when it hit the floor. Sitting there with his pencil hovering over his Spanish workbook, Pup could feel a dark charge in the air, even though she didn't say anything, even though he couldn't hear what was being said on the other end of the line. Then she ordered Jack to call an ambulance, to let her know as soon as it arrived. "Don't leave him," she said. "Not even for one second. Don't let them tell you that you can't ride in the ambulance." Her voice was calm, capable, full of authority, but as soon as she hung up, she turned to Pup and her face melted into a puddle of terror.

"Pat's sick," she said. Then, she said it again. "Pat's sick." Before he had a chance to ask what she meant by that vague word, *sick*, which could describe anything from a case of the sniffles to stage-four cancer, she had grabbed her car keys off the counter and was running wildly through the house looking for Pup's dad, who was out in the garden, weeding as usual. When she finally found him, Pup witnessed but could not hear their conversation through the window, his mother waving her hands frantically, his father nearly keeling over in the grass, and then they were running through the yard to the garage, his mom without a jacket despite the October chill, his dad still wearing his gardening kneepads. Pup looked down at his workbook. He was still holding his pencil. Looking back on it now, he realized that he knew, even then, how it would end. The words on the page blurred in front of him. *Perder* was the word he was trying to conjugate. *Pierdo. Pierdes. Perdemos.* I lose. You lose. We lose.

"So now you know," Luke murmured into the basketball, "that I'm the reason why he's dead. If I'd told him to go to the infirmary. Or urgent care. . . . If I'd gone downstairs and asked Mom what she thought. . . . If I'd acted even a little bit less like the hotshot asshole older brother I've always been, he'd still be alive. He'd be twenty-three years old. He'd be out here with us right now, shooting free throws with his terrible

Joakim Noah form, and we'd be making fun of him for it, and somehow he'd still be beating us. But instead he's dead, because I killed him."

"Luke," Pup whispered. "You didn't kill Patrick. He just died. It was an infection. It—it happens to people, sometimes. Even young people. They get sick and they die."

"It does *not* just happen. Do you know *one* other person who died when they were twenty years old? *Do* you?"

"Izzy's brother," said Pup. "Teddy. He didn't even make it to twenty. He was only *eight*."

"That's different. That poor kid had some horrible kind of incurable cancer. What Patrick had wasn't like that. They could have cured him, if they'd had enough time. And maybe they would have, if it wasn't for me." He was trembling all over, despite his hoodie and the eighty-degree night. "He should have called you that morning instead of me. If he had called you, he'd still be here. What you did last night— tracking me down, calling the cops on me—you think I hate you? You saved my life, Pup. You saved me. Because that's what brothers do. That's what *strangers* do. But not me." He shook his head slowly. "Not me. My brother was calling me for help. My brother was dying. And what did I do? I told him to sack up and take an aspirin." He was crying so hard now that snot leaked from his nose and he didn't bother to wipe it away. "And I *love* you, Pup. I love you so much. I love you so much and I'm so sorry because now you hate me, but I'm *glad* you hate me, because I don't deserve you. I don't deserve anything. Not family, not success, definitely not love. I gave up my right to all those things the minute I hung up on Pat that day and let him die."

"No," Pup said softly. "No. No. No. No." This was the one argument he would not let Luke win. As he repeated that one word again and again, until it became a chant, a hushing soothing sound, a lullaby, he was remembering Patrick's advice when he'd been training to make the freshman team at Lincoln. *You don't have to be the best,* Patrick had said, flipping him the ball as they ran through their hundredth shell drill of the morning. *You just have to be the most tenacious. You just have to outlast them.* "No," Pup said again. He would outlast Luke's words with his chant, his refusal, his *no*. And it worked. At last, Luke gave up. He collapsed against Pup's shoulder, his ragged breathing evening, and the basketball fell from his hands and rolled away down the alley.

COLOR:

one of the most dominant elements;

it is created by light

36

THE WEEK AFTER LUKE RETURNED to them, Pup's mother did something unprecedented: she moved Sunday dinner to a Tuesday night. It was the eve of the Fourth of July, and while Carrie and Pup's older sisters busied themselves chopping tomatoes and slicing watermelon in the kitchen, Pup and Declan wandered the backyard, supervising the younger nieces and nephews as they threw Snaps at each other's feet on the concrete path leading to the garage. Jeanine and Mary had made an executive decision that it was too hot for Bolognese and had made a trip to Costco for crates of frozen hamburger patties and giant bags of corn chips. Inside, Noreen's husband, Dan, sweated before the stove, slowly stirring a large pot of honey-baked beans, while Mike and Frank, two more of Pup's brothers-in-law, dragged two huge coolers out to the deck. They filled up the coolers with ice and drinks—but nothing stronger than pop, bottled water, and juice boxes for the kids. Pup's mother, who was usually the sole cook for their weekly family parties, sat idly on the deck, her eyes hidden by a pair of prescription sunglasses, her slinged arm tucked into her body, and watched her grandchildren play. His father, seated next to her, was quiet too. He didn't speak to anybody, except to occasionally remind the children not to trample his vegetables. They both seemed preoccupied, nervous, as their eyes drifted again and again to the alley gate, waiting for the arrival of their invited guest.

This wasn't an intervention, because Luke was already in rehab. Thirty days of inpatient treatment, followed by another month of outpatient, followed by enrollment in an aftercare recovery program. He'd been there for six days now, and nobody knew how it was going because Luke wasn't allowed to speak to anybody on the outside. All they knew was that he was still there, that he hadn't checked himself out or snuck away in the middle of the night, and, lacking any other kind of information, they had all decided to take this as a good sign.

So, no, it wasn't an intervention. But it wasn't a normal family dinner, either, and not just because they'd changed the menu and moved it to a Tuesday and Carrie was there but Luke wasn't. Once the counselor at the hospital had heard Luke's story, she'd suggested family therapy as an important piece of his recovery. Pup's parents had immediately refused. "I don't want some *stranger* coming into our home, poking around in our lives," his mother had said. His father had agreed with her, and so had Jeanine and Matthew. And that probably would have been the end of it, if it hadn't been for Pup's idea.

"What if," he'd suggested tentatively, the morning after Luke shared his awful secret, "it wasn't a stranger?"

And that was how Mrs. Barrera ended up as the special invited guest to their Sunday-dinner-on-a-Tuesday, balancing a paper plate on her knees and accepting offers of more baked beans, more fruit salad, another pickle, a Sprite?

That first session of family therapy was not as painful as Pup had imagined it would be. While the dusk settled over the neighborhood and the younger nieces and nephews ran around in the yard, waving their sparklers and trailing glitter in the darkening air, the older family members—Pup and his sisters and their spouses and Carrie and even Declan and his fourteen-year-old sister, Clare, sat in a circle of lawn chairs on the deck and talked about what they could do for Luke once he was out in the world again, how to help him cope, how to help him avoid the temptation of alcohol, which, Mrs. Barrera warned them grimly, would be everywhere. It was a painful and long-overdue conversation, and it was a good thing Mrs. Barrera had brought a "listening stick"—an old broom handle that she'd hot-glue-gunned all over with sequins—so that Jeanine and Matthew couldn't commandeer the conversation.

After that, spurred on by some gentle prodding by Mrs.

Barrera, they talked about Patrick. They talked about his death, for a little while. But then, for much longer, they talked about his life. They unearthed their memories, they aired out their love for him. They cried a lot. They laughed a lot more. The sun finally sank completely and as soon as true darkness settled over the neighborhood, the booms and pops and fizzes of the alley fireworks began, the air thickening with sulfur and grill char. Smoke filled the dark sky. Above the rooftops, the people who just couldn't wait one more day began blowing off their grand finale fireworks. Red and silver and blue showers, low, rumbling booms, crackling fountains of light arced across the sky like man-made stars.

It was late before that first session of family therapy ended, before they took turns hugging Mrs. Barrera goodbye and, one by one, Pup's older sisters gathered up their children and pushed their strollers or drove their minivans back to their own corners of Flanland. His parents, as usual, fell asleep five minutes into *Antiques Roadshow*. He switched the television off and covered their legs with the lightweight blanket folded over the back of the rocking chair. Then he went up to bed.

On the seventh step, Pup lifted his arm, out of rote habit, to flip off the fat angel in its frame, but before he had a chance to extend his middle finger, he froze.

The angel was gone.

Someone—his mother, his father, he didn't know—had

taken it down. In its place was Patrick's high school graduation photo. He'd switched out his Cubs hat for a stiff black mortarboard, perched at a jaunty angle on his head, and he was smiling hugely, completely unselfconscious of his crooked front tooth. His eyebrows were black and thick and almost touching above his wide blue eyes, which looked eagerly into a future he must have believed—had every right to believe—would last many years, decades, half a century or more.

Pup stepped back. He looked at his brother's face. Then he leaned his forehead against the glass, living eyes gazing into pixelated eyes, a one-way stare, living breath fogging the plate between them. He'd once feared that his memory was fading, that the day would come when he could no longer remember Patrick the way he wanted to. But he had fought against the fading, and he would keep fighting. They all had, and they all would, all of the Flanagans, all in their own private way. The years would spool onward, but as Pup stood before Patrick on the seventh step, he swore to do whatever he could to shorten the distance between the linear measurement of those lengthening years and the feeling of them, a feeling that didn't move in lines at all, but in waves, sometimes moving forward toward healing, toward happiness, but other times drawing back upon itself so that the ache felt fresh as ever. What could he do but keep swimming?

37

THE FIRST THING PUP NOTICED about the green room
was that it was not actually green. It was a long, narrow space
with yellow walls and a white tile floor. On one end was a
table lined with trays of cookies and sandwich wraps and
fruit salad turning into mush where kids lined up to fill their
paper plates. On the other was a row of folding chairs that
remained empty because everyone was too nervous to sit. For
the first time in his life, Pup couldn't eat. He strode the length
of the room and back again, grabbing at his stranglingly tight
Chicago Cubs tie and listening to the low murmur on the
other side of the wall grow louder as the crowd began to fill
up the auditorium.

"Sup?"

Pup almost didn't recognize Qurt, his partner from the
state competition, because he had shaved off his mustache
and his eyes looked different.

"Oh, hey, Qurt," Pup said. "How's your summer?"

"Insufferably boring, as all summers of my life have always

been and will always be until next year when I finally break out of my shitbox town and move to Paris." He lifted Pup's tie with a thumb and forefinger, turning it back and forth to inspect it. "I see you're still dressing like a middle-aged dad."

"Hey!" Abrihet appeared by Pup's side, carrying a tray of mini desserts. "I bought him that tie." She put her free hand around Pup's waist and he felt the blush blooming up his neck. Even though they'd been official for three weeks, he wasn't used to it yet, this whole girlfriend thing. Every time Abrihet touched him, it still felt like a miracle. She was wearing her red floral dress, her dangly earrings, and a pair of leather sandals with a bunch of straps going up the ankle. She had an easy style that allowed her to fit in with this crew of artists. Pup had a rumpled poly-blend dress shirt and a belt that didn't match his shoes. Qurt's eyes flicked to the place where her hand rested on Pup's hip, then flicked back to Pup. For a moment, he actually looked impressed. "Well," he conceded, "I guess it's a good strategy. Dressing like you're taking your kids to a daddy-daughter dance at the local mall will force the judges to focus on your work, not your look. I should have thought of that myself."

"But that would mean taking off your fabulous purple cape," Abrihet pointed out. "And the cape matches your eyes perfectly."

"No," Qurt corrected her. "My *eyes* match my *cape* perfectly." He lifted two fingers to his face and pulled his contact lenses to the side, showing her the brown pupils beneath.

"Amazing."

"I know." Qurt smiled at her as the lavender lenses slid back into place. "Well, I better go score a chicken Caesar wrap before they run out. Good luck out there, you two." He turned then, shaking out the cascade of satin that hung down his back, and disappeared into the crowd.

"I think I'm gonna barf," Pup said, running a hand over his gel-encrusted hair. "Something's wrong with my stomach."

"Nothing's wrong with your stomach." Abrihet chose a mini fudge brownie from her paper plate and popped it into her mouth. "You're just a little nervous."

"Why did I eat that Canadian bacon breakfast sandwich?"

"I seem to recall Mr. Hughes warning you not to eat gas-station meat on the drive up here."

"I know, but I just figured that was his anti-corporation, anti–Big Oil, anti–Big Agriculture prejudice coming through."

"No, it was his anti-diarrhea prejudice coming through."

Pup winced.

"James." She handed him the dessert plate and rested her two hands on his shoulders. "Your photographs are beautiful and you deserve to be here. Okay?"

"Okay." Pup sighed. "What about you? Are you doing okay?"

She shrugged. "I talked to her this morning. I wish she

was here. I wish she'd change her mind." She plucked another brownie off the dessert plate. "But I'll be all right. The chocolate is helping a little bit."

"And the rest of your family is coming, right?"

"Oh yeah. And I just *know* they're going to sit right up in the front row, too. That's how they are." She looked at him. "Is your family coming?"

"Nah." Pup looked down at the big shiny dress shoes that were already starting to pinch his toes. "They're proud of me and everything, but they're not really, like, comfortable with me sharing our private family stuff in public."

"Well, I can respect that." She thought for a moment, chewing her brownie. "You did *show* them your portfolio, at least, though. Right? So at least they know how talented you are?"

Pup nodded. The night before, he'd sat with his parents in the kitchen with the windows open to the late summer wind and watched quietly as they put on their reading glasses and leafed through the images one by one. His mom had brushed tears away before closing the folder.

"Oh, Pup," she'd said. "We're so proud of you."

"Good or bad," his dad added, his voice gruff, "you got us right, kid."

The door to the green room opened, and most of the kids in the room turned around expectantly. But it was only Mr.

309

Hughes, dressed in his finest Hawaiian shirt.

"I'm not supposed to be back here," he said, dribbling his coffee all over the floor as he hurried over to them. "But I just had to see how you two were holding up."

"I think I'm gonna barf." Pup yanked at his tie while his stomach blooped and gurgled.

"I *told* you not to eat that gas-station meat."

"I told him it's just nerves," Abrihet said.

"*Nerves?* What the hell *you* got to be nervous about? It's all these *other* kids who should be nervous. They've got nothing on you two!" He was making no effort to lower his voice, and a couple of the other contestants were now glaring over at them. "Anyway, I wanted to give you a heads-up." He fished a booklet out of his back pocket. "I snagged a program when I came in. Thought you might want to know your order. Abby, you're going eighth. Pup, you're first."

"First?" Pup said faintly. He felt the inside of his mouth get sweaty. He really *was* going to barf.

"That's great!" Abrihet gave him an encouraging smile. "It means you can get it over with and just enjoy the rest of the program! I've got to sweat through seven people before it's my turn."

"If you get nervous, just look for my big goofy head in the crowd. I'm easy to find. Front row." He winked at Abrihet. "Your dad saved me a seat."

"I *told* you they'd be in the front row." Abrihet rolled her eyes at Pup.

"They brought signs, too," Mr. Hughes added. "And possibly an air horn."

"Oh, god." Abrihet covered her face, but Pup could tell that she was just as pleased as she was embarrassed. He knew how painful it was for her not to have her mom there, and that her family was going over the top to make her feel loved, to protect her, to make the absence a little easier.

Suddenly Pup's heart filled with dread. How could he share his own family's story of loss, and all the pain that had rippled afterward, with a room full of strangers? The acid surged in his throat, and as he turned around to bolt for a bathroom in which he could evacuate his Canadian bacon biscuit, a woman in a black blazer with a short sweep of pink hair and a clipboard appeared, blocking the doorway.

"Okay, everyone," she said. "We're ready to begin. Feel free to hang out back here until your name is called. Best of luck to all of you!" She looked down and consulted her clipboard. "Now," she said, "if I could just have James come with me. Is there a James here?"

Pup swallowed the vile burp that was bubbling up his throat and raised a trembling hand. It was too late to quit, no matter how much he wanted to.

His hand was on the velvet corner of the curtain and then he was stepping out onto the stage. There was a small lectern where he'd been instructed to stand, and he hurried to it, the soles of his too-tight dress shoes plunking hollowly on the hardwood. He'd been expecting one of those big wooden podiums like the ones his teachers used at school, the kind that would at least conceal half of his body from the hundreds of eyes in the packed auditorium, but no such luck. It was one of those modern things, more like a music stand, and all that stood between Pup and the room full of onlookers was a thin metal pole and five empty feet of stage. Behind him, hanging from the ceiling rafters, was a screen where his photographs would be projected, eight by ten feet high. The stage lights were hot and glaring in his face, but he could make out Mr. Hughes and his parrot-covered Hawaiian shirt in the front row. Abrihet's dad was there, and her *amoui* and brother and a gaggle of cousins, too. Mr. Hughes had not been joking: they were all carrying signs decorated with her name, rolled up and wedged beneath their seats or placed across their laps, and that made him relax just the tiniest bit, because he knew that even if she pretended otherwise, she was going to love those waving signs. He took out his notes from the breast pocket of his dress shirt. The crinkling sound they made as he unfolded the paper was picked up by the mic, and carried out all the way to the back of the room.

"My project," he began, after a shriek of microphone feedback, "is called *The Emergency Inside*." There was an expectant silence from the audience. Mr. Hughes and Abrihet's family watched him, their posters on their laps. Here he was, Pup Flanagan, a boy who couldn't command attention at his own family's Sunday dinner, and now every person in a very large, very crowded room, was waiting for him to speak. It was too much. *I can't do this*, he thought. He was a fraud, a joke. Just a few months ago, if you'd asked him what a silver halide was, he'd have guessed it was one of the cool new drugs the popular kids at school were doing. He'd heard some of the contestants talking in the green room. Some of them had been taking photography classes since elementary school. He had no right to be here. He folded his notes back up—again, their crinkling was amplified by the stupid super-sensitive mic—and turned back toward the safety of the curtain. But before he'd taken his first step, a loud squeaking far at the back of the auditorium broke the silence.

One of the double doors was opening, but the lights were glaring in Pup's face and all he could see was the silhouette of a person hurrying down the aisle in search of an open seat. The metal door closed with a bang, and was immediately thrown open again with another loud squeak, this time by two people, hunched arm in arm and hurrying down the aisle behind the first latecomer. Now, a family with young children was squeezing through the door. The woman was holding a shrieking baby in her arms and by now the rest of the auditorium had turned away from Pup to check out this rude mob of people who were interrupting the competition. But Pup was standing stock-still, one hand clutching the lectern, because he'd know that baby shriek anywhere. It belonged to his niece Chloe. He put a hand over his eyes and squinted out past the stage lights. One by one, stepping over people, hushing apologies, shushing their children, waving proudly at Pup as they took their seats, was the entire population of Flanland. Twenty-six people, twenty-seven if you counted Carrie, which Pup did, because as she gave him a small smile before hurrying into her seat, he knew exactly why she was there: because Luke, in his last week of inpatient rehab, couldn't be.

So there they were, scattered throughout the auditorium, all those pale-blue watching eyes. Had they rented a bus? Had they caravanned? Were his parents planning on staying overnight in Ann Arbor, paying money for an actual hotel? And what would they say when he aired their deepest sorrow to a room full of strangers? After all, he'd shared his pictures with his parents, but he hadn't shared a word of his speech. If there was ever a time to abandon ship, it was now. But when Pup ranged over the rows and rows of people and found Annemarie's steady eyes, then his mother's, his father's, and even his oldest sisters', he understood that the fact that they were there meant that they believed it was okay. And so he took a deep breath and began.

He started at the bottom of the sea. The abyssopelagic zone, the most unknown and feared and foreign place on the planet, less habitable, less explored than even the moon. The place that Patrick had dreamed of seeing for himself one day.

When you are in this zone, Pup told them, surrounded by creatures made mostly of slime and water, and the pressure is crushing and everywhere is utter darkness, you grope your way around, terrified and desperate for the sight of something familiar.

But nothing is familiar and so you do things to beat back the fear.

Pup clicked the little button the pink-haired woman had given him. You might distract yourself with quiet routines, he said, as the first photograph appeared on the projection screen: his mother, aged far beyond her years, shading carefully in her adult coloring book.

Or you cheapen a tragedy into a stupid little ghost story.

He clicked again, to the forlorn room at the Sig Sig house, dust on the empty desk and broken glass scattered on the floor.

Or you drink.

On the screen, huge enough for even those in the back to see, came Luke, passed out on the roof in the early morning light.

But all of these things, Pup explained, are shortcuts; they won't work. You're trying to swim up too fast, and you're going to get compression sickness. You're going to bleed from your nose and ears, and maybe even from your deeper organs if you're not careful. Don't be reckless. You have to come up slowly, expecting no miracles. You have to outfit yourself with the proper gear.

The first thing you need, if you want a shot at getting out of this alive, is strength. Find somebody who already has it, and let them teach you. Pup clicked to a photo of Annemarie in a short-sleeved work blouse, tattoos twining up her arms, staring down the camera behind her big desk on the twenty-third floor of the Aon building.

The next thing you need is hope. You can't keep swimming if you've stopped seeing the point.

Onto the screen flashed a photo of Mr. Hughes. His body was hunched forward with intensity, his glasses slipping down his nose as he lectured a group of Abrihet's cousins about *Guernica* over steaming plates of *dorho* and rice. Mr. Hughes, who had believed in him. Who, after a year's worth of terrible art projects, had taken a chance on Pup because of a single photograph.

The next thing you need—and this is a big one—the next thing you need is love.

He clicked to the photo of Abrihet in her red dress, the center point of light in the lobby of the university hotel. He glanced quickly to stage left, where she was standing in the small space between the curtain and the wall. He saw her freeze, saw her hand squeeze the velvet fabric of the curtain tighter. Maybe it was too soon to tell her that he loved her, but he didn't care. Patrick would have supported a romantic gesture like that. And Patrick was a philosopher, so he would know.

The last thing you must search for is forgiveness.

Pup clicked to the fight, that terrible portrait of his parents squared up against Luke like boxers in a late round. They had forgiven him for everything, but that only meant something if he could find a way to forgive himself. If he could make it through rehab and stand clear-eyed on the other side, Pup hoped, then the love of his family, which had never wavered, could see him the rest of the way.

In the end, Pup explained, if you work hard, and fight, and are lucky, you might start seeing it. Just a glimmer at the end of a long, watery tunnel. Don't expect miracles. You will still be you, and there's no way of undoing the things that have happened. These things are the raw materials of your life now, and you have to find a way to work with them. You have to find a way to keep being you.

As Pup clicked to the final photograph, his self-portrait in the alley, he found that it was easy now. The photographs were stories without words, but they had given words to his story. He cleared his throat. He was almost finished. He looked down at his notes and realized he'd barely looked at them. He hadn't even needed them.

And then you'll feel it.

It's not anything concrete, of course. There is nothing— not time, not family, not even love, that can give you that, and you know better than to hope. No, it is just a sudden and acute sense you have that all the energy in the world is converging in this one place, in these waves and this sky, in this darkness and light. It is converging in you, he is converging in you, he is buried and ticking in your heart, and you can feel him as you swim, pushing you onward, burning in your lungs, pumping your blood. Pushed on by the converging energies around you and in you, you propel yourself up and up, and soon the water turns from black to green to blue, and the blue is the place where the light finally begins to pierce. But you are still so far underwater and there is still so much work to do. Despite all your progress you are a long way from breathing on your own; you are not a fish and you were not made for this environment. But the one thing you know for sure is that the blue is the light and the light is where you are headed. *Can you see it?* you feel him asking as he urges you on. *Can you see it?* You tell him that you do, and this time you're not just lying to yourself. You really do see it. With a final tremendous kick, your arms reach up and out and grab at the sky. You want to tell him how dazzling it is. You want to tell him, but you don't have the words. But then you understand that you don't need the words because he already knows. After all this time, these years of searching and yearning and waiting for a sign, you've finally found him: a beautiful latent image curled up inside of you this whole time, just waiting to be developed.

ACKNOWLEDGMENTS

Thank you to the following people for guiding me through the creation of this book:

My editor, Alexandra Cooper, who has pushed me, in her gentle way, to be the best writer I can be. I'm forever grateful for our partnership.

My agent, Barry Goldblatt, who never gave up on this project, even through the cringeworthy early drafts. I'm so grateful to have you in my corner.

Thank you to the entire team at HarperTeen for their tireless work on this story. Special thanks in particular to Alyssa Miele and Rosemary Brosnan. Thank you also to David Curtis and Catherine San Juan for the gorgeous book design, and Brenna Franzitta, Alexandra Rakaczki, and Christine Corcoran Cox for their excellent copyediting and proofreading.

Deep gratitude to Samrawit Areki for our many conversations throughout the writing of this book—I'm so excited to see all the amazing things you do in your college career and beyond. Thanks also to Amilia Tsegai, Bsrat Negassi, Sarah Kennedy Bennett, and Kristin Keglovitz Baker.

To the following friends, thank you so much for sharing your many growing-up-in-a-giant-family stories: Jenny Callahan, Michelle Hynes, Sarah McDermott, and Bridget Quinlan.

Special thanks to one of my oldest and dearest friends, Dr. Alicia Pilarski, for always being up for answering my many medical questions.

Mike Howe, the biggest Cubs fan I have ever met (and that's saying something): thank you.

Thank you to Danielle Owensby and Maisie Lothian for sharing their art and their knowledge of photography with me, and to Tina Capodanno for scoping out the auditoriums of Ann Arbor on my behalf.

Special thanks to Dan and Nora, who have taught me many lessons about death metal, thrash metal, the wonders of marine life, and the special joy only siblings can provide, all of which have made their way into this book.

To Mom and Dad, do you remember the very first reading I ever did, in an abandoned storefront, where there was no heat and a shirtless man in overalls was guzzling warm lemonade out of a mason jar? I don't even remember what I read; I only remember that you were there. Your support and love still means everything. And to all the other Morrisons, Brennans, and Gillespies: I wrote a book about family because I've got one of the best.

And most of all, to Roisin, Sheila, and Aine, *mo chroí*, and Denis, the measure of my dreams: I love you.